DESTROYER

ALSO BY BRETT BATTLES

The Jonathan Quinn Thrillers

Novels

BECOMING QUINN

THE CLEANER

THE DECEIVED

SHADOW OF BETRAYAL (US)/THE UNWANTED (UK)

THE SILENCED

THE DESTROYED

THE COLLECTED

THE ENRAGED

THE DISCARDED

THE BURIED

Novellas

NIGHT WORK (Originally Published as FLIGHT 12)

Short Stories

"Just Another Job"—A Jonathan Quinn Story
"Off the Clock"—A Jonathan Quinn Story
"The Assignment"—An Orlando Story
"Lesson Plan"—A Jonathan Quinn Story
"Quick Study"—An Orlando Story

The Rewinder Thrillers

REWINDER
DESTROYER

The Logan Harper Thrillers

LITTLE GIRL GONE
EVERY PRECIOUS THING

The Project Eden Thrillers

SICK
EXIT NINE
PALE HORSE
ASHES
EDEN RISING
DREAM SKY
DOWN

The Alexandra Poe Thrillers
(with Robert Gregory Browne)

POE
TAKEDOWN

Stand-Alones

Novels

THE PULL OF GRAVITY
NO RETURN

Short Stories

"Perfect Gentleman"

For Younger Readers

The Trouble Family Chronicles

HERE COMES MR. TROUBLE

More at BrettBattles.com

DESTROYER

BRETT BATTLES

Published by 47North, Seattle
www.apub.com

Amazon, the Amazon logo, and 47North are trademarks of Amazon.com, Inc., or its affiliates.

ISBN-13: 9781503951594

ISBN-10: 1503951596

Cover design by David Drummond

Printed in the United States of America

To DeeDee Li, Derek Rogers, Christine Buckhout, and Gar Haywood.
Thank you for keeping me sane(ish).

CHAPTER ONE

I live in fear.

Fear of my past.

Fear for our future.

Fear that I've paid too high a price to save my sister's life.

Fear that I will be held accountable for altering mankind's destiny.

Don't think destinies can't be altered. I've done it more than once.

The first incident was an error, but not the second.

Time travel. It can be . . . problematic. Even the smallest of errors can result in, well, a place like this.

Don't thank me, though. What I've done carries with it the guilt of millions of erased lives. Maybe billions.

Believe me or not, but the truth is the truth.

My name is Denny Younger, and I am a rewinder.

JUMP.

CHAPTER TWO

This is not the first time I've seen the man in the gray suit, but it takes me a moment before I place him.

Ruby's Coffee Shop.

The café is near my apartment, and I often go there for an early coffee while my sister is still sleeping, so I've come to recognize many of the regular customers. The man is one of them, though I'm pretty sure he's only started coming around in the last couple of weeks or so.

The thing is, I'm nowhere near Ruby's right now. I'm downtown walking toward the San Diego Central Library. It's a place I go to expand my knowledge about this time line. Though, as my girlfriend, Iffy, has shown me, I can do a lot of my research on the worldwide Internet, physical books are what I'm used to.

The man is standing off to the side of the open glass wall that serves as the building's entrance. He's holding a brochure as if studying it, but he's not. He's watching me approach. When I glance in his direction, he looks back at his pamphlet, suddenly interested in it again.

It's possible he's having the same "I've seen this guy before" moment that I just had, but the tingle I feel at the back of my neck makes me think otherwise. I see no hint of surprise or even confusion in his eyes. He's interested in me.

Acting like I haven't noticed anything special about him, I causally walk into the library's large lobby, but casual is not how I feel. The desire to hurry to someplace private where I can slip my hand into my satchel, press the go button on my chaser, and make a time jump away from here is nearly overwhelming. Only that's not an option. The device's battery strength continues to decline with every trip I make. Until I have a way to recharge it, I decided to limit my jumps to only those that are necessary, and have left the chaser in my safe at home. It seemed like a good idea at the time. Now, I'm not so sure.

I take the escalator up to the second floor, where I position myself so that I can discreetly watch the entrance below. A few moments pass before the man finally saunters inside. By the way he hesitates near the base of the escalator I know he's aware of where I have gone. Instead of following me, though, he heads deeper into the first floor where I can no longer see him.

I frown in annoyance. I'd been hoping he'd come up so that I could sneak around him and make my way out of the building unseen. But now I assume that if I try, he'll spot me. So, for the moment, I'm trapped.

Two months ago while Iffy and I were walking around Coronado Island, I saw someone I swore I knew—a veteran rewinder named Carla Manning. She was walking in front of us and hadn't seen me yet, so we followed her all the way to a restaurant. Through the glass door we watched as two teenagers greeted her, their features clearly indicating they were her children. With much relief, I realized it wasn't Carla at all. Or, at least, not the version of Carla from my world.

I'm feeling the same panic now that I felt then. It's the cost of living in fear of being discovered. Some days I can almost pretend I'm like everyone else here, that this is the world I was born into.

But it's not.

I have no idea if anyone else from my old world survived the change, but if they did, they'll be looking for me. What I can't figure out is if the man is one of them. Though there's something familiar about him, I'm positive that prior to the first time I noticed him at Ruby's, I'd never seen him before. That doesn't mean he's not from my former life, though. There were, after all, many rewinders I never met.

I retreat to a table from where I can keep an eye on most of the second floor, pull out my laptop, and pretend to work on it. Nearly twenty minutes pass before the man rides the escalator up. I tense the moment I see him, but stay my urge to get up and run. He walks into the area where I am sitting and chooses the open table farthest from mine.

Once more I really wish I'd brought my chaser. Who cares about the miniscule power drain a quick jump would cause? Yes, perhaps the man is harmless, but why take the chance?

I close my computer and shove it back in my satchel. There's no reason to put off my departure any longer. If he's here to take me, I'm already lost.

As I rise, I innocently glance around the room and once more catch him looking in my direction. With a sense of calm I don't feel, I return to the escalator and head down to the lobby.

The entrance area is considerably more crowded now than when I first arrived, and I have to weave through a mass of patrons to get to the exit. This actually allows me to shoot a quick look back. I expect to see the man descending the escalator or at least standing at the top, but he is nowhere in sight.

Does this mean he's used his own chaser and is already waiting for me outside?

I head back into the daylight, my body tense in the anticipation of someone grabbing my arm, but I make it to the sidewalk without any interference. Looking around, I don't see the man anywhere.

What I do see, however, is a city bus moving toward the nearby stop. It's not heading in the direction I want to go, but I don't care. I run over and jump on just before the doors close. Taking a seat a few rows back, I watch the library as we pull away, but once more see no sign of the man in the gray suit. Just to be sure, I scan the other passengers in case he is already here, but he's not.

As I slump against the window, I tell myself it's just a coincidence. He's not after me. He's not a rewinder.

For the most part, I believe it.

◆ ◆ ◆

When I arrive home, I find Iffy sitting at the dining table. I don't like to leave my sister alone in the apartment if I'm going to be gone for more than thirty minutes, but while Iffy doesn't officially live with Ellie and me, she's here more often than not and is able to play guardian when I need to get away.

"How is she?" I ask as I pull off my satchel and set it on the dining table.

"Still asleep." Iffy tilts her chin up and we kiss. "How did the research go?"

"It didn't." I tell her about the encounter with the man in the suit.

"Are you sure he wasn't one of them?"

"If he was, I doubt I would have made it home."

She looks unconvinced, which is understandable given her own encounter with one of my fellow institute members back in early April. "I don't think it's a good idea for you to leave the chaser here when you go out."

Though I've been feeling the same, I say, "You know why I can't take it."

She's silent for a moment, and when she speaks, I know what's coming. "Please, let me call RJ."

She has been pushing her friend on me for a while. Raymond Johnson is someone she grew up with, who is now attending one of the local universities, UC San Diego, where he is studying something called information technologies. She has repeatedly told me he can help with the chaser's power problem.

To this point, I've rebuffed the suggestion. Now, though . . .

"Can we trust him?"

Clearly she's been expecting me to shut her down again and looks surprised at my question. "Absolutely."

I think for a moment longer and then, with the hope that I don't regret what I'm about to say, tell her, "Let's talk to him."

My chaser sits on the table in front of us. It looks like nothing special, just an old wooden box that could as easily be from 1015 as from 2015.

Iffy's likened it to a cigar box in size, and from the pictures she's shown me, that seems about right. It even has a similar lid. When opened, though, instead of revealing rows of cigars, it uncovers a control panel.

The device was developed at the Upjohn Institute, a place that now never existed, and yet I walked its halls, studied in its library, and slept in its dormitory. The device is what allowed rewinders such as myself to travel through time.

It was Sir Gregory, one of the institute's administrators, who told me during training that the chaser is the most powerful thing on earth. "In the wrong hands, can you imagine the devastation one of these could cause?"

I don't need to imagine now. I've done it. But that's the past. What we're doing now is trying to figure out the future.

Iffy sits beside me. Across from us is her friend RJ.

While technically I'm no longer employed by the Upjohn Institute, and therefore am not bound by their rules and regulations, I can't ignore the sense of panic growing in my chest. Revealing the truth about who I really am to an outsider and explaining what a chaser allows me to do are two of the institute's cardinal sins.

To this point, I've shared these secrets with only two others. Iffy, when I thought she was about to be erased forever and telling her wouldn't matter; and my sister, Ellie, who I brought to this reality so she could receive medical treatment our former time line denied her.

Bringing a third person into our circle—someone I have just met at that—is beyond merely difficult. I'm in a mental battle with myself to keep from picking up the chaser and racing out of the room. But like it or not, I need Iffy's friend.

My chaser's battery *will* eventually run dry, rendering the device useless. I can't allow that to happen. I may be the last of the rewinders, but if I'm not, others will be searching for me so they can force me to bring back the original time line. Without a working chaser, I can easily be taken. The machine gives me the ability to hide if necessary, or, if I must, fight them on an equal footing.

RJ looks at the box and then at us. "So?"

"We're hoping you can help us figure out how to charge it," Iffy says.

When he lifts the chaser off the table, I nearly leap out of my chair to snatch it back from him. Sensing my unease, Iffy grabs my thigh and gives it a squeeze. This does little to calm me, but it does keep me in my seat.

RJ turns the box around, studying each side. Finally he asks, "What do you mean charge it? It's a box."

"It's more than a box," Iffy says.

He looks at Iffy, waiting for her to elaborate. I can feel her glance nervously in my direction, prompting RJ to turn his attention to me. "So, what is it?"

It takes me another couple seconds before I can say, "I don't see how that's important."

Iffy squeezes my leg again and then asks RJ, "Will it help if you know?"

"Um, yeah. I need to understand what I'm working with here." He turns the chaser around again. "I don't even see a place to plug anything in."

My discomfort is reaching maximum. "I'm not sure I'm ready for this."

"Look," RJ says, setting the device down, "I don't know what the big deal is, but Iffy said you needed my help. If you don't want it, fine. No worries." He stands.

Iffy scolds me with her glare as she says, "Denny?"

I close my eyes for a half second and then let out the breath I've been holding. "I'm sorry . . . yes, we do need your help."

"Then you're going to have to tell me what that thing is."

After another quick glance in my direction, Iffy says, "Actually, it'll be easier if we show you."

The plan is one she proposed after she finally convinced me to have the meeting. Reluctantly, I then worked up the information per her instructions and input it into my chaser. What I didn't do was openly agree to executing her plan.

While I know in principle this will be the easiest way to convince him, going through with her plan means yet another major institute rule broken. So when she stands, I'm not so quick to do the same.

"What's wrong?" she asks.

"I've never done it with three before." This is a weak argument at best. Marie, my personal instructor during my training period at the institute, told me a rewinder could jump with as many as five people in a pinch, and that once someone had taken a journey with seven. Three won't be a problem.

"Never done what with three?" Wariness has crept into RJ's voice.

Iffy gives him a reassuring smile before saying to me, "I'll stay. You can go with him by yourself."

This is not the response I expected, and while RJ seems nice enough, if we're really going to do this, I'd much rather have Iffy along. "Never mind. I'm, um, sure it'll be okay."

RJ's concern has only intensified. "What are you guys talking about?"

Iffy hands me the chaser as we move away from the table and then waves RJ over. "Join us."

He hesitates.

"RJ, don't be an idiot. Get over here."

Reluctantly he walks over.

Iffy puts her arms around me from the left. "Grab on to Denny on that side just like this."

"Whoa, whoa, whoa," he says. "I think it would be better if—"

"Quit being such a baby and do it."

"You guys are messing with me, aren't you?" He looks around. "Are we on one of those practical joke shows? You're streaming this live online, aren't you?"

"RJ!"

Looking like he's sure he's being set up, he very tentatively grabs my right side, leaving a gap between us.

He's probably close enough, but I'd rather not take any chances. "Move in a bit."

"Oh, sure. Move it." He steps right next to me and hugs me tight, like he wants to crush my ribs.

"I'd like to be able to breathe."

"Too much? Sorry, man." He loosens his hold, still smiling like he's in on the joke.

"Everyone set?" I ask.

9

As Iffy nods, she locks eyes with RJ. "Don't freak out."

"Freak out about what?" he asks.

I raise the chaser and press go.

◆ ◆ ◆

At Iffy's suggestion we go for the dramatic.

RJ apparently has a passion for all things space related, so I jump us to a hill in the Mojave Desert within the boundaries of Edwards Air Force Base. The date is April 14, 1981, and as per the protocol I learned during my rewinder training, we arrive in the dark of the early morning.

RJ gasps as he pulls away from me, cringing from the headache of the trip. We all experience one, but we haven't gone that far back, so it's not very intense. Since I do this a lot, I barely notice it and am able to immediately assess our surroundings.

In the west, a quarter moon rests just above the horizon, providing more than enough light to see the dry lake in the plain in front of us. At one edge of the lake is a large rectangular area filled with cars and campers and RVs, many with lights on. I have never seen so many vehicles parked in one place before. Surely there are more than a thousand. As for the hill where we stand, we are alone. I look around and spot some large rocks that should hide our presence during daylight and then use the chaser's calculator to adjust the location number so that we will pop out behind the boulders next time.

"Where . . . what . . ." RJ stutters as he rises out of his crouch and looks around, wide eyed.

"Grab on," I say. "We're not done."

"What are you talking about? We're not done what? I don't understand."

"RJ," Iffy says, "do you want us to leave you here?"

I know he's desperately trying to find an explanation for what has just happened, but he's obviously coming up empty. The thought of being abandoned, though, is enough for him to scramble back over and grab on to me again.

A push of the button, and we travel physical backward forty feet and forward in time several hours to 10:05 a.m. The bright sunlight forces me to squeeze my eyes shut. Once I feel them starting to adjust, I slowly open them again. The good thing is, with a trip this short, the accompanying headache is all but nonexistent for all of us.

RJ has once more moved a few feet away from me. He blinks rapidly as he stares up at the sky. "But . . . but . . . how . . . we were just . . ."

Iffy moves quickly to his side, but as she puts an arm around him, he jerks away and looks at her, terrified.

"It's just me," she says.

He swallows hard, and when her hand touches his shoulder again, he doesn't shake it off.

"I told you not to freak out."

"You drugged me, didn't you?" he asks. "This is some kind of hallucination."

"What? No. We didn't drug you."

"This can't be real."

She touches the rock we are now hiding behind. "Feel it. It's real."

He moves a hand toward the boulder as if he or it or both might explode if actual contact is made. When his fingertip brushes the surface, he freezes for a second and then shoves his palm against the rock.

He turns to me. "Where's your apartment?"

"A couple hundred miles south," I say, almost adding that I'm pretty sure it hasn't even been built yet. Better to ease him in. "We're in the desert, north of Los Angeles."

His brow wrinkles as he tries to process this. After a few moments, he sneers and begins shaking his head. "No, no, no. We're still in your apartment. That box, it's some sort of VR rig, isn't it?"

Now I'm the confused one. "VR?"

"Virtual reality. I have no idea how it could work without goggles, but holy crap, this is great!"

"It's not VR," Iffy says. "Feel the wind and the heat. Smell the dirt. We're not in Denny's apartment."

RJ shakes his head, snorting a couple laughs. "So, what? That's some kind of transportation device? Very funny, Iffy. But I'm not stupid."

"Oh, it's more than just a transportation device."

He cocks his head, his mask of denial cracking a little. "What do you mean?"

Iffy glances at me. "How much time do we have?"

I check the chaser. "Just a few more minutes."

"Come on," she tells RJ. "There's something you're going to want to see." She starts climbing up the rock.

"Oh, no. You tell me what the hell is going on, or I'll—"

"Trust me, you're not going to want to miss this."

"This is insane," he says as he starts up after her.

Once I put the chaser in my satchel, I head up, too.

I'm still a long way from understanding all the intricacies of Iffy's world, but I'm sure our presence here is breaking some kind of United States law. We're on a military base without permission, after all, on what is a very important day. When Iffy told me her idea, she assured me that while security might be tight, it wouldn't be anywhere near as strict as it becomes after the New York terrorist attack in 2001. I hope she's right. While we could easily escape by jumping if we're spotted, I would rather the military not see us disappear in front of their eyes.

For this reason, I urge caution as we reach the top and peer over it.

The dry lake bed lies before us. Permanent lines are drawn into it, mapping out what look like several wide roads. Off to the side, in the area where all the vehicles are parked, a crush of people now line a barrier on the edge closest to the lake. They're pressed together a dozen deep at the least, like a giant amorphous snake with one very straight edge.

"What is this?" RJ asks. "Where exactly are we?"

"Edwards Air Force Base," Iffy tells him.

His mouth opens several times as if he wants to ask something else, but each time it closes again without a word.

After a few minutes, Iffy points at the distant sky. "See it?"

Both RJ and I look to where she's indicated. At first I see nothing but blue, then slowly I begin to make out a white dot.

"Is that a plane?" RJ asks.

"Not exactly," Iffy says.

The dot grows and begins to take shape: wings and a tail connected to a fat body.

I glance at RJ. His expression is a battle of wonder and confusion. I look back to the sky and see that two smaller aircraft have joined the first. At that moment we hear the distant sound of the thousands gathered on the lake cheering.

"This can't be," RJ whispers.

Down the aircraft travels, its shape becoming more and more distinctive.

"This can't be."

I worry that RJ is going to jump off the rock and run, but he stays where he is, transfixed by the event unfolding in front of us.

Iffy pulls her phone out of her pocket and points it toward the aircraft. Using the camera, she magnifies the image until the vehicle rests prominently in the middle. The iconic image is impossible to mistake for anything other than what it is—a space shuttle. We are witnessing the return of the very first one to orbit the earth.

RJ stares at the camera for a moment and then quickly returns his gaze to the sky so he can watch with his own eyes.

The shuttle is so low when the landing gear deploys that I've begun to wonder if the aircraft is going to crash. I am not familiar with the details of this event, but I do know at some point there is at least one disaster involving the shuttle program. I only hope that I'm not about to see it. But the gear does drop down, and the aircraft touches the dry lake bed with a puff of dust.

As the orbiter slows, RJ finally looks back at Iffy's camera.

"That's . . . that's the *Columbia.*"

I look at the screen, but the only thing I can make out on the shuttle is a red, white, and blue rectangle next to the barely readable words *United States.* "How do you know?" I ask.

He points to a line of black on the front half of the fuselage. Letters or numbers, maybe, but impossible to read.

"The *Columbia* is the only one that had its name on the cargo bay doors," he explains. "All the others were closer to the cockpit. They even moved *Columbia*'s there later, too."

As if just realizing what he's said, he jerks back from the phone and climbs quickly off the rock. When we join him, he backs away a few feet, creating a buffer between us.

"I don't understand," he says. "What just happened?"

Iffy smiles sympathetically. "RJ, you saw it with your own eyes."

"I don't know what I saw."

Iffy lifts the flap of my satchel and says, "May I?"

After I nod, she pulls out the device that has brought us here.

"It's called a chaser," she says. "It allows Denny to travel through time."

RJ spits out a solitary laugh. "You're crazy."

"You just witnessed the landing of the very first space shuttle mission, *in person*." She looks around. "We're standing in the middle of the desert, hundreds of miles from where we were twenty minutes ago. Not to mention when we left San Diego it was evening, and now it's midmorning."

"No, it's some kind of . . . some kind of trick," he says, though he sounds far from convinced that he is right.

"All right. What else can we do to prove it to you?"

He frowns skeptically. "Right. You'll take me anywhere."

"We can."

"Okay. Let's go see, um, the signing of the Declaration of Independence." He crosses his arms as if he's thrown down a challenge he knows we can't deliver on.

In a way, he's correct. There are so many things wrong with this request—from the clothes we are wearing to the type of money we don't have, not to mention that RJ's African American ancestry could create its own set of dangerous problems—but it's the proximity of the signing to the point in history where I already changed the time line on multiple occasions that concerns me the most. "We're not prepared for a jump that far," I say. "Plus it would use up too much of what is left in the battery. Which is what we're trying to get your help with, after all."

Looking at me for approval, Iffy says, "How about something a little more recent? Say within fifty years of 2015?"

"That we can do," I say with a nod.

RJ is silent for several seconds before saying, "1977?"

It is near the far end of the time frame, but doable. "Okay," I say. "Do you have an exact date and location?"

A mischievous smile grows on his face. "I do."

◆ ◆ ◆

The total time of our journey into the past was several hours longer than I had anticipated, but I don't adjust for this when we jump home, and instead return us to my apartment only ten minutes after we left.

Being in the opening-night audience for a movie called *Star Wars* has turned RJ into an enthusiastic supporter of the—as he calls it— "Juice the Time Machine" project. While he and Iffy take detailed measurements of the chaser and the power slot, I check on my sister, and am surprised to find her sitting up, a book in her hand.

"When did you wake?" I ask.

"A few minutes ago."

I sit on the bed beside her and touch her forehead, happy to find it cool. "How are you feeling?"

"Okay."

"Tired?"

"I've been sleeping all day."

"I'll bet you're hungry."

Her eyes light up. "Yes. Very. How about a hamburger?"

I made the mistake of letting Iffy pick up a hamburger for Ellie one night, and now my sister can't get enough of them.

"I'm thinking soup tonight."

She grimaces. "I don't want soup."

Knowing even if I win this argument, I'll lose, I say, "I'll see what we have."

I tilt my head and read the title off the spine of her book. *Oliver Twist.* Charles Dickens. He was a writer in our time line, too, though his canon of work is different than it is in Iffy's world. Ellie likes reading this version of him better, she's told me. Even though his stories are more than 150 years old, she says there are things about them that remind her of home and the friends she will never see again. These are the same friends who stopped visiting her as she grew more and more sick, but Ellie doesn't know this. That occurred to the version of her I watched die when I was still a boy. I grabbed this Ellie before her friends turned their backs on her.

"Where did you go?" she asks as I stand up again.

"Go?"

"Someone was knocking on the door. I went to check, and you and Iffy and her friend were gone."

"Did you open it?" I ask, instantly concerned. When she is here alone she is, under no circumstances, supposed to talk to anyone.

She shakes her head. "Just peeked out the window."

"Who was it?"

"I don't know. By the time I looked, no one was there."

With the exception of Iffy, who has a key, and this evening, RJ, the only visitors we usually get are either our landlord, Mr. Castor, or people trying to sell us something. I assume it must have been one or the other, though my sense of unease does not completely disappear.

"You didn't answer my question," she says.

"We took a quick trip."

"Back?"

"A few years."

Ellie still struggles with the idea that I jump through time. The only trips she has taken with me were the jumps we made when I brought her here, and she was basically unconscious through all of them. But she realizes that the world here is completely different than the one we were born into, and she can't ignore that the brother who had once been two years younger than she is now five years older. It's actually surprising that she hasn't had a mental breakdown. Thankfully, she's only fourteen and still has a bit of wonder about the world.

"Let me go see what I can whip up for dinner."

"No soup," she says.

"No soup," I agree.

When I return to the other room, RJ is looking over several pages of notes.

"How's it going?" I ask.

He looks up, surprised. "Great. You wouldn't consider letting me open it up, would you? I'll be very careful."

"No way."

While I've opened one of the smaller interior cavities to disconnect my chaser's companion function, I've never opened the main area. And with the very real possibility that this is the last chaser in existence, I wouldn't want anyone else to do it either, unless there was absolutely no other choice.

"Figured as much," he said. "It's okay. I have a couple ideas that might do the trick. We'll have to do a little testing, though."

I frown. This is treading into the same waters as opening the box.

Before I can respond, though, he says, "Don't worry. Nothing invasive. I just need to check power levels and make sure we're sending the right type of electricity in so that we don't fry any circuits. I assume it uses DC, but who knows? Don't suppose you'd be open to bringing it by the lab at school? They've got everything I need there."

"I'd rather we do what needs to be done here." I can't chance others getting curious about what RJ is working on.

"You're not making this easy, are you?" He thinks for a moment. "Give me a couple days to see what I can come up with."

"Sure," Iffy says. "Call me when you're ready, and we'll set up a time to meet again."

For months, the weight of the chaser's diminishing power problem has been sitting squarely on my shoulders, but now, at least for the moment, it's almost gone. So it's with relief that I offer him my hand. "Thank you."

"Thank *you*," he says, smiling broadly. "'May you live in interesting times.' Sure fits, doesn't it?"

I cock my head. "What?"

"It's something a friend told me once. Said it's some kind of Korean or Chinese curse. I can't remember what. It doesn't sound like a curse to me." He nods at the chaser. "And with that, man, you get to live in multiple interesting times."

His words are truer than he even realizes.

He starts to turn for the door, but then stops. "Oh, I'll, um, probably need to get some parts. They might not be cheap. And, well . . ." He points a thumb at himself. "Student."

"Of course. How much do you think you need?"

He considers the question for a moment and then says, "A few hundred?"

"Wait here."

I go into my room and open the safe I keep in my closet. It's where I put the chaser when I'm not using it. It's also where I keep some of the cash I've collected on hand. Usually there's between $5,000 and $10,000, but I've recently had another bill from Ellie's doctors, and at the moment there's only $1,800.

I pull out ten one-hundred-dollar bills and return to the other room. "If you need more than this, let me know," I say, handing the money to RJ.

His eyes widen when he sees how much it is. "This should be more than enough. I'll bring you receipts and change."

"Don't worry about it. Whatever you don't spend, you can keep."

"I can't do that," he says uneasily.

"We're not asking you to do this for free. Keep the money."

"You're sure?"

"I'm sure."

"Thanks, man." He walks over to the door, but hesitates before opening it. "So, um, if we can power that thing up, any chance we might be able to go back and watch an Apollo launch?"

"If you fix the charging problem, I'll take you *anywhere* you want."

CHAPTER THREE

I would rather not use the chaser again until RJ's given us a working charger, but the lack of adequate cash in the safe means it's time to go on another collection run.

Over the past few months, we've created a long list of potential "donors" by searching through newspaper databases and online archived news footage. Each entry has been chosen carefully, but none are without their dangers.

The list is broken up into groups based on how much cash I should expect to find. The higher on the list, the larger the potential haul. To this point, I've stuck to the lower half, with the occasional venture near the middle, but today I'm selecting a name from the top five. In the event that something goes wrong with RJ's attempts to alleviate the chaser's power problem, it makes sense to stockpile enough money to cover Ellie's upcoming medical bills and the rent through the end of the year.

Exhausted from a day that has been stretched even longer than normal due to our trips with RJ, and knowing that my task ahead will require my total focus, I decide it's best if we wait until morning and get some sleep first.

◆ ◆ ◆

Upon waking, I pack my satchel with the items I think I'll need, grab some clothes, and then head into the bathroom for a shower. Moderately refreshed, I grab my satchel and carry it over to the closet. Along with the standard med-kit and notebook I usually take on a mission, I add in a few specialized items I think I'm going to need and then head out into the living room.

There, Iffy gives me the once-over. "You might want to change shirts. Something with a crew neck."

I'm currently wearing a dark gray, V-neck T-shirt, which, apparently, will stand out in the year we're headed to.

After I change, I check in on Ellie and am happy to see that she's sound asleep. Again, I'm not concerned about leaving her alone. While the trip might take several hours, we'll be gone from our home time no more than a minute.

Back in the living room, I make sure my new T-shirt meets with Iffy's approval and then pick up the chaser. "Ready?"

She puts her arms around me. "Ready."

◆ ◆ ◆

The year is 1998, and I am walking through a building in Tampa, Florida, that is under construction. I've left Iffy in 1996, where she will be safe from any shifts in the time line if something goes drastically wrong. I wish we could bring Ellie with us, too, but I don't want to do anything that might affect her recovery, so to prevent any time line problems, we never tell her specifically where we go or what we will be doing.

In exactly six years, two months, and seventeen days from this moment, a joint task force of federal and local law enforcement officials will surround this building. A shoot-out will result in the deaths of two police officers and seven of the gunmen inside. The remaining four occupants will be arrested. In the days that follow, their boss, Victor Munoz—who, until then, had been running a very successful drug distribution operation—will flee the country and spend the following five years fighting extradition from Guatemala. Ultimately, he will be unsuccessful.

I witnessed the shoot-out already and watched Munoz sneak away from his house as he began his journey out of the country. The latter was unnecessary on my part, but the historian in me is ever curious, and sometimes I just can't help wanting to see things for myself.

I am back on task now, though.

It is the middle of the night, and there is no construction crew on-site. There is, however, a solitary guard stationed in a hut by the gate of the temporary fence surrounding the property. Periodically he walks through the building to fulfill his duties, but I already know his schedule. I watched each time he left on his rounds and documented them in my notebook. He will not be venturing out of his hut again for another twenty-three minutes, more than enough time for me to do what I need to do.

While the outer walls of the building have already gone up, most of the rooms inside have only been framed out. I draw a rough map of each floor in my notebook.

The largest rooms are on the third level and will eventually be accessed by a hidden elevator at the back of the building. From the newspaper stories that Iffy discovered detailing the raid in 2004, I know these are the rooms in which the illegal product will arrive in bulk and be prepared for distribution.

The fifth floor is the one I'm most interested in, and part of me wants to rush right there. It's the floor where the money will be counted and where Munoz's private office will be located. But information is the key. One small detail could be the difference between my success and my never going home again, and for that reason I take my time on each of the lower four floors before finally making my way to the top.

Those same newspaper articles that described the workrooms noted that the building contained a safe, but though Iffy and I searched through everything we could find, we never discovered a mention of its exact location. Logically, it will be on this top floor, too, so I search for anything that might indicate where its future home will be.

Outside the space that will become Munoz's office is a long room. If I had to guess, this will be where the money is counted. In addition to the doorway into the boss's office, there are two others. One leads to the central hallway, while the other opens into what will either become a small office or a large closet. Off this room is yet another, even smaller, space—three feet deep by four wide. Unlike elsewhere in the building, the floor of this tiny alcove has been reinforced and stands a good three inches above those in the other rooms. Clearly, it's intended to hold something heavy.

The safe. What else could it be? It's easy enough for me to check for sure, however.

I pull out my chaser, use the calculator to determine the location number for the exact spot I am now standing, and store it in the machine's memory. I then call up the locator for a hidden position a block away from the building and set the time for a forward jump to exactly 3:00 a.m. three months from now.

After checking my notes and satisfying myself that I've collected everything I need, I hit the go button.

◆ ◆ ◆

Iffy once showed me an old movie called *The Time Machine*, in which images of the world whip by as the traveler moves forward or backward through time.

What a nightmare that would be. If that happened to me every time I traveled, I would squeeze my eyes shut for the whole trip. Thankfully, the only thing I see is a gray mist or nothing at all.

The street is quiet when I arrive. I walk silently to a position from where I can see Munoz's building. The construction fence still surrounds the property, but the building itself appears to be almost done. I look for lights in the windows but see none. Just to be safe, I walk around the block and check the other side. The only illumination is the flicker of a television set in the guard's hut. I can see the man on duty sitting in front of it, and from his profile am pretty sure it is the same guy I saw twenty minutes earlier or, from his perspective, three months before.

I make a few quick hops to check when he goes on his rounds and then select the location number of the room on the fifth floor and jump there.

Turning on the flashlight on my phone, I think I've made an error. The reinforced space that should be right in front of me is not there. In its place is a painted wall. After I softly rap on it and hear the echo of an open space beyond, I run my fingers up the two strips of molding that appear to parallel the edges of the hidden space. About three quarters of the way up the molding on the left side, a small piece moves a fraction of an inch sideways as my hand touches it. When I push the segment farther, the wall suddenly swings out.

I shine my light into the opening and find—surprise, surprise— a large metal safe sitting on the raised floor.

My next jump takes me six months forward to late spring, 1999, and back on the street, where I can first safely check the building. The fence is gone, and while there are a few lights on inside, the top two floors are dark. A second jump, and I'm once more inside the storage room.

A metal door now shuts off the main entrance to the room; it is secured by multiple locks, while heavy-duty metal shelves sit along the walls. Each shelf is filled with shoe box–size plastic-wrapped packages.

I try not to think about what the bundles must hold, but it's impossible. I don't need any research to tell me that over the next several years, people will become addicted and many will die because of the drugs passing through this place. My rewinder training would instruct me to just let it go, but I don't work for the Upjohn Institute anymore, and, especially in cases such as this, I am more than willing to operate under a modified set of rules. The drugs, however, are something I can deal with later. Right now it's the cash that's important.

After opening the false wall and revealing the safe, I mount the tiny camera I've brought with me from 2015 inside the top of the doorframe. The device is motion-activated and has a battery that— as long as it isn't in constant use—should last about three days. The elevated position isn't the greatest, but putting it anywhere else will increase the chance of its discovery. I'll just have to make it work.

My next jump takes me to the street again, three nights later. When all looks quiet, I return to the storage room. Many of the plastic-wrapped packages are gone, further deepening my hatred of Munoz's operation.

I open the secret panel and am happy to see my camera is still there. On an empty shelf, I set up my laptop computer and hook the camera into it. There are four video clips, each of the same man opening the safe. In two of the clips, he blocks my view, but the other two are clear. Well, relatively anyway. The angle of the shot means that I'm seeing only the top of the dial, not the actual number of the combination, which, in this case, lines up with a mark on the right side. But I can use the number I do see as my guide, and soon the safe is open.

As I hoped, it holds considerably more cash than I've come across on previous missions. Before, my record take for a single trip was around $9,000. From the stacks of bills in front of me, I know I will shatter that number.

I pull out a balled-up duffel bag, the last extra item I'd included in my satchel, and start stuffing money into it as fast as I can.

It is nearly three quarters full when I hear a key slip into one of the locks on the main door. I suck in a surprised breath and momentarily freeze. I was so sure I would be undisturbed.

My heart racing, I decide to forgo the remaining cash. I zip up the duffel and grab my chaser. As I am reselecting the location and date for the very first place I went after leaving my apartment, the final dead bolt slips free, and the door swings open.

It's Munoz himself. I recognize him from the newspaper articles. Even though he is clearly startled by my presence, it doesn't delay him from reaching for what I assume is a gun. Before he can draw it, however, I disappear.

◆　◆　◆

I arrive just a block away from where I was moments before, at almost the exact same time of night, only instead of June 12, 1999, it is July 17, 1996, and on the lot where Munoz's building will be erected is a rundown house that has sat there through much of the twentieth century.

"How did it go?"

Iffy stands right where I left her. Though she is well aware that I have done much in the time I've been gone, from her perspective I left only moments ago.

I hand her the duffel bag. "Munoz came in before I could fill it all the way."

"Didn't you do a check first?" she asks, not hiding her concern.

"The top floors were dark. I thought no one was there."

She looks me up and down. "Are you all right? Did he hurt you?"

"I'm fine," I say, though my nerves are still on edge. It was the closest call I've had on one of these missions. "Let's get this over with and go home."

She wraps her arms around me, and we jump forward to January 20, 1999, a mere few weeks after Munoz's drug operation has moved into its new quarters. Pay phones are much easier to find here than they will be in 2015. The one we locate is in front of a closed liquor store and is covered in stickers and scratches. Thankfully, though, when I pick up the receiver, there's still a dial tone.

From my experience on previous money-gathering trips, I know the call I'm about to make doesn't need a coin. I also know this is the moment I'm about to once again break the institute's number one rule: never knowingly alter the past. Of course, this won't be even close to my largest transgression. While my actions will cause changes to the time line, it's unlikely any ripple will affect my or Iffy's future life in California.

Well, there *would* be one exception if I had left Iffy in 2015. In that case when I returned, she'd have no memory of where I had gone or why. A small change, perhaps, but who knows how it might affect our relationship? That's why I always bring her along and leave her a few years farther in the past while I work, just to be safe.

The line rings several times before a woman answers, "Nine-one-one, what's your emergency?"

I give her the address of Munoz's building and tell her about the drugs and the money before hanging up. Iffy and I then jump home.

Before I even move, she grabs her laptop from me and plops down on the couch. After a minute, she smiles. "It worked."

She turns the screen so I can see the news article she's located.

"Munoz and his men were taken into custody three weeks after the phone call," she says. "He was convicted and sentenced to thirty years in prison. Which means he's still behind bars."

This was but a minor blip on the current time line, but a change nonetheless. The six-plus years Munoz would have remained in business had he not been arrested have now never happened. I'm not fool enough to believe my actions put a big dent in the central Florida drug scene, but I am hopeful that a few people might have been helped.

Iffy opens the duffel bag and counts the money. When she's through, she says, "Seventy-nine thousand, three hundred and forty."

I definitely shattered the record.

Here's where stealing from criminals and changing time lines work well together. The money I've taken from Munoz's safe was now never there in the first place. He was already in jail, his operation dead, by the date I popped into his drug closet. Yes, I know, it messes with your mind. All you need to remember is that *I* am the constant. It's the path of the traveler that must be followed. When I took the cash, the old time line still existed, and when I made the call that changed Munoz's future, the money was already in my possession, so it didn't just disappear. It does mean that each bill I've taken has a duplicate out there somewhere, but it's unlikely to cause us a problem.

Iffy and I have talked about other ways of increasing the amount of money we have, such as depositing everything in a bank several years in the past so that by now it will have earned considerable interest, or even traveling back and investing in stocks that we know will do well over time. But the truth is, I know very little about finance, especially here, and worry that some detail will be missed that will expose us, so taking these steps makes me uncomfortable. I grew up at the bottom of the caste system in my world, where saving money, let alone investing it, was never an option. Perhaps someday we'll do it, but for now I'm satisfied with putting the cash we collect—cautiously and not all at once, of course—in a bank here in 2015.

CHAPTER FOUR

The next morning RJ calls Iffy and says he has a few things he'd like to try out and will be here in the evening. My impatience for his return makes the day drag on forever. It doesn't help that he still hasn't arrived when the sun begins to set.

Iffy and Ellie are on the couch watching some kind of drama on the television. I try to follow along, but my attention is on the breezeway outside our front door as I wait for the sound of footsteps and the first hint of a knock.

"Maybe you should call him," I say to Iffy. "What if something happened?"

Without taking her eyes off the screen, she says, "He'll be here when he gets here."

"You said early evening. It's not *early* anymore."

"Would you two be quiet?" Ellie says. "I can't hear."

Iffy whispers, "I never said 'early.'"

I take a breath and then try to concentrate on the television, but the images are making no more sense to me now than they were a few moments earlier, so I push off the couch and head for the door.

"Where are you going?" Iffy asks.

"For a walk." I grab my phone off the dining table. "If I'm not back before he gets here, call me."

"Shhh!" Ellie says.

Stepping out of the apartment, I look around, hoping I'll see RJ walking toward our door, but there's no one else there. I head over to the stairs and down to ground level, then walk out to the street.

The western sky holds only a hint of deep orange as it fights its losing battle against the coming night. I scan the street, once more looking for RJ and once more not seeing him. Disappointed and anxious, I head west toward the beach.

While there are still a few open spaces here and there along the curb, most of the spots have been claimed for the night. If RJ doesn't arrive soon, he'll be forced to park several blocks away.

I pick up my pace and tell myself not to think about RJ or why he's running late or where he'll park his car. To give my mind something else to do, I focus on the vehicles I'm passing and attempt to determine the make and model of each just from sight. This is one of the subjects I've been recently studying. Cars, I have found, are very important to the people here in San Diego. So, gaining more understanding of the automobile culture will, I hope, help in my continuing quest to understand this world. Unfortunately, I'm still very bad at the identification game, and at best succeed in recognizing only one or two cars out of every ten.

I've made it down four of the six blocks that separate my apartment from the beach when Iffy calls to let me know RJ has arrived.

"I'll be right there," I tell her as I whip around and start jogging back the way I came.

When I'm only half a block from our place, movement in a parked car just ahead catches my eye. At first I think I must have been mistaken, but as I near, I notice that a man is in the driver's seat, and am thinking he probably created the movement I saw. I assume he's getting ready to start his car and leave, but my caution makes me take a longer look at the driver as I go by. Unfortunately, it's too dark to see anything more than his shadowy form, but since he doesn't jump out and try to grab me, I assume he's not a threat and hurry on to my building.

When I enter the apartment, the others are gathered in the dining area. Two hard-sided suitcases sit on the table—one large and one small, like a fat briefcase. RJ has the larger one open and is pulling out wires and small metal boxes.

When he sees me, he says, "Where's the chasing machine?"

"Not a chasing machine, a chaser," I say.

"Chaser, right. You have it?"

I head into my bedroom.

The combination I use for the safe is the date I was accepted into the Upjohn Institute. It's one I'll never forget. While I was in training, I thought that day had changed everything for the good. I'm not so sure about good or even bad, but I do know it *did* change everything, and not only for me, but for everyone.

The chaser sits in a cloth-lined cubbyhole at the top of the safe. In the large section below it are the stacks of cash we took from Munoz. I grab the device, shut the safe, and return to the others.

The thick briefcase is now also open, but instead of containing more bits and pieces of electronics, it holds tools. There are movable dividers, with slots on each side filled with screwdrivers and wrenches and the like. There are also several electronic devices with meters on the front. One of the devices is sitting on the table next to the items RJ had removed from the other case.

"Ah, great." RJ extends his hands toward me. "May I?"

I touch the spot that unlocks the lid and then give him the device. "Be careful."

"Yeah, yeah. Don't worry."

Like he did at our first meeting, he examines every inch of it. When he is through, he sets it down and picks up the black box with the meter on it. There are two wires leading out of it, each ending in a metal tip.

When he starts to move the tips toward the power socket on the chaser, I say, "That's not going to hurt anything, is it?"

"This? No. It only receives. Doesn't emit anything."

Iffy slips her hand into mine and gives me a squeeze. Her message is loud and clear. We asked for RJ's help, and we should let him do what he needs to do.

For the next several minutes, we watch him take measurements with the meter and write things down in a black-covered notebook. When he finally finishes, he picks up a two-inch-square, clear plastic pouch that is sitting next to the pile of wires. Inside are several small metal items. He opens the top of the pouch and pours the pieces into his hand.

"If I'd had some modeling clay with me last time, I would have taken an impression," he tells us. "But since I didn't, I had to make some guesses."

I'm not sure what he's talking about until he takes one of the metal pieces and tries to fit it into the chaser's power socket. He eventually works his way through each piece and then drops all but one back into the bag. He holds up the remaining piece for us to see.

"It's not perfect and I'm not sure if it's going to work, but it's in the right ballpark," he says.

He demonstrates by placing the selected connector into the socket. It fits well enough, but does appear to be a bit loose.

"Shall we give it a go?" he asks me.

"I don't know. You're the expert."

He laughs. "That was rhetorical. Of course, we're going to try it." He sorts through the wires and picks one out. "This is going to take a few minutes. Any chance I can get a Coke or something?"

"I'll get it," Ellie says.

In my concern for getting the chaser powered up, I forgot that my sister is also here. The brightness in her voice surprises me, and I'm equally taken aback by the way she seems to almost drift into the kitchen. When she returns a few minutes later, she's holding a soft drink can.

With a smile that seems almost hopeful, she holds the can out to RJ and says, "We only have 7-Up. Is that okay?"

"Better than nothing," he says, taking it from her with only a quick glance.

It takes me a moment before I realize what's going on. My fourteen-year-old sister is infatuated with Iffy's nineteen-year-old friend. I don't even know how to react to this. Should I be the disinterested brother or the overprotective parent?

RJ seems to barely even notice her, which is a relief and yet somehow annoying. Yes, she is *way* too young for him, but doesn't he find her attractive? She has always looked older than her age, and though my opinion might be biased, I think few would disagree that she's beautiful.

In a moment of clarity, I mentally slap myself. What am I thinking? She's my sister. I'm *glad* RJ isn't paying her attention.

I consider suggesting that she should go lie down for a bit, but I'm pretty sure she'll just ignore me. I decide to let her have her little fantasy. As long as it stays only in her head, where's the harm?

I force myself to focus back on what RJ is doing.

Using some melted metal—soldering, he calls it—he attaches one end of the wire to the special connector, and does the same with a different type of connector to the other end. This then is all hooked into a box about the same size as a small tin of mints, with a dial on top.

As he grabs the end of the wire with the connector that fits into the chaser, he says, "Do you know what the power level is at right now?"

I turn on the chaser's display screen and point to the spot where the number is shown. "Forty-six point seven three percent."

"Okay, moment of truth."

He slots the connector into the chaser and looks at the display.

"Is that it?" I ask.

"We'll know soon enough."

All four of us stare at the battery level number. For nearly a minute nothing happens, then the number suddenly jumps to 47.19.

"It works!" Iffy says.

I'm numb and relieved and excited all at once.

RJ, on the other hand, looks annoyed. He keeps his gaze on the power number until it changes again, this time to 47.51, and then turns on the screen of the rectangular device at the other end of the wire chain.

Whatever he sees there increases the depth of his frown.

"You did it," I say. "It's working. The level's going up."

"Give me a moment."

He turns the dial on the small box between the two wires, and looks back at the chaser's display. The power number stays at 47.51 for a few more moments and then changes to 47.83. He stares at it until it changes a half minute later to 48.07.

He turns the dial again and once more watches the display. The number increases in a similar pattern to what it's been doing to this point. Another turn of the dial doesn't seem to change anything, including RJ's frown.

"What's wrong?" Iffy asks.

He unplugs the wire from the chaser. "It's the connector. I just don't have it right."

"But it's charging," I counter.

"Yeah, but it should be doing it a lot faster. I started with a low power input, but even when I pushed it to the highest my rig can handle, it didn't make a difference. The loose connector is making it take forever." He picks up the rectangular device at the other end of the wire and then scoffs. "And then there's the fact that the one and a third percent increase ate up nearly three times that from my power source. We'd have to recharge this battery again at least once just to get your chasing machine up to one hundred percent. Not very efficient."

"But we *can* charge it."

"I can do better," he says. "This time I brought clay. I'll make an imprint and build a better connector. Might be a couple days before I'm ready to come back."

He disconnects everything and starts putting it all back in the suitcase.

"Hold on," I say. "Can't we use that in the meantime?"

"This is just a prototype. I'll make the real thing sturdier and easier to carry around." He thinks for a moment and then shrugs. "But you're paying the bills, and if you want to use this until then, have at it."

He pulls out the items that make up the prototype device and reconnects them. When he's done he picks up the rectangular battery.

"Two ways of charging this. You can plug it into the wall with this." He hunts around in the large suitcase and pulls out an adapter. "But I was also thinking you might find yourself someplace where conventional power's not available. You know, when you . . ." He pauses and shoots a glance at Ellie, then points behind his back a few times.

It takes Iffy and me a moment to realize he means travel into the past.

"RJ, she's Denny's sister," Iffy says. "His *older* sister. So she's clued in on the time travel thing."

He looks at Ellie and then at me and then back at Ellie. "How old are you?"

She looks reluctant to tell him, but finally whispers, "Fourteen."

He turns to me. "And you?"

"Nineteen."

He looks between us again before focusing back on me. "She's your older sister?"

I nod. "By two years."

"That's messed up, man."

He doesn't know the half of it. "You were saying there's another way to charge the battery?"

"Right. Uh, so this side"—he turns the battery over so we are looking at the side opposite the display screen—"is covered with small solar cells. Just set it in direct sunlight, and it'll charge up. Not nearly as fast as plugging it in will, but when you don't have that option, it'll do the job for you."

"This is genius," I say, meaning it.

A way to charge a chaser via the sun? It's a wonder someone at the institute hadn't thought of that. Of course, I hadn't even heard of solar power until I came here. While some form of that technology might have existed in my world, I never saw evidence of it at the institute, and it certainly never trickled down to us in caste Eight.

"Thanks," RJ says, a sheepish smile on his lips. He hands me the charger. "Be careful. It's just thrown together and not built to last."

He puts the rest of his stuff away and takes an impression of the chaser's power socket with a small bit of clay from his tool kit.

"I'll let you know when I have it ready," he says and heads for the door.

"Good-bye. Nice meeting you," Ellie says.

RJ pauses long enough to turn and say, "Yeah. Same." And then leaves.

Both Iffy and I turn and look at my sister, our eyebrows raised.

Her expression all innocent, Ellie says, "What?"

CHAPTER FIVE

The next morning I accompany Ellie to an appointment at the hospital while Iffy runs some errands for her mother.

It's a quick visit, Dr. Roseth wanting to make sure she isn't having any complications from the latest treatment she received. Like the past handful of times we've seen him, he's very pleased with her progress, and while he doesn't come out and actually say it, I get the strong sense he's convinced she's going to beat the disease.

This experience is completely different than when she was sick in our original time line. I was twelve when the cancer had begun to affect her, and just a year older when it had taken her life. As lowly members of caste Eight in a North America still ruled by the British, proper medical care was not an option for us. The truth is, though, I have a feeling that even if we'd been born into the nobility, the empire's doctors still wouldn't have been able to save her. There was an inertia in our old world that throttled progress, much like the dial throttles the power output on RJ's charger, and I don't think medicine had come anywhere near as far there as it has here.

I am feeling particularly optimistic as Ellie and I leave the hospital and take the bus to the restaurant where we will be meeting

Iffy for lunch. The two things I've been most worried about are both moving in positive directions—Ellie, of course, and the power situation of my chaser. The latter is currently showing a battery level of 76.44 percent after I left it hooked to RJ's charger all night. Even if RJ isn't able to make a better connector, the problem has been solved.

The restaurant in the Gaslamp Quarter of downtown San Diego has become a favorite of mine, and Iffy is waiting outside when we arrive.

"So?" she asks Ellie.

"He said I'm on track. I just need to keep doing what I'm doing."

"That's great." Iffy hugs my sister and then me.

The hostess offers us our choice of tables, either on the front patio or inside. While Ellie wants to sit in the sunlight, I worry that the warm day will drain her too much so, much to her disappointment, we take a place in the middle of the dining area.

I can't remember the last time I felt as relaxed as I do now. The conversation as we eat focuses mainly on things Ellie wants to do when she's finally given a clean bill of health—places she wants to go, foods she wants to eat, and activities she wants to try. She's obviously been doing some research of her own about this world, because it's actually quite a list. As little as three weeks ago, I would have steered the conversation in another direction, fearing we would otherwise be tempting fate. But it appears fate has decided to give us a winning hand, and I now see no harm in letting her dream a little.

I'm feeling so good when we leave that I almost overlook the gray-suited man from the library sitting at a patio table. His presence is such a surprise that I can't help but stare at him for a few seconds before grabbing Iffy's arm and putting a hand on Ellie's back so that I can hurry them out to the sidewalk.

"What's wrong?" Iffy asks.

I say nothing until we walk around the corner and are no longer in the man's line of sight. "It's him."

"Him who?" Ellie asks.

I hesitate. My sister knows nothing about the man shadowing me, and though I don't want to unduly worry her, it would be better if she knew the truth. "A guy I think is following me."

"What?"

Iffy asks, "Where was he?"

"Sitting outside the restaurant."

Ellie starts to turn like she's going to head back to the corner and take a look, but I gently grab her arm and stop her. "Why don't you two go home?" I say. "I'm going to figure out who he is."

Ellie looks worried. "Is that a good idea? What if he catches you?"

"He'll never even know I'm around."

Iffy is trying to act unconcerned, but I can't miss the unease in her eyes. I kiss her and whisper in her ear, "It'll be fine. I'll be home before you are."

"You'd better be."

While I earlier wrote off seeing the man at the library as a coincidence, I realize now that was a mistake. His presence at the restaurant cannot merely have happened by chance. He's tracking me.

So it's time I return the favor.

I find a spot behind a dumpster where no one can see me and set my chaser for a backward jump of seventy minutes. When I reappear there is a slight change in the angle of the sunlight and some of the cars parked along the street are different, but otherwise everything is exactly the same as when I initiated the journey.

I make my way to a sandwich shop that sits almost directly across the road from the restaurant where we ate. I purchase a bottle of water and a bag of chips and then sit at one of the tables at the front window.

Nine minutes later, I see Iffy arrive, and four minutes after that, Ellie and the earlier version of me join her. There was a time when seeing myself like this was unnerving, but I've had plenty of interaction with other Dennys since then, and it doesn't faze me anymore.

Thirty seconds later, I spot the man coming down the street from the same direction Ellie and I just did. He pauses a couple of storefronts away until the three of us go inside the restaurant and then begins walking.

I watch as he is shown to the outside table where I will later spot him. When he's occupied giving his order to the waitress, I slip out of the sandwich shop and find another quiet spot.

This time I jump back fifteen minutes and position myself near the entrance to a liquor store, a half block from the bus stop Ellie and the earlier me will arrive at. I know the man wasn't on the bus with us. Even in my good mood, I didn't neglect to check my surroundings, and I'm sure I would have seen him. But he must have been following us.

If he is from the institute, he would be using rewinder techniques and could very well already be somewhere nearby waiting for our bus to get there. I carefully scan the road but see no sign of him, so as the bus finally approaches, I focus on the vehicles behind it.

There. He's in a sedan two cars back.

As soon as the bus pulls away and reveals Ellie and me walking down the sidewalk, the sedan swerves into the spot where the bus had been and pauses. Most of the parking spots along the street are filled, but at the curb not far from where I'm watching everything, a car is pulling out. The man notices this, too, and is starting to swing his vehicle into a U-turn that will bring him over here.

I duck inside the liquor store and pretend to be interested in the magazine rack next to the window. As soon as the man parks, he jumps out and jogs across the street after my sister and the earlier me. When he reaches the corner, he stops and looks down the road toward the restaurant, just like I'd seen him do when I was in the sandwich shop. Once he disappears, I exit the store and approach his car.

Letters on the back spell out LEXUS. This is a luxury brand belonging to one of the large carmakers, but I don't recall which.

I pause momentarily as a memory flashes in my mind. Last night, when I went out for my walk, there was something . . .

A car, with a man sitting in it. Right. I'd forgotten about that. His vehicle was a nice sedan. I didn't check the brand, but an uncomfortable feeling on the back of my neck is telling me I'm looking at the same car now.

Who *is* this guy?

Looking through the windows, I spot three square white boxes in the backseat, and a toppled stack of loose paper in the well where a passenger's feet would go. A gym bag and several files sit in the front passenger seat, while on the floor are several crumpled-up paper sacks from various fast-food establishments.

I try the door, but it's locked. Unfortunate. I was hoping I could learn his name from the vehicle's identification papers. I could time hop inside, but the car is exposed and I can't chance someone seeing me suddenly appear in the front seat. There is another way, though, a method I've utilized several times on my missions to obtain more money. I use my mobile phone to take a photograph of the Lexus's license plate and then find an empty alley.

My jump takes me into the office of Mason Evans, a supervisor at the Department of Motor Vehicles facility in the town of Oceanside. I've arrived in the middle of the previous night, and, as expected, am alone. Mr. Evans's office has become my go-to destination for vehicle information. After searching around several bureaus, I've selected his for two reasons: the smaller town means less security than in San Diego or Los Angeles, and most importantly, Mr. Evans keeps his login password on a piece of paper taped underneath his keyboard.

Moments after I input the Lexus's license plate number, I am presented with the name Vincent Kane and an address not in San Diego, as I'd hoped, but in Los Angeles. To be sure I have the right person, I look up Kane's driver's license information and am presented with a picture of my unwanted shadow. The address listed matches the one on the car registration.

I've seen Kane in San Diego for a few weeks now, and it makes me wonder if he's made a move south but has not yet reported a change of address. That would complicate my task. If I'm going to find out why he's so interested in me without tipping him off, I need to get inside his home and see what I can learn. If that place is now in San Diego, I'll need to follow him to find it, a task far from easy, even with my chaser.

The logical move is to check out the Los Angeles address first.

When the world rematerializes around me, I am standing on a hiking trail in Griffith Park, with the city of Los Angeles sparkling in the night below me. The time difference between my last location and here is only five minutes, so it's still the early hours of morning.

The park is a few miles from Kane's address, but as I've been trained, I always choose a place I'm confident will be unoccupied for my initial arrival point. The home is located in an area just northwest of downtown that the map on my chaser tells me is called Myer Hills. But that map is of my old world. According to the one on the smartphone, here the place is referred to as Echo Park.

The quick route would be to follow Sunset Boulevard, but even at this hour there is traffic and my chance of being seen is too great. So I take a more circuitous route, making a series of what are called visual jumps—meaning I can actually see the place I'm jumping to before I hit go. Short hops, in other words, and safe. I pass through backyards and empty lots and quiet side streets. It takes me thirty actual minutes to get there, but I alternated between jumping forward and backward thirty seconds, so, by the clock, I arrive in Kane's neighborhood at basically the same time I left Griffith Park.

While I did spend a considerable amount of time in downtown Los Angeles several months ago when I first realized I'd changed the worlds, I have never been in this specific area before. It's a small valley bisected by a road called Echo Park Avenue. The home is near the east end of the valley on a street halfway up the north side.

As I approach, I see that it sits on a lot a good fifteen feet higher than the level of the road, and is reached via a stairway that runs up the side of the street-accessible garage. There's a mailbox at the bottom of the stairs—no name on it, only the house number.

I move to the other side of the street so I can actually see his place. Even then, it's only a partial view, but it's enough to see that the place is a two-story Spanish-style home. Like in the other homes in the immediate vicinity, I see no lights on inside.

Cautiously I return to the stairs and make my way up, then sneak through the small front yard to the house. Much to my relief, the night remains quiet. In my world, people often had small plaques mounted beside their front doors engraved with their family name. It would be nice if Iffy's world also embraced this practice. I would hate to jump inside and find that it is not Kane's home. I maintain an oddly stitched-together set of morals now, I guess, that includes it's okay to steal from criminals, that sometimes it's acceptable to enter someone else's personal property without permission and sometimes it's not, and, top of this list, it's okay to erase untold numbers of lives to be with the woman I've fallen for and to save my sister.

Yeah, there's a lot of gray area in my life.

One more jump puts me on the other side of the door, in a living room filled with old, overstuffed furniture. A large television sits on a cabinet against one wall, while mounted to another are shelves filled with books and framed photographs.

On the other side of the room is the opening to a hallway that appears to go all the way to the back of the house. I know I should probably check to make sure no one is there first, but the photos draw me over.

I turn on my phone's flashlight and narrow the beam with my hand so that no unnecessary illumination escapes. Immediately I can confirm that I have not made a mistake by coming here. In many of the pictures is the man who's been following me, meaning I can officially label him as Vincent Kane.

There are other people in the shots, too—friends, I suppose. There is an older couple who both, in differing ways, bear a resemblance to Kane. His parents most likely. In three of the shots is an even older woman, who is always accompanied by the woman I assume is Kane's mother. She looks as if she could be a hundred years old. I've never seen a face so wrinkled and worn, like it's long overstayed its welcome. Only her eyes, blazing with keen awareness between her aged lids, speak of a life not yet ready to give up.

The thing I take most from the pictures is that if the couple are indeed Kane's parents, then he was born in this world and is not, as I feared, another rewinder. While on the one hand that's a relief, on the other it begs the question why would a person from this time line be interested in me?

Hoping I will find my answer somewhere in this house, I begin searching.

The back hall leads to an open room that is part kitchen and part second living room. The furniture and television are newer than what's in the front room, leading me to believe this is the space Kane uses most. Along the back wall are several large windows, one of which appears to be able to slide open. Though it's too dark to see much of anything beyond them, light from a handful of homes on the hillside glows here and there. The view during the day must be beautiful.

The only thing of any real interest I find, though, is a note on the refrigerator door held in place by a "See Grand Canyon" magnet. On it is written the name *Vince*, followed by a phone number. And below this is what appears to be a schedule:

Monday – Lorna

Tuesday – Lorna

Wednesday – Theresa

Thursday – Theresa

Friday – Peggy

Saturday – Lorna

Sunday – Lorna

I have no idea what it could mean. The phone number, however, is the prize here. I take a picture of the note and then return to the front of the house and take the stairs to the second floor.

Along the upper hallway are five doors—two on either side and one at the far end. The two nearest me are closed. I leave them for now and check the ones that are open. The first I come to leads into a bathroom that—from the items I find on the counter—appears to be used by a woman.

The next open door is on the other side of the hall. Technically it's probably considered a bedroom, but it's been converted into an office and is cluttered with more of the white boxes I saw in the back of Kane's Lexus.

I remove the lid from one of them and find it stuffed with files. After a quick look through a couple of folders, I get the sense that Kane is involved in some kind of financial work.

This guess is confirmed when I find a business card in his desk with his name on it and the job title of: CERTIFIED PUBLIC ACCOUNTANT. There is no company name, and the address given is a post office box. It makes me think that it is likely Kane is self-employed. I pocket the card, and as I start to leave the room, I see a large, six-month calendar pinned to the wall. There are over two dozen dates circled. When I realize the day I saw Kane at the library is one of them, I try to recall all the other times I've noticed him. To the best of my recollection, every single one of those dates is circled. To say that realizing this is upsetting would be an understatement. But what troubles me even more is the fact that there are other dates marked for which I don't remember seeing him. Was he watching me those days, too?

Then I notice the outlier, and a shiver runs down my back. The marked date is more than three months before the other circles begin and has a very special significance to me.

April 4, the very day I returned to this world with Ellie.

The day I made Iffy's time line permanent.

He can't know that.

There's no way he can know that.

Stop! You've seen the pictures, I tell myself. *He's not a time traveler. There is no way he can know the importance of April 4.*

I take several breaths to calm down. While the other circled dates may or may not represent all the times our paths crossed, the April date must have nothing to do with—

I pause, staring at the calendar as an answer dawns on me. If the other dates are times he saw me, then maybe the same is true for the first one. *Maybe* he was in the park where I appeared with Ellie. To this point, I thought that our arrival had gone unseen, but there *were* others in the park. Many had come running to see if they could help when Ellie collapsed. Had he been in the crowd? Could that be what this is all about? He could have been freaked out by what he saw and searched until he found me again. And when he did, he started following me to see if I would disappear.

This possibility fits the facts, but while I want it to be true, it's still speculation. And it's always better to know for sure.

I exit the room and move to the one at the end of the hall.

The moment I step inside, I freeze. I'm in the master bedroom. A door off to my right leads to what I'm sure is an en suite bathroom. It's the bed, however, that's caught my attention, or more specifically, the shape of the single person lying on it.

When I'm sure there's been no change to the deep, rhythmic breathing I heard upon entry, I quietly move into the room until I'm close enough to see the sleeper's face.

It's Kane.

This is unexpected. In less than twelve hours, he will follow Ellie and me to our lunch with Iffy. Which probably means he will follow us first to the hospital and then to the restaurant. With the way morning traffic is in Los Angeles, he'll need to leave within a few hours to be able to do that. Add in the possibility that it was Kane I noticed parked on my street last night, and I would have thought he'd have found a hotel in San Diego. Now I'm wondering if he actually comes home every evening, even if just for a few hours. That's a lot of driving and doesn't make much sense.

Unfortunately, any search of his bedroom will have to be done when he's not here, so I go out as silently as I came in. I also ignore the two rooms with closed doors at the other end of the hall and add them to my "check next visit" list, which, for me, will be in only a few minutes.

I'm tempted to jump right into his living room midmorning, when I know he will be gone. But caution, as it almost always does, overrides this whim. There could be others sleeping behind the closed doors after all. I hop back out to the porch and then choose a spot in some bushes around the side of his house that can be seen only by someone standing a few feet away. I set my arrival time for 10:00 a.m. and jump.

When I pop back into the world, my eyes are closed to slits in anticipation of the morning sun. As soon as my irises adjust, I head toward the front of the house. Logically Kane can't be here and still make it to San Diego, where the earlier me will see him in a couple hours, so my hope is that the house is empty, but I'm stopped at the corner of the building by a voice coming from the front yard.

"Here we go. Lemonade, nice and cold." The speaker is a woman with an accent I believe is Hispanic.

She's obviously talking to someone. I wait for a second voice, but there's no reply. Kneeling down, I peek around the corner. A chair has been placed in the middle of the small front yard, and in it sits an old woman, a glass raised to her lips. I have only a partial angle on her profile, but it's enough to see that she's the same wrinkled woman from Kane's photographs. Standing beside her is a middle-aged Hispanic woman with shoulder-length dark hair. She's wearing a colorful shirt and a pair of white pants, and sees the world through brown plastic-framed glasses.

The older woman lowers the glass again and hands it to her companion. "Not sweet enough. More sugar."

"No more sugar," the Hispanic woman says. "It's not good for you. This is okay."

"More sugar."

"Mr. Kane would not want you to have more sugar. You know that."

"Do you see Vincent here? I don't."

"That doesn't matter."

"Lorna."

My eyebrow raises slightly. Lorna is one of the names on the schedule I found in the kitchen.

The Hispanic woman—Lorna—raises her free hand in surrender. "Okay, okay. More sugar. I'll be right back." She heads inside the house.

So the schedule is a list of . . . attendants? I think for a moment, trying to recall what this kind of person is referred to as here. Caregiver. That's it. The people on the list must be the ones who watch over the old woman while Kane is gone. Which must mean he comes home every night to take over.

Without looking, I reach for the wall to steady myself so that I can lean out and get a look at the front door, but I misjudge the distance and my palm knocks into it harder than I expect it to. The sound isn't loud, and when the old woman starts turning in her chair, I assume she's easing an ache, but she twists all the way around until she is looking directly at me. I hold as still as possible, hoping her ancient eyes are not strong enough to pick out the part of my head sticking around the house. Her blank expression seems to confirm this is the case at first, but then suddenly her lips curl in a smile and I can't help but think that it's aimed at me.

My hand automatically moves into my satchel and finds the combination of buttons that will trigger an emergency escape, but there's something about her face that keeps me from pushing anything yet. Maybe it's the intelligence burning in her eyes, or maybe it's the fact that I can see some of Kane in her. Whatever the case, I'm unable to figure it out before the groan of a hinge signals the door opening again.

The old woman turns back around as Lorna returns. I listen, sure that she is going to say something about seeing me, but instead she takes the glass, gives the lemonade another taste, and says, "Now, that's better."

I back out of sight and pull my chaser out. Instead of hitting the escape combination, I select the locator number for the living room of my apartment and a time that will put me there not long before Iffy and Ellie arrive home from lunch.

As much as I would like to conduct a more thorough search of Kane's home, I would be a fool to do so when someone else is here, which, from the looks of things, might be all the time.

The only thing I can do for now is go home.

CHAPTER SIX

As planned, I'm waiting in the apartment when Iffy and Ellie walk in. Immediately I notice dark circles under my sister's eyes. Though it isn't even midafternoon yet, it's been the busiest day Ellie's had in a while, and it's clearly taken a lot out of her. I mentally kick myself for adding the lunch onto our schedule. It was obviously a bad idea.

"Are you feeling okay?" I ask her.

"I'm fine," she says with more energy that I'm sure she feels. "Did you find out who the man was?"

"You don't look fine."

"I am. I swear. Just . . . a little tired is all."

"Then you should go lie down."

Frustrated, she says, "Denny. The man."

I take a breath, then nod. "Yes. I got a name."

"What is it?"

"Doesn't matter. You wouldn't know him."

"Well, of course, I wouldn't know him. But so what?"

I frown. "Vincent Kane. Happy?" I glance at Iffy. "The name familiar to you?"

She stares off for a moment, thinking, then says, "Never heard of him."

"So, who is he?" Ellie asks.

"Why don't we talk about it later? Right now I want you to get some rest."

"I don't need a rest."

"Oh, really? Then why are your eyelids half closed?"

"You're worse than dad."

I know our experiences with our father were not the same. Ellie was his favorite. Her death took whatever happiness was left in him with it. From that moment on, he and I were just doing time together. So from her point of view, there is some warmth in the accusation, but for me, it is damning.

After a few moments of awkward silence, she says, "Maybe I am a little tired. I think I will lie down for a few minutes."

The sudden tension I've been feeling ebbs as she starts walking toward the hallway. I know she realizes she's stepped across a line, but she doesn't fully understand why so it's easy enough for me to let it go.

Just before she disappears, she stops and looks back. "Thanks for lunch. That was fun."

I notice a brief flicker of excitement in her eyes. Most of her time is spent either in the apartment or at the hospital, so perhaps going somewhere new for lunch hasn't been such a mistake after all.

Once she's gone, I tell Iffy about my trip to Kane's house.

She is as unnerved as I am by the circled dates on his calendar, especially the one on April 4.

"And you're sure he's not one of your friends?"

Friends is not exactly the word I'd use to describe other time travelers, but I say, "He's not. There are pictures of him when he was young. He grew up here."

"So what's his deal then? Why is he interested in you?"

These are the same questions swirling around my mind, but I'm no closer to any answers now than I was at Kane's house.

"Can you stay with Ellie for a while?" I ask.

"Where are you going?"

"If I can't get into his house, maybe I can get into his car. There's got to be something there that will help us understand what he wants."

"You're not going to confront him, are you?"

"Of course not."

She stares at me, her eyes narrowing slightly.

"He'll never see me," I promise.

◆　◆　◆

I previously witnessed Kane arriving in the Gaslamp Quarter and following us to lunch. What I didn't check is what he did after we left. So I return to there, arriving in the same alley I used before, only closer to the time we finished eating.

I find a good spot where I can watch the action unnoticed and then wait. No more than ten minutes pass before I see Iffy, Ellie, and me coming around the corner. I observe the brief conversation where I tell them I've seen Kane—though at the time I didn't know his name. We then split, Iffy and Ellie heading for the bus stop, and Earlier Me hurrying over to the alley where I had arrived a few minutes ago.

To avoid any unnecessary conversations, I make sure I'm not seen by Earlier Me. He isn't off the street for more than thirty seconds when Kane strolls around the corner. About halfway down the block, my follower suddenly halts, his gaze focused on the bus stop where Iffy and Ellie are waiting. There are four other people standing near them, none of whom—as Kane's obviously just realized—are me.

He scans around, and even looks behind himself as if expecting to find me standing there. There's no missing his sense of panic, and I can't help but get a little pleasure from this.

A bus is approaching the stop. When Kane looks back toward Iffy and my sister, he notices it, too. This seems to only deepen his confusion. After a few seconds, though, he makes a decision. He takes one last look around before rushing across the street to his car.

To the honks of annoyed motorists, he makes a sweeping U-turn as soon as the bus has passed by and falls in behind it. I wait until they disappear and then make a jump back to the apartment, making sure to arrive several minutes before the version of me returning from Kane's house will get there.

As I've mentioned before, I've seen multiples of me many times, and have even interacted with them on occasion, but I find that unless absolutely necessary, it's best to avoid surprising myself. I head out to the street and make my way to a place where I can keep an eye on the bus stop where Iffy and Ellie will be arriving.

Before the bus even gets there, though, I see Kane's car. He passes the stop and then takes a parking spot almost directly across the street from my building. He sits in his car for a few moments before finally getting out. He looks left and right, his gaze even sweeping past my position, but I'm tucked in the shadows beside the entrance to another apartment building, making it impossible for him to pick me out. He then jogs across the road and disappears down the side of my building.

I check my watch. The girls won't be entering the apartment for another thirteen minutes. The walk from the bus stop will take only four minutes at most, meaning the bus won't be arriving for about nine. Depending on how long Kane is away from his vehicle, this might be my opportunity to search it. I keep an eye on the spot where he's disappeared, expecting him to return at any moment. So when the bus arrives without his reemergence, I'm curious as to what he's been doing.

I slink farther back into the entryway to prevent Iffy and Ellie from accidentally spotting me. When they're gone and Kane has still not returned, I decide to put off checking his car for the moment, and instead, find out what he's up to.

Avoiding the street, I pass all the way through the complex and the parking area in the back to the alley that runs behind all the buildings. Carefully, I move from place to place until I am only one structure from my building.

Kane had walked down the side of my building using the long driveway that serves our covered parking in back. Since it's still daytime, most of the slots are empty, making it easy for me to see that Kane isn't there.

Thinking he might be somewhere along the driveway, I slowly lean around the edge of the wall for a look. It's deserted. He must have gone through the back breezeway into the courtyard of my building; either that, or we've crossed paths and he's already back at his car.

As I step out of cover, intending to sneak over to the parking area of my complex, I catch movement at the top of my vision and hear a shoe scrape against something rough. Ducking back behind the building, I hear the thump of something heavy landing on the roof of my building's carport.

A few more scrapes followed by someone taking a deep breath and then what I assume are feet landing on asphalt. As the person begins jogging down the driveway toward the street, I allow myself to peek after him.

Kane.

He'd been on our roof. But why?

I watch him run across the street and out of sight. Using the chaser's calculator, I figure out a location number that will put me on the roof of my complex without having to climb, and touch go.

There are certain things a chaser does flawlessly, such as if your destination is at ground level but there's a surface that covers it—like a sidewalk or a road—the device will compensate for this, and you will arrive feet solidly placed. Where it has issues is with artificially elevated locations. If your location number is even just slightly off, you're in trouble. That's why getting the calculation right is so important.

In my rush to find out what Kane was up to, I've apparently made an error, and materialize two feet above the actual roof. Fortunately when I hit the white grainy surface, I'm able to keep from falling flat on my face by catching myself with a knee and a hand. And while my landing is loud, I'm above a unit rented by one of our neighbors who works during the day. So, in theory, my arrival and walking around should go unnoticed.

Still, I place my steps with care as I head over to the section of the roof above Ellie's and my place. It takes me only a moment to spot that there's something that shouldn't be there. A palm-size silver box sits at the base of the retaining wall that runs around the roof, on the side where the driveway is. A wire runs out from it and over the top of the lip, out of view.

I kneel down next to the box and pick it up. Though I haven't held this type of device before, it's easy enough to figure out from the control buttons that it is a digital recorder. I follow the wire, and find, as it starts down the outside of the building, that it's been painted a color very similar to the wall, making it all but invisible to anyone more than a few feet away. With this knowledge, I can see that it goes all the way down to my bedroom window.

What in God's name is going on here?

I coil up the wire and shove it and the recorder into my satchel. What I want to know is, did Kane put this device here just now, or has it been in place for a while?

I set my chaser to take me back thirty minutes before Kane showed up, and use a more accurate location number so that I forgo falling from the sky.

A recorder sits in almost, but not quite, the same spot as the first one I found. I pull out the confiscated device and compare the two. From a scratch along the left side, I can see that I am holding two versions of the exact same recorder. The only difference is what's displayed on the small digital screen. On the device I took, the main readout sits at 00:00:04, while on the one I just found—the earlier version—the number is 01:47:32.

I hit PLAY on this second device but hear nothing, so I rewind a little bit and try again. My voice and Iffy's from earlier that morning come out of the speaker, and I listen for a few seconds as we talk about our plans for the day. I rewind some more and hear another conversation, this one not nearly so easy to pick out because it took place in my hallway.

Anger boiling under my skin, I check the other device. The only thing recorded on it is four seconds of a man saying today's date and the time that coincides with Kane's upcoming visit to the roof.

Though it's true I still have much to learn about this world, I haven't just been sitting around in ignorance. I check the devices and find a cover that, when open, reveals a memory card. When I remove the one that has the recordings of Iffy and me on it, the number on the display screen switches to 00:00:00. I hadn't anticipated that. Kane will be expecting to find a full recording, but since I don't want to leave the card with our conversations on it, there's little I can do except hope he thinks the recorder malfunctioned. To complete the illusion, I slide the card that has yet to record any of our voices into the slot.

Time now to check his car.

I take a carefully planned jump that puts me in the driveway of the apartment building across from me moments before Kane parks in front of it. From there, I watch him ease to the curb and then head across the street. As soon as he disappears from sight,

I head over to his car and then kneel next to it, pretending to tie my shoe. I know from previous observations that there is a woman walking a dog somewhere behind me, but she's going in the other direction. None of the apartment buildings in my neighborhood contain more than twenty units, and there are only a handful of windows from which I can be seen. I check them all to confirm there is no one watching and then take a thirty-second micro hop inside the car.

I arrive on the driver's seat in a crouch, the wheel a half inch from my ribs. Once I stretch out, I hunt through the central console and find a few receipts, a plastic container holding mints, some pens, and a screwdriver, but that's it.

I turn my attention to the dash box in front of me—the glove compartment, as Iffy calls it. There's a soft fabric case containing a manual for the vehicle and a copy of the registration. The information on the latter matches what I already know. The only other things inside are a few more pens and some auto service records.

This, so far, has gotten me nowhere.

I lean between the seats and lift the lid of one of the white boxes sitting in the back. Similar to the box at Kane's house, it's full of files that seem to pertain to his job. The same is true of the other two boxes. I open a few of the loose files sitting on the front seat and see that they are also work related.

I grunt in frustration. There is nothing here that sheds any more light on my follower. The only place I haven't checked is the trunk, but I can't risk opening it as he might see me from the roof. Nor can I jump inside. It could be full, in which case my chaser's emergency function would kick me fifteen feet to the side and likely land me in the middle of the street.

As much as I would prefer to avoid it, I see no other choice. I'm going to have to confront Kane directly. While I am just over six feet tall, I am thin and not particularly intimidating, so it will be important for me to set the where and when of the encounter.

And if there is anything I could be considered an expert at, it would be controlling time and place.

◆　◆　◆

My plan is to visit Kane in his bedroom after he has gone to sleep and catch him off guard.

I could go back to a previous evening, but that would cause a time ripple I would rather avoid. If I did that and succeeded in scaring him off, then everything he does after our discussion will be different than what it has been. Even just that one night would mean he wouldn't follow us to the restaurant, which in turn would mean that while the events as I know them will always be part of my memory, Iffy's and Ellie's memories will change, and in their minds Kane wouldn't be sitting at the patio table and I wouldn't go to his house. In fact, they won't even know Kane's name. Perhaps in the grand scheme this isn't a big deal, but I'll know the break between our memories exists, and as I've said before, that's the kind of thing I'd like to prevent from happening.

I return to my home time—a time that corresponds with the actual days and minutes and seconds I've been alive, in other words, as far forward as the chaser will ever allow me to go. This puts me in the apartment about forty-five minutes after I promised Iffy I wouldn't confront Kane.

She and I talk through my plan. She's naturally concerned, but feels as I do that we need to get to the bottom of this.

My intention has been to wait until 11:00 p.m. before jumping to Los Angeles, but by ten o'clock I'm too anxious to hang around any longer and decide to go.

Unlike when I visited Kane's street in the early morning hours, there are lights on in many of the houses. Unfortunately, one of these is Kane's. To eat up time and burn off some of my nervous energy, I take a walk around the neighborhood.

When I return twenty minutes later, Kane's house is dark. Still, I force myself to wait until 10:45 p.m. to make sure he's had enough time to fall asleep, and then from my list of previous jumps, I select the locator that will put me just inside his front door.

The living room looks no different than it did on my last visit. I glance down the hall to the back of the house. It's dark and quiet in that direction, and I see no reason to check it out again. I am here for a single purpose, and *he* is upstairs.

The two doors at the near end of the second-floor hallway are closed again. I realize now that one must belong to the old woman from the yard. I ease past them and continue on until I am just outside the master bedroom.

I allow my anger at Kane's intrusion into our lives to grow, hoping this gives me the confidence I will need when I confront him. When I am as ready as I will ever be, I step inside and quietly close the door.

Like before, I see his shape on the bed, under the covers. Since he's facing away from me, I move around the side so that when I wake him, I will be the first thing he sees.

As I crouch down beside the mattress, though, I realize something isn't right. Hair lies across his face, but Kane's hair is short, cropped on the sides and not much longer on top.

I look around for something I can use to move the hair away from his face, and that's when I spot the pair of brown-framed glasses on the nightstand. I've seen them before, but not on Kane's face. I look back at the bed and realize the shape of the person is too small to be my follower.

This isn't Kane. It's the woman who brought the old woman the lemonade. The caregiver called Lorna.

I wonder for a moment if she might be his wife, but quickly dismiss this thought. She'd called him Mr. Kane when she was talking to the old woman. Not something a wife would likely do.

So where *is* Kane? Did he get held up in traffic and is still on the way home? Or is he not coming at all?

Perhaps my previous assumption was wrong and Kane doesn't come home every night. This I can check, either by going back and following him to see where he went earlier this evening, or by popping back into his house later tonight to see if he's returned.

It's been a very long day for me, though, and I can no longer ignore the exhaustion I feel. So whatever I decide to do needs to wait until after I get some sleep.

I open the bedroom door again so, if for some reason, the old woman needs help during the night, Lorna will be able to hear her, then I move into the hallway and pull out my chaser.

Like I did earlier, I make a home time jump, and am in the present when I arrive in my darkened apartment.

I'm a little surprised Iffy isn't sitting in the living room, waiting up for me. It's not that late, after all, and we often stay up long past midnight watching television shows and movies I have never seen before. But then again, even though her day has not been as long as mine, it has been stressful, and I can't blame her if she's already fallen asleep.

I slip the chaser back into my satchel and head toward my room. The door is closed but not latched, and through the crack between it and the jamb, I see only darkness. I carefully push it open so I don't wake her, but as I step inside, I hear Iffy let out a soft moan.

"That's far enough."

It's not so much the harsh male voice that stops me from moving as the barrel of the gun that's suddenly pressing against the base of my skull.

CHAPTER SEVEN

"Hands in the air," the man whispers behind me.

I raise my left, hoping the movement will distract him as my right hand shoots down to my satchel and starts to push the flap away. But before my hand can slip inside the bag and find my chaser, the gun moves away from my head and slams into my wrist.

I cry out in pain. Any harder, and I'm sure it would have broken a bone.

The cold circle of metal presses against my neck again. "Put your hands in the air and don't touch the bag!"

Two seconds, that's all I need. If I can just get to the chaser's control buttons, I can hop backward and deal with this problem before it even begins.

"Do it!" the man says. "Or would you rather I shoot you in the head? There's no way you can disappear before I pull the trigger."

Part of my mind is screaming at me to just do it, but the rational part is yelling even louder that I would never make it.

"Well?" he asks.

I raise my hand in the air.

As the metal leaves my neck, I hear a faint exhale of breath behind me that sounds almost like relief. As soon as it ends, though, a hand pulls the strap of my satchel over my head and off my shoulder.

It feels as if a pit to the center of the earth has opened under my feet. If never altering the past was the institute's number one rule, then never let anyone take your chaser would be 1A.

"Turn around. Slowly."

I do as ordered. Like I know will be the case, the man pointing the gun at me is Vincent Kane. My satchel hangs over his shoulder, and he's taken a few steps back so that he is out of my reach.

"Denny Younger," he says in an odd mix of disbelief, disgust, and reverence.

"I know your name, too," I reply in a voice that comes out with less strength than I intend.

A nervous smile. "I'm sure you do."

I need to keep him off balance in hopes that he'll make a mistake that will allow me to grab back my bag, so I tell him, "I was just in your house."

His smile falters.

"I've seen the old woman you live with."

His eyes narrow.

"Is she your grandmother?"

His face tenses, and even in the dim light, I can see that his cheeks are growing red.

"I know she's sick and that you have Lorna there taking care of her tonight."

While I know there's a chance he might follow through with his threat to pull the trigger, what I'm trying to do is provoke him into physically attacking me. He may be heavier than I am, but he doesn't look like he's in all that great of shape. And I've had some instruction in self-defense, so at least in theory, I should be able to use his momentum to my advantage.

"Did you know Lorna is in your bed tonight?" I say, attempting to push him over the edge. "Or is that where she usually sleeps?"

A roar leaps from his throat, but instead of rushing at me as I expect him to, he turns and runs into the hall.

I shoot a glance at Iffy, fighting the urge to check her, but if I can stop this whole mess before it begins, then whatever Kane has done to her will be moot. I sprint into the hall and see that the door to my sister's room is opened a few inches. I thrust it open and run inside.

The only one there is Ellie. As with Iffy, the noise Kane and I have been making has not woken her up. I want to check her, too, but again, the most important thing I can do right now is get my chaser back.

I head quickly into the living room and find the front door is wide open. I sprint outside and pause on the breezeway just long enough for a quick listen. Running steps, downstairs near the front of the building and growing fainter. I reach the stairway in seconds and fly down it three steps at a time and then race around the pool to the entranceway at the front of the courtyard. I stop to listen again when I reach the street, but I don't hear running this time.

I wildly scan left and right for any sign of Kane. How could he disappear so quickly?

At the sound of a motor starting, I turn and am just in time to see a sedan pull from the curb and speed toward me. Its bright head-lights prevent me from getting a good look at it until it is almost parallel to me.

It's the Lexus sedan I searched earlier. Kane sits in the driver's seat, his hands locked on the steering wheel. When he looks at me as he passes, there is both fear and hatred in his eyes.

I know it's ridiculous, but I rush into the street as if I might be able to grab onto the car and jerk it to a stop. I even run after him for several seconds before my mind finally forces my legs to stop.

He's gone, and he's taken with him the one advantage I have in this world.

◆ ◆ ◆

As I hurry back to the apartment, the one thing I know for sure is that I am living in temporary time. Every moment that has already occurred and will occur since I arrived back from my unsuccessful trip to Kane's house is just a placeholder. I will get my chaser back, and I will erase all of this. It no longer matters if Iffy's and Ellie's and my memory will then differ. There is no other option.

Whoever Kane really is, whatever his plans are, I cannot—no, *will* not—let him get away with them.

I have no idea if he realizes what he's taken from me, but whether he does or not, my chaser is basically a piece of junk in his hands. Sure, if the flap was unlocked—which it's not—he could scroll through the menus and do some calculations, but he could never jump. To do that, he would need to rekey the machine to recognize him. That's not a simple process, and very few know (knew/have ever known) how to do it. I know how only because my instructor Marie thought it important to train me in more than just the official curriculum. So even if Kane *is* a rewinder—which the evidence I've seen so far does not support—he's highly unlikely to have the technical knowledge to use my device.

Still, the sooner the device is back in my hands, the better I'll feel.

Without another chaser at my disposal, however, I'm currently like everyone else in this world, bound by the common laws of time and space. And since I don't know how to drive a car, I'm going to need help.

I check on Ellie first. Though she's still unconscious, her breathing sounds normal, and I am hoping whatever Kane has done to her has not harmed her in any lasting way.

Iffy, too, is still out, though she's restless.

I shake her shoulder. "Iffy. Wake up."

She answers with a moan, so I rock her a little harder.

"Iffy. Come on. Open your eyes."

Her breaths become pants, like she's in the middle of a bad dream.

"Wake up!"

I lift her into a sitting position, and immediately the pants become a moan again and then a "Wha . . ." as her eyes flutter open for a brief moment and then close.

I gently tap her cheek. "Hey, it's okay. Wake up."

Her lids blink a few times, and she then squints at me. "Denny?"

I have no experience with people who've been drugged. The only ones I've seen are those in movies Iffy has shown me. Coffee seemed to be something that is often given, so I carry her into the living room, put her on the couch, and run into the kitchen.

When I return a few minutes later with a cupful of French roast, Iffy has fallen back asleep. As soon as I get her eyes open again, I place the cup against her lips. She automatically takes a sip, then pulls back, her eyes widening.

"Too hot," she says, blinking.

I blow on it.

"What am I doing . . . out here?" she asks, her voice breathy, dreamlike.

"Try this," I say, holding the cup up again.

She takes a more tentative sip this time. "Still too hot." Her brow creases, and she suddenly looks around in a panic. "He's here! Kane. He's in the apartment!"

"Was here," I tell her. "He's gone now."

"He's gone?"

I nod.

It takes several seconds for her confusion to ease enough that she begins to relax.

"Can you tell me what happened?" I asked.

There's a delay before she looks at me. "Huh?"

"How did Kane get inside?"

She looks confused, the drug still affecting her. "Kane?"

"Yeah."

"Oh, um, front . . . door."

"You let him in?"

She squeezes her eyes shut before stretching them wide for a second and then shakes her head. "Not me. Ellie was up. We were talking when he knocked. Said he was with the police. She . . ." Her head dropped as she ran out of steam.

"She got to the door first?" I asked.

A nod.

This wouldn't be the first time Ellie rushed to answer the door before anyone else could get there. It's a moment of excitement in her usual, boring day.

"He shoved his way . . . in," Iffy whispers. "Asked where you were."

"What did you tell him?"

"To get out." She starts to lean against me, but then sits up straight, her eyes widening again. "He asked about . . . about your chaser. Wanted to know if you had it with you." She takes a breath. "Had to tell him. He . . . pulled out a gun, pointed it at Ellie. I'm sorry."

"Don't be sorry."

She puts a hand on the couch and tries to push herself up. "We have to check on her."

I put an arm around her. "She's okay. She's sleeping."

"You're . . . sure?"

"Uh-huh."

Iffy relaxes a little. "He made me give, um, give her some of her sleeping pills."

"Do you remember how many?" I ask.

"He said four, but only gave her . . . two. Dropped the other two under her blankets."

"He made you take some of them, too?"

"Gave me the same. I spit most of them out when he wasn't looking."

"I need you to wake up. Can you do that?"

"Am . . . awake."

"I mean really awake. I need your help." In as few words as possible, I tell her about my encounter with Kane and how he's gotten away with my chaser.

The last part is what finally seems to get her heart pumping again. She grabs the cup of coffee and downs the whole thing.

We discuss our options and come up with the outline of a plan that is 90 percent desperation, but neither of us know what else to do. We figure that Kane is either still in San Diego or is heading back to Los Angeles. There is just no way to know for sure. But what we do know is that the old woman is in LA, and she's clearly important to him. He has to return to her at some point. At least, that's our hope. So that's where we decide to go.

Since Iffy is in no condition to drive us north, she calls the only other person who knows my secret, and convinces RJ to help us out.

We are heading up the coast on the I-5 freeway in just under thirty minutes. I'm in the front with RJ, while Iffy is in the back, Ellie's head in her lap. As much as I would like to leave Ellie at the apartment, there's no one we can trust to watch her there. LA is a different story, though.

It's not long before Iffy is leaning back in her seat, lightly snoring, essentially leaving RJ and me alone together for the first time.

Initially, we simply ride in silence. It's as we're passing a sign for an upcoming exit to the town of San Clemente that he finally says, "What's it like?"

My head has become so filled with thoughts of Kane and why he has forced himself into our lives that it takes me a moment to realize RJ has spoken. "What's what like?"

"Alternate earth. Where you're from."

I look out at the road ahead. "*This* is alternate earth."

I sense his confusion long before he says, "What do you mean?"

I purposely kept details light during our previous talk. After all, seeing the shuttle land and being in the opening night audience of *Star Wars* meant there wasn't much more I needed to do to convince him of the chaser abilities.

"This world right now isn't the one that's supposed to be. There was a change in the time line. An accident."

"Wait. I thought we were talking about parallel worlds. Isn't that where you're from? Isn't your world still out there?"

"No," I say, though a more accurate answer would be, "I don't think so."

"Then what happened to your world?"

"It doesn't matter."

Though I know he wants to ask more, he's apparently understood from the tone of my voice that I don't want to discuss it, and we fall back into silence.

I've read some on the theory of parallel worlds. As far as I know, it's not a concept that was ever developed in my world. It was certainly not something we were ever taught. Here, though, it's seen as a real possibility.

If I were merely stepping between the worlds, it would certainly remove the guilt over the millions (billions?) of erased lives I know

I've caused. But while the parallel world theory might very well be true, the world that fills this particular cosmic groove is the one that should be occupied by the massive British Empire and the Upjohn Institute, the same world where my sister once died from cancer and where I should have accepted my lot and become a librarian. I made the change to *this* time line. I played god with *this* world. Because of me, Iffy's and RJ's reality has crashed the groove.

Perhaps there is a parallel world out there like the one I was born into, but it ends at the similarity. It is not mine. I'm not a scientist and can't prove any of this. But I know at my very core that this is the truth.

◆ ◆ ◆

Before leaving San Diego, Iffy made one other call, and it's to the Los Angeles home of its recipient that we head first.

We reach the old Craftsman house in the middle of Hollywood a little after 1:00 a.m. With the exception of the porch and the living room, the rest of the home is dark. The old wooden door opens as we pull into the driveway, and Marilyn Bryant, Iffy's former landlord, steps onto the wide stone porch.

RJ helps me ease my sister out of the back, but I carry her across the yard alone. Iffy follows behind, carrying the bag of Ellie's things we threw together before RJ picked us up.

Marilyn meets me at the top of the steps and lightly caresses Ellie's cheek. "She looks better than the last time I saw her."

We had to bring Ellie to a hospital in LA for a special test not long after I brought her to this time line, and we had spent the night here at Marilyn's. While it hadn't been the easiest of trips for my sister at the time, I'm thankful now that we'd taken it. Ellie knows Marilyn, so when she wakes and sees that neither Iffy nor I are here, she won't completely panic. At least I hope.

"Where would you like me to put her?" I ask.

"She'll be using my room."

I hesitate. "There's no need to put yourself out. There must be someplace else she can use."

"Don't worry. You won't be putting me out. I promise. Besides, she'll be most comfortable there."

"Thank you," I say and carry Ellie into the house.

As I am tucking her into bed, Iffy gives the bag to Marilyn and goes over my sister's pill schedule.

When she's finished, I say, "I'm not sure how long we'll be gone. Hopefully, we'll be back first thing in the morning, but—"

"But you might get delayed," Marilyn finishes for me.

"Yes."

The truth is if everything goes as planned, we won't be back at all, because I'll use the chaser to stop Kane before we'd ever come to LA.

Temporary time, remember.

"Ellie will be fine," she says. "Just tell me you two haven't gotten yourselves involved in something stupid."

"We haven't," Iffy says.

RJ is waiting for us in the car when we return. "Where now?" he asks.

I pull out my phone and bring up a premarked map. Touching the digital pin that points to Kane's house, I say, "There."

CHAPTER EIGHT

At my instructions, RJ parks around the corner and up a block from Kane's place.

As much as I would like Iffy to stay in the car with her friend, I know I may need help, so we leave RJ alone and make our way down the street.

The faint *whomp-whomp-whomp* of a helicopter fades in and out over the valley and soon disappears completely. Just before we reach Kane's street, a set of headlights turns onto the road at the bottom of the hill in front of us.

Not wanting to take any chances that it might be Kane, Iffy and I duck behind some rubbish bins at the curb. Instead of turning at the intersection, the car keeps going straight and drives right past us without slowing.

After a quick check to make sure no other vehicles are coming, we make our way to the corner and turn down Kane's street. Pausing, I scan ahead. Like I'd previously observed, Kane's garage door is closed. Though I can't see much of his house, what I can see appears dark.

I motion for Iffy to stay close and then jog down to the garage. The door is old and warped just enough that there is a gap between it and the cement wall. I shine my phone's flashlight through the crack to see if the Lexus is inside. The angle isn't great, but it appears the space is empty. Out of habit, my hand starts to move toward the satchel I'm not carrying so I can use my chaser to hop inside and know for sure. The reflex is just another demonstration of how reliant I've become on the device.

I silently chastise myself and then whisper, "Let's check the street and see if he's parked nearby."

While there are over a dozen cars lining the road, none is Kane's. Given that there are still plenty of open spots available, I think it unlikely he's left the Lexus on another street.

Yet again, it feels as if the world has dropped out from under me. I've been counting on him being here, and am now wondering if we've just made a huge mistake leaving San Diego.

The dark corners of my soul are whispering that I've lost my chaser forever. I could live with that, I guess, but only if I knew the box had been destroyed and no one else could ever use it. And though I'm still convinced Kane doesn't possess the knowledge to rekey the device so it'll work for him, I can't help wondering, *What if he figures it out?* Highly unlikely, I know, but not impossible.

Will the world suddenly change again?

Will Kane create a break far enough back in time that it will erase me?

And what of my sister?

And Iffy?

And Marilyn and RJ and everyone else?

In my downward spiral, I've lost all sense of where I am. It's Iffy's hand slipping into mine and her words "Let's check the house" that start to bring me back.

I blink until the fog in my mind clears enough for me to see Iffy looking at me.

"Don't worry," she says. "He'll show up. And if he doesn't, wherever he is, we'll find him."

She's right, of course. While the weight of all humanity is my constant companion, I can't let it overwhelm me. I need to stay focused. After all, the world around me is still as I made it, and until I suddenly wink out of existence, I must do all I can to get my device back so that the time line remains intact.

We head over to Kane's house and quietly take the steps up the side of the garage to the raised front yard. I can see now that the whole house is dark. I study the front windows for signs of movement, but there are none. There *is* something odd about the front door, though. Right in the middle at eye level is a square patch that's lighter in tone than the rest of the door. When I last stood next to that door, there was no light patch.

As Iffy starts toward the left side of the house, I grab her arm and motion for her to follow me to the small front porch. At the base of the steps, I hold up a hand, telling her to stay, and then quietly make my way up. As I reach the top, I flick on my phone's flashlight again, and use my hand again to focus the beam, this time so that it doesn't spill through any of the nearby windows.

The patch is a piece of paper that has been folded in half and taped to the door. Written large on it are two words:

DENNY YOUNGER

I yank the paper down, quickly unfold it, and read the message inside.

You will call me at 10 a.m. tomorrow morning. Don't waste time trying before then because I won't answer.

Stay in Los Angeles.

Instead of a signature, there's a phone number.

"What is it?" Iffy whispers behind me.

I silently read the note again and then move back down the steps and hand it to her. While she's looking at it, I punch in the number from the bottom of the note into my phone. The line rings at least a dozen times before a generic message tells me that the subscriber has not yet set up voice mail.

The note did warn me he wouldn't answer, but the fact that it proves true makes me want to slam my phone into the ground. Though I doubt he's inside the house, I march up the steps and pound on the front door.

"Kane!"

Iffy rushes up behind me. "Quiet," she whispers. "You'll wake up the whole neighborhood."

"I don't care," I say and then yell his name again.

Iffy looks through the window and then says, "I don't think anyone's here."

At the very least, Lorna or the old woman should have come to investigate the noise by now. We should have heard the creak of the floor or even seen a light come on, but neither has occurred.

Kane has been here and gone, taking the women with him.

I knock again, but instead of yelling this time, I growl in frustration with the final slam of my fist.

Concerned that Kane might somehow be keeping tabs on us, we don't go back to Marilyn's house for fear of leading him to Ellie and instead take a room with two lumpy beds in a cheap motel on Sunset Boulevard just ten minutes from his place.

While RJ and Iffy seem to fall asleep almost immediately, I stare at the ceiling for at least an hour before I finally drift off. I'm not sure that I'd use the word *sleep* to describe my state over the following five hours. It was more a weave of different levels of semiconscious that were all far from restful.

When my eyes open for good, it's a little after 7:00 a.m., and I'm more exhausted than I was when I lay down.

I can hear Iffy in the bathroom, taking a shower, while RJ is nowhere to be found. I grab my phone and try calling Kane's number again, but the result is the same. This time I'm too tired, however, to even work up the urge to throw my phone on the ground. I lie back down and stare at the familiar spots on the ceiling.

The front door opens several minutes later, and RJ comes in carrying bags in each hand. I smell coffee and immediately sit back up.

"Hope you like doughnuts," he says.

I shuffle over to the dingy dresser where he's set everything down, and grab a coffee from one of the bags, dump in some cream, and take a sip. It's hot but not unbearable.

"Thanks," I say and take a longer drink.

RJ pulls out a long, chocolate-covered doughnut and plops down on the other bed. Between bites, he says, "I called a friend of mine from school while I was out." Another bite. "He works part-time at Verizon. Asked him if he could dig up any info about the number from your note. Maybe even tell us where it is."

I stop drinking. Verizon, I know from commercials, is a phone company. "He can do that?"

"He said no promises, but he'd check. Oh, and it's going to cost five hundred bucks. That's okay, right?"

I get to my feet, excited. "Absolutely. When will we know?"

"Whoa, relax. He doesn't go in until noon."

Noon? I was hoping we'd have the information before my ten o'clock call with Kane. "No way he can go in early? I'll give him another five hundred."

"He's already a little skittish about doing me the favor. If we push him, might back out."

My shoulders sag. That is a possibility we can't chance.

I wander over to the window and pull the curtain back. Another beautiful day in California. I just hope this place is still called by that name when the sun goes down.

We leave the motel at nine thirty, and park on a street just a couple blocks from Kane's house. None of us really think that's where he'll be, but on the off chance he is, we'll be close.

I try the number at 9:50 and again at 9:55, each time hearing the same recording. The second it turns to ten o'clock, I try again.

One ring.

"Hello, Denny." Kane. It's a voice I think I'll never forget now.

"What do you want?"

"Right to business, huh? Okay then," he says, nervous, almost as if he's unsure of himself, "tell me, why is your chaser machine not working?"

His phrasing is odd, but the mere fact he calls the device a chaser means he must have something to do with the institute, right? Of course, if he is from the institute, he should know why the device doesn't work. But what about the pictures in his house? Pictures of a much younger Kane taken here, *in this world*. This is his time line, isn't it? Or are they fakes?

"You're institute security, aren't you?" It's a stab in the dark, but the best guess I can come up with.

"What?"

"Administration, then."

A pause. "Oh, I understand. No to both."

This leaves only the possibility that I've already dismissed, but I say it anyway, "A rewinder?"

There's almost a boylike quality to his voice when he says, "I wish."

Clearly he knows what a rewinder is. But if he's not one, and not security or administration, then *what* is he?

"Then what—"

"No," he says, suddenly truculent. "It's *my* questions that need to be answered. Not yours. Why isn't it working? I know it should. You used it yesterday."

I don't answer.

"Maybe you think I don't know what your machine does, but I do. It's a time machine. You even used it to check up on me yesterday."

Again I remain silent.

"I know you found my recording device on your roof and changed the memory card because you goofed up. If it had been completely blank, I would have thought there'd just been a glitch. But you left my tag with the date and time at the beginning. Only *I* hadn't recorded that tag yet."

I'd put the card in so that he might think the recorder had failed to work properly, but I had forgotten about the recording at the beginning. If I'd erased that, we'd probably still be playing our game of hide-and-seek in San Diego, and I might have even already gained the advantage on him.

It's the little things. The twelve-second mistake I made in 1775 that allowed George Washington to live, and now the four-second recording I should have erased but didn't.

"Why isn't the device working?"

There's a way I can make everything right, I realize, and it even involves telling the truth. "Because it's keyed to me."

"Keyed?"

"It'll only work if I am the one who activates it."

Now it's his turn to remain silent.

"It's no use to you," I tell him. "Just give it back to me and we can go our separate ways."

"Oh, you'd like that, wouldn't you? Once you were alone with it, you'd go back to some point where you could make sure I wasn't a problem for you, maybe even keep me from being born." He pauses. "Which is kind of funny if you think about it, since I wouldn't be here if it weren't for you."

I don't know how, but he knows I'm the one who brought this world into existence.

"I promise you that I won't do anything to harm you."

"I know you won't. What you are going to do, though, is help me."

"Help you what?"

"Keep your phone close, Denny."

"Help you what?" I repeat.

But the line has already gone dead.

I try calling back, and am sent once more into the land of a dozen rings and generic messages.

◆   ◆   ◆

Having no choice but to wait for Kane to contact us again, Iffy has RJ drive us to the Alcove Café, a place she used to frequent when she lived in LA, and where, she tells us, we can hang out for several hours without anyone telling us to leave.

We sit out front at a table under the trees, but say very little. I've forced myself to set my phone on the table and not clutch it in my hand, but I can't stop looking at it every few seconds.

At 11:40, RJ's friend calls. He's apparently gone to work a little early to see if he can find out anything for us. I try to glean what I can from RJ's side of the conversation, but he's mostly saying, "uh-huh" and "all right" and "okay." When he hangs up, Iffy and I look at him expectantly.

"The number belongs to a pay-as-you-go phone," RJ explains. "It's not a Verizon phone but from a smaller niche phone company that specializes in disposable devices."

I can't hide my disappointment. "So he can't track it down?"

"Hold on. Apparently there's some kind of reciprocal informa-tion deal between a lot of these places. He snooped around a bit and found that the only time the phone's been on and traceable was at ten when Kane called you."

"Where was he?"

"Hollywood. My friend says it looks like he was walking around."

"Where in Hollywood?"

"Near the Chinese Theatre."

"So that's all we know?" Iffy asks.

RJ grimaces. "Sorry."

"We should go there," I say, reaching for my phone.

"He'll already be gone," Iffy says calmly. "We'd just be wasting our time. We should wait here until he calls again."

Though I agree with her on principle, I'm growing antsy just sitting here.

Sensing this, Iffy strokes the back of my neck. "Save your energy for when we'll really need it."

I hold on to my nervous tension for a few more moments before I let out a long breath. I give Iffy a thankful half smile and then say to RJ, "When you talk to your friend again, please thank him for trying."

"When you give me the $500 you owe him, I will."

Iffy squeezes my shoulder and then pushes her chair back. "I'm going to the restroom."

As she stands, RJ does the same. "And I think I need a piece of chocolate cake," he says. "You two want anything?"

Both Iffy and I decline, and then she and RJ head inside the café.

The first eighteen years of my life, I never once considered the possibility of time travel. The important things for me were school and chores and avoiding my father as much as I could. But in the past year and a half, traveling wherever and whenever I want has become such an ever-present part of my life that it's hard for me to remember how to live without the ability. Not having access to my chaser feels like I'm missing a limb.

These are the selfish thoughts I have. And as guilty as they make me feel, they pale in comparison to my potential guilt over what Kane might do if he somehow gains control of the device.

I start to pick my phone up, but quickly force my hand away. "Come on," I whisper. "Call me."

RJ rejoins me a few minutes later, carrying a new cup of coffee and a piece of cake on a plate. *He must live on sugar,* I think. I didn't even touch the doughnuts he'd brought to the motel, and know that Iffy had only one, but the bag was all but empty when we left. And now dessert.

I must have been staring at his plate, because he says, "Want a bite?" He holds a forkful of the pastry toward me.

"I'm fine. Thanks."

With a shrug, he shoves it in his mouth and then proceeds to devour the rest of the slice.

As he's putting his fork down, I look past him at the café, thinking Iffy should have been back long ago. "Was there a line for the bathroom?"

"Don't know," he said, glancing over his shoulder at the building. "Want me to go check?"

I need to do something other than sit here, so I push myself up. "I'll go."

Grabbing my phone, I head inside. The bakery is on the right-hand side of the building, with a full bar—empty at this early hour—on the left. Another customer directs me to the restrooms, which are located in an interior seating area farther back.

There is no line in front of the woman's restroom. I hesitate and then knock on the door.

"Iffy?"

"The men's is the next one over," a woman sitting at a table behind me says.

"Just looking for my friend."

"You won't find her there. Been empty for a couple minutes."

I turn. "Are you sure?"

"You can check for yourself. Should be unlocked."

I pull the door open. The room is designed for one occupant at a time, and is currently not in use.

I approach the woman I've been talking to. "The last person who left, was she a small woman, dark hair? Wearing a, um, pale green T-shirt?"

The woman thinks for a second and then shakes her head. "A blonde, I think. Maybe about forty years old."

"What about before her?"

"I got here about the same time the restroom freed up."

"Oh, well, thank you."

I look around. The only other person in the room is a man at a table against the far wall, working on a laptop and wearing earbuds. I hurry over to him.

"Excuse me."

It takes a moment before he looks up and removes one of the earbuds. "Yeah?"

I ask him about anyone he might have seen coming out of the women's restroom.

"Wish I could help, but I'm kinda focused here, so . . . um, sorry."

He quickly puts the bud back in his ear and returns his attention to his screen.

I look around and spot a door leading to an outdoor area along the side of the building. It's the only other direction she could have gone. If she'd come out the front of the building, I would have seen her. Maybe she ran into a friend and stopped for a few minutes to catch up.

When I exit, though, I find that only half the tables are full, and Iffy is not sitting at any of them. From the lack of plates and glasses in front of the majority of people who are there, it's obvious most have just sat down.

I quickly scan the area. To my left, the seating area feeds out into the front portion, where our table is. And to the right, the patio soon narrows to a pathway that leads to what looks like a driveway.

If she went left, then she's probably already back at our table, so I go the other direction, and in my rush toward the back, I bump against one of the tables and nearly knock over a glass of water.

"Hey, buddy. Slow down," a guy with a full dark beard says.

"Sorry," I reply, but I'm already two tables away, and it is unlikely that he hears me.

Thankfully, the pathway is clear, and I get to the other end in only a couple seconds. I was right. A driveway. It curves between the café and another building to a small parking area.

"Iffy," I call as I move into the lot.

All but one of the slots are filled. Two women are getting out of a car that's just pulled in. When I call Iffy's name again, they glance in my direction, then just as quickly dismiss me as someone they don't know.

I go clear to the back of the area to make sure I check everywhere, but Iffy isn't there.

I missed her in passing, that's all, I tell myself. *I'm sure she's with RJ now, wondering where I am.*

I head back to the café and weave through the side patio. The man whose table I hit glares at me, and I apologize again, making sure he can hear me this time.

When I reach the front area, I find RJ at our table, still drinking his coffee and still alone.

"Did you see her?" I ask.

He looks up at me, brow furrowing. "You didn't find her?"

I shake my head. "She's not back there."

"Are you sure?"

As I say, "Of course, I'm sure," my phone rings.

I pull it out and see Kane's number on the display.

Not now, I think, but I accept the call and say, "Yes?"

"There's a building on Casitas Avenue in Atwater Village." Kane recites the address. "Be there in twenty minutes."

"I need a little more time than that." There's no way I'm going anywhere until I find Iffy.

"You have twenty minutes."

"Please," I beg.

"Twenty minutes. Just you. Make sure your friend stays in his car."

Not only has he said friend instead of friends, he has identified RJ as male. He must have been hiding near his house when we were there last night and followed us to the motel and then to the Alcove. My phone pressed hard against the side of my head, "You have her," I say, my voice barely controlled.

"Don't be late."

Click.

◆ ◆ ◆

On one side of Casitas Avenue are businesses and warehouses and parking areas, while on the other sit homes and apartment buildings and townhomes. The address Kane has given me corresponds to a building on the business side that has a FOR LEASE sign attached to the front. There's a fence around the adjacent parking lot, with a car entrance gate that's closed and locked. The pedestrian one beside it, however, has been left partially open.

"Let me out here," I say as soon as we pass the building.

"I don't think you should go in there alone," RJ says as he pulls to the curb. "Maybe we should call the police."

"And tell them what? That Kane took my time machine and won't give it back?"

"If he's really got Iffy, that's kidnapping."

He has a point about that, but I can't chance the chaser falling into the hands of the authorities. Who knows who'd get hold of it then? As much as I wish it weren't true, the device's safety is more important than any of our lives. Besides, I don't think Kane is interested in hurting Iffy. He wants me. She's just the lure.

I open my door. "Wait here. I'll get her out, then you two get as far away from here as you can."

It doesn't really matter where they go. Once I'm inside, if I can get my hands on my chaser—strike that, *when* I get my hands on my chaser—I'll rewrite all of this, and this period of temporary time will finally be erased.

The only windows on the front of the building are too high for me to look in, but even if I could, they are so covered with dust that I wouldn't see much anyway. As I pass through the gate, I note the dusty windows continue down the side of the building. Below them at various points are several closed doors.

At the very back of the parking lot, in the shadows, is a car. Even at this distance, I'm sure from its shape that it's Kane's Lexus.

I try the doors to the building one by one, but it's only the entrance closest to the car that's unlocked. The hinges creak as I push the door open. The area inside is dim but not dark, the dirty windows letting in more than enough light to make out details. The entire space—side to side, front to back, floor to rafters—is open. A warehouse, though one that clearly hasn't been used in a while. At precise points, metal columns rise from the ground to support the roof, but otherwise the floor is empty.

Well, not completely empty.

Forty feet in front of me, Iffy sits in a chair, Kane standing behind her. Wide silver bans encircle her ankles and her chest. Duct tape—a name I know thanks to Iffy—holding her in place. There is a small table, too. On it are two bags—a dark-colored backpack and my satchel.

"Please close the door," Kane says. He's trying to sound calm, but the shake in his voice is even worse than it was when we talked on the phone.

Perhaps that should give me some hope, but what it does is make me worry he might do something stupid and unexpected. The smartest thing *I* can do at the moment is play along. I close the door and turn back to him.

"Now come over," he orders me. "Slowly. And keep your hands where I can see them."

My steps echo off the cracked cement floor. As I draw nearer, I lock eyes with Iffy, trying to silently ask if she's okay. If she's responding, though, I can't tell. She just looks scared to me, further fueling my anger toward Kane.

"Stop," he says when I'm about fifteen feet away.

As soon as I halt, he steps out from behind Iffy's chair. In his hand I see that he is once more holding the gun he threatened me with in the apartment.

I raise my hands out at my sides, fingers spread, to drive home the point that I'm unarmed. "I came just like you told me to. Now let my friend go."

With a speed that surprises me, he whips his gun up and points it at me. "Shut up. You only speak when I tell you to speak." He takes a step in my direction. "Here's your first question. Where were you born, Denny Younger?"

"Here," I say. "In California."

He glares at me and shakes his head. "No. The truth."

"It is the truth."

"It's not!" His voice has started to shake again, only this time it also has an edge of desperation. "*Where* were you born?"

I try to swallow, but my mouth has gone dry. "The Shallows," I finally say. "New Cardiff."

For a few seconds, he starts and stops a smile several times, as if he's forgotten how to actually do it. "Say it again."

"The Shallows in New Cardiff."

"And where is New Cardiff now?"

I see no reason to lie. "It never existed."

"Like the Upjohn Institute?"

The cotton that has soaked away all the moisture from my mouth has moved into my throat. "Yes."

"Like the magnificent world where the British still ruled here?"

My voice fails completely, so I only nod.

He stares at me for what seems like hours before he says, "I didn't believe it, didn't believe the stories about you." His voice has taken on an almost dreamy quality, and I sense that he's talking as much to himself as to me. "How could anyone? And yet you're actually real. I've been waiting to find out the truth for a long time. A long, long time."

Waiting for a long time? What's he talking about? I've been here only since early spring. It makes no sense.

The only thing that *is* clear is that though he knows about my world, he's not of it. I thought it impossible to be more confused about what's going on, but I was wrong.

He walks over to the table, removes my chaser from my satchel, and sets it down. "You're going to help me with a mission."

"What kind of mission?"

That half smile again, there and gone. "A mission of mercy." He places the muzzle of his gun against the back of Iffy's skull. "Approach the table. But be warned, any trick you try won't be fast enough to stop me from pulling this trigger."

I wish he was wrong, but he's not. Even if I were to activate the emergency escape combination, he'd likely know something was up and would shoot Iffy before I could disappear.

Yes, I know. Ultimately it wouldn't matter. I'd be able to go back and stop Kane long before we ever got to this point and avoid Iffy's death. But I would always remember that I let him kill a version of her. Despite all the lives I have already erased—once even Iffy's—I'm not strong enough to be even tangentially responsible for her outright murder. What I must hope is that he will drop his guard at some point for long enough that I can make my move without risking her life.

When I reach the table, Kane says, "Open it. Nice and slow. No sudden movements. Tell me you understand."

"I understand."

I reach out and touch the plate that unlocks the lid and then move the top out of the way.

"Step back," he barks. "Ten steps. Big ones."

The buttons are right there, so close. Three seconds, four tops is all I need. But Kane needs only one to pull the trigger, so I move away.

Once I stop, he lowers the gun and drags the chaser closer to him. From inside the backpack, he removes an old, leather-bound book. I'm close enough that I can see there's no title on the front or spine. A bookmark sticks out of the top, and he opens the book to that page. When he sets it on the table next to the chaser, I can see just enough to know that the text is not commercially printed, but rather handwritten. A journal?

After studying the page, he shoots me a look to make sure I haven't moved and then does something I'm not expecting. Looking back and forth between the book and the chaser, he enters information into the device.

"What are you doing?" I ask.

"I told you to be quiet," he says.

I don't care what he told me. He could damage the machine, and this period of time that I've been thinking is only temporary might become permanent. "You shouldn't be playing around with that."

"I know exactly what I'm doing."

He takes another look at the book, and enters something else into the chaser.

"So to use this, I just press GO, right?"

"It won't work."

"Let's see."

He picks up the chaser and taps the go button. But as I've already warned him, nothing happens.

Looking disappointed, he says, "Because it's keyed to you?"

"Yes."

Kane considers the box for a moment before setting it back down. "But you *can* take someone with you, correct?" He taps the journal. "Says here you can take someone. Which I'm guessing is how you got your sister here, right?"

I nod, momentarily unable to speak.

Kane glances at Iffy and back at me. "What about three?"

I don't like where this is going at all so remain silent.

Kane picks up the journal. "You don't need to answer," he says, flashing the book in my direction before putting it in his backpack. "That's in here, too, so I already know you can."

If the journal was a curiosity before, I absolutely must get my hands on it now.

Kane pulls my satchel over his head so that the strap drapes across his chest, removes a hefty collapsible knife from inside the backpack, and dons the bag, effectively securing the satchel in place. He then uses the knife to cut away the tape holding Iffy's ankles to the chair.

Before he does the same with the loop around her chest, he says, "This is very sharp. I wouldn't try anything if I were you."

Once the tape is off, he closes the knife and slips it into the small pocket on the side of my satchel just below where the strap connects. He then pulls out the chaser.

"It's my understanding that we need to be in close contact," Kane says. "Is that correct?" Even if I wanted to answer, he doesn't give me enough time before he starts talking again. "I'm sure you're thinking this is your chance to overpower me, but don't forget I'm the one holding the gun. Now, we will do this in exactly the way I describe."

I'm instructed to stand a few feet in front of Iffy and then turn my back to her. As I do this, I catch a glimpse of the chaser's control panel. Kane has input a number into the destination box at the top that appears to conform, at least in length, to a standard location number. The glance I get is too quick to memorize each digit, but the last four stick with me—3928—because they're familiar, but at the moment I'm too occupied to figure out why. I also note he's input a date, but the only number I catch is a 2 at the end.

Once I'm situated, he has Iffy stand up and press against my back.

"I'm sorry," she whispers as she puts her arms around my chest. "He surprised me."

"It's okay. Don't wor—"

"No talking!"

From the sound of Kane's voice, he's right behind Iffy now. I feel a bump as he moves against her back.

"Just so you know," Kane says, "I've got my gun to your girl-friend's head again."

He has obviously given this considerable thought. To further prove this, he grabs my hand and pulls it back toward him, out of my sight.

"Extend your finger and keep your hand right where it is," he says.

I do it, though it's hard to remain completely still in such an awkward position.

He grabs my wrist and says, "Here we go."

The words are barely out of his mouth when I feel the chaser's go button press against my outstretched finger.

CHAPTER NINE

The gray mist of the journey swirls around me like a cloud. I think I still feel Iffy behind me, but it's hard to tell. The sensations of touch and pressure within a jump can be misleading.

No more than half a minute passes before the shroud begins to fade and the world takes shape around us. It's nighttime, so at least Kane's done that part right. Without seeing the chaser, though, I have no idea of the exact hour. It's also significantly colder than it was in the warehouse. I feel Kane's hand slip from my side, and hear him grunting in pain as the price of the time trip is extracted in the form of a headache.

I, too, am feeling it. Even though it's far from the worst I've ever had, it still takes me a moment to realize this is my chance to grab the chaser.

I try to twist around, but Iffy is still clinging to me, her face contorted as she works through her own internal torture.

"Stay here," I whisper as I pry myself loose. "I'll be right back."

By the time I'm free, Kane is weaving and stumbling away from us, and is already a good thirty feet away. I head toward him, intending to run but barely able to manage an ugly jog. We are on an open surface that crunches strangely under my feet. I can't get a sense of what exactly it is or tell how far it goes on because my eyes are still accustomed to the relative brightness of the building in LA.

I'm only a few feet away when Kane lurches around, his gun slicing through the air like a club. The only way I can keep from being hit is to arch backward as I skid to a stop, the ground crumpling loudly under my feet.

Kane seems to find his balance, and aims the weapon at me.

There's nowhere for me to hide, so I yell, "You'll never get back if you kill me!"

I can see him thinking about this for a moment, and then he shakes the end of the gun at me. "Stay there." He watches me, daring me to defy him.

I hold my ground.

After a few moments, Kane's gaze moves beyond me, and then he starts scanning the area. "Where are we? Where's the city? Where's the damn city?"

Keeping my voice calm and low, I ask, "Which city?"

"Which city? Los Angeles! What do you think?"

He spins around, taking in our surroundings, but as I can see from my position, there are no city lights in that direction, either. In fact, except for the stars above us, there are no lights anywhere.

He focuses on me again. "Where *are* we? What did you do? Are we even in the right time?"

I have no idea where we are, but I know what's causing his confusion. Not only have we been traveling disconnected from a companion—a human grounding point that rewinders at the institute used to keep their chasers on course—we have also been affected by the three of us jumping together. Either factor alone would be enough to throw us miles off course. Together, who knows how far we are from his target? As for the date, though, whatever he input is the date we arrived. That is always accurate.

None of this I tell him, however. I simply say, "If you let me see the chaser, I can figure it out."

He clutches the device against his chest, panicked. "I'm not that stupid."

Taking a step toward him, I say, "Then just show me the display and I can—"

He points his gun at my chest. "Get back!"

"You won't hurt me," I say. "The chaser is useless without me."

I take another step.

"I said get back!"

A gust of wind suddenly blows past us, making the already chilly air feel like ice. We are all dressed for a warm summer day in Southern California, not for the freezing night we've ended up in.

"You tricked me, didn't you?" he says, his gun hand shaking, from fear or the cold or likely both.

Fighting hard to keep my teeth from chattering, I take another step. "I didn't trick you. I don't know where we are. You said Los Angeles. Is that where we were supposed to arrive?

"When is this?" he asks as if he hasn't heard me. "*When*?"

Another step takes me to just a couple feet from the outstretched weapon. "When is it supposed to be?"

I'm close enough now that I can see his eyes narrow. "She warned me you couldn't be trusted."

I have a terrible feeling that despite the fact that he can't use the chaser without me, he's about to shoot me anyway. Knowing I need to act first, I dip down and lunge forward, then slam upward into his wrist. As my shoulder connects, the gun fires into the night sky, the boom of the weapon temporarily destroying the hearing in my right ear. My left isn't doing much better, and picks up only a muffled yell as Kane screams in anger.

I barrel forward, intending to knock him to the ground, but he twists to the side, and instead of connecting with his chest, I glance off his ribs and stumble past him.

"Denny! Watch out!"

Iffy's voice is barely discernible above the ringing in my head, but I heed the warning and whirl around. Kane has heard her, too, and has abandoned whatever he was about to do and has started running toward her.

She's my weakness. I can't let him get control of Iffy again, so I push off the crumbling earth and thrust myself after him.

Glancing at me over his shoulder, he shouts, "Stop or I'll kill her!"

His words might be tough, but the fear in his eyes tells me his threats are just bluster.

I cover the last few feet in an angled leap that crashes me into his side. Down we go, hard to the ground, but in a direction that keeps him from landing on the chaser. Any hope that the fall stunned him quickly dissolves as he scrambles out from under me and tries to get back up.

I reach out to grab him, but only manage to snag the strap of my satchel. I expect to see the muzzle of his gun at any second, but while Kane stills hold the chaser to his chest with one hand, the other is now empty. At least the fall has done some good and jarred the weapon loose.

He grabs the strap a few inches above my hand and pulls at the bag, trying to break loose my grip. I see something peeking out around the edge of the small flap that covers the side pocket and then remember the knife.

I rip it out and flick the blade open. As soon as Kane sees it, he jerks back as if expecting me to stab him. I lunge a few inches forward like that's exactly what I'm going to do, but instead yank the knife back and slice through the satchel's strap.

Kane tries to pull the bag with him as he scrambles to his feet, but I've got too good a hold on it. He kicks out, hitting my knife hand, but ultimately the satchel slips from his grasp. Apparently unwilling to fight for it any longer, he starts to run.

I push myself to my feet to chase after him but immediately fall back down from unexpected pain radiating up from my right thigh. I think at first I pulled a muscle when we fell, but when I touch the spot, it's sticky and wet.

The cut is not much more than a quarter inch deep, but it is long and painful. I was so focused on Kane that I didn't feel the knife slice through my skin after he'd kicked it.

I look in the direction he's gone and can barely make him out in the distance. In my current condition, there's no way I can catch him.

Iffy stumbles over, still wincing. "Did you get the chaser?"

I shake my head and try to keep the pain from my face, but fail.

"What's wrong?" she asks, suddenly concerned. When she spots the gash in my jeans, she kneels and leans in for a closer look. "We need to get you to a hospital. You need stitches."

"No hospitals," I say. I don't know where we are in time—in fact, there may not be any hospitals here—but whether there are or not, minimizing the chances of being remembered by the locals is basic training, so automatic for me. "You'll have to do it."

She looks at me as if I've gone insane. "You mean the stitches?"

"Yes."

"I, I can't do that."

"Sure you can."

It would be easier to just cut through my pants, but it's the only pair I have with me, so with Iffy's help, I pull them down to my knees, gritting away as much of the hurt as I can. I then remove the med-kit from my satchel. Once I clean out the wound with a packet of disinfectant, I give Iffy the suture kit.

Looking dubious, she says, "I'm not even good at putting a button on a shirt.

"You have to do it and fast. If you don't, Kane gets away, and we're stuck here forever."

The potential of being abandoned in time turns out to be just the motivation she needs. I clench my teeth and try to think about anything else—a task at which I'm only partially successful—as she sews up my wound. When she's done, she coats her handiwork with more disinfectant and then covers everything with a couple of gauze bandages and tape.

After she puts away the med-kit, I hold out my hand. "Help me up."

Iffy is considerably smaller than I am, and it's a bit of a circus act getting me back on my feet. Keeping most of my weight on my left leg, I tie together the cut ends of my satchel's strap and then swing it over my head, draping it so that it falls on my left hip instead of my usual right.

"Maybe you should rest a little first," Iffy suggests.

"He's already got ten minutes on us. We can't waste any more."

I point in the direction Kane had been headed, and take the first step. The pain from my newly stitched wound is so acute I nearly stumble back to the ground, but I force myself to stay upright, and with each successive step the discomfort eases a little.

"Where are we?" Iffy asks.

"I have no idea."

"Do you at least know when?"

I shake my head.

After a while the ground under our feet stops crunching and becomes packed dirt. My eyes have adjusted enough that I can see the dark shapes of vegetation not too far ahead, but there is still nothing but the flat surface in the area we're passing through.

Another breeze blows by, and Iffy presses herself against me, shivering. I put my arm around her and rub my hand over the exposed skin below the sleeve of her T-shirt. We need to find someplace out of the cold, but given how empty the area seems to be, the chances of that aren't great.

By the time we reach the brush, I'm walking almost normally. I'll pay for this later, I'm sure, but I can't worry about pain yet to come.

"This is sagebrush," Iffy says, touching one of the plants. "We're either in a desert or close to one." She looks back the way we've come. "I think we were on a dry lake."

I look back, too, and can see that the area we've just left is lighter than that which surrounds it, much like the lake bed where we saw the space shuttle land. I wonder for a moment if we've somehow ended up back there, but the silhouettes of the tall mountains both ahead and behind us are definitely different. We're in a valley, not the edge of the desert plain where Edwards Air Force Base is located.

Before we start walking again, I listen for Kane's footsteps, but the only noise comes from the breeze tickling the tops of the sagebrush.

I look up at the stars and pick out Polaris. I should have done this upon arrival, but Kane has stolen my focus. I now know that we are heading basically west and that the valley we are in runs north and south.

As I tilt my head back down, I catch a glint out of the corner of my right eye, like another star, only at ground level. Though at first glance it looks like a single light, it's really two. After a few moments, it disappears, only to reappear again seconds later, incrementally closer to us.

"Is that a car?" Iffy asks when she looks to see what's captured my attention.

"I think so."

This at least gives me some idea of when we are. Motor vehicles started showing up in the early 1900s, but I don't think that's how far back we are. At the rate the headlights appear to be traveling, I'm thinking anywhere from the 1920s to the 1960s.

The vehicle is several miles to the north and heading in our general direction. While it's possible the road it's on will turn toward the east or west before it reaches us, if the route continues south, the car is likely to pass within a mile or two of our current position. Though my default is to limit our interaction with the people of this era, we need help getting some place warm and back to civilization.

"Run," I say, and start loping due west as best as my injured leg will allow me. If the road is two miles away, there's no chance we'll reach it in time, but if it's one, maybe.

Iffy matches my hindered pace, but I know she could go faster.

"Just run," I tell her. "Don't wait for me."

She looks unsure.

"Go! I'll be right behind you."

"You better be," she says and then sprints ahead.

I try to follow the same path she takes, but soon she disappears into the night, leaving me to pick out my own way. Looking to my right, I see the lights are much closer now. If Iffy doesn't reach the road in the next two minutes, we're going to miss our chance.

The terrain has steadily inclined since we reached the brush, so it's with some surprise I see that it suddenly dips down into a narrow wash. It's only because I throw out my arms to maintain my balance that I don't fall as I come over the top. Once I'm up the other side, I search ahead for Iffy and spot a shadow moving quickly toward the road much farther away than I thought she would be.

I push myself as hard as I can, but there's only so much my leg will give me. The headlights are less than a minute from being directly in front of me. I'll never make it on time, but I now think there is a good chance Iffy will.

Once more the terrain dips through a wash. When I crest the far side, I can pick out the dark line of the road. The vehicle is all but in front of me now, and I can tell it's not a car but a truck. I search for Iffy and spot her about a hundred feet shy of the blacktop. As I adjust my route to take me directly to her, I notice another shadow, this one only about a few hundred yards ahead of me.

I curse under my breath as I realize the error I've made. The person nearing the road is not my girlfriend. It's Kane.

He reaches the highway twenty seconds ahead of the truck and moves into the middle, waving his arms. I can hear the vehicle's engine roar as the driver uses it to stop. Kane runs up to the door. It's too far for me to hear anything, but then I see him race around the front of the truck to the other side.

"Hey!" I yell as loud as I can. "Hey! Don't leave!"

Ahead of me, I can hear Iffy doing the same, but when the motor revs up again and the truck starts to move, it's clear our shouts have gone unheard.

◆ ◆ ◆

It's at least a half hour before we see another set of headlights. Iffy and I have spent the intervening time huddled together among the bushes on the side of the road, trying not to freeze to death. Iffy jumps to her feet to flag down the vehicle, but I'm slow to follow, my wounded thigh stiff and unforgiving from the prolonged crouch.

Unfortunately the vehicle is headed north, opposite the direction Kane has gone, but we can't afford to be picky at the moment.

When I finally join her, Iffy stands in front of me so that she's blocking the view of my ripped pants as we wave our arms and shout.

The car that rolls to a stop beside us is a sedan. It's rounder and larger than most of the cars in Iffy's world, so it's a safe guess it's from several decades earlier than 2015.

The window rolls down, and a man old enough to be my grandfather looks out. "Car trouble?"

It's as good a cover as any, so I nod. "Any chance you could give us a ride to the nearest town?"

"I could do that, or I could also take a look at your engine and see if we can get it started."

"We, um . . ." I pause, trying to think of something that won't make him too curious, but it's Iffy who comes up with a good response.

"It's the gas tank," she says. "We were driving down a dirt road a little ways back. We think a rock punched a hole in it."

His eyes narrow slightly. "What were you doing off the highway at this time of the morning?"

Iffy slips her hand in mine and says, "My husband wanted to show me a place his dad used to take him camping when he was a kid." She smiles. "Took us a while to walk back to the highway."

The moment she says "my husband," I notice a change in the man's demeanor. His suspicion has disappeared, leaving in its place a sense of sympathetic understanding.

"Hop on in," he says, pointing at the backseat.

Neither of us can resist sighing in relief as the warmth of the interior wraps around us.

The moment we settle in, the man presses down the accelerator. "I'm heading all the way up to Bishop, but I can drop you in Lone Pine. It's only about fifteen miles ahead."

Iffy squeezes my hand, and from the look on her face, I know she's familiar with the names. At least we are no longer completely lost.

"Thank you," I say. "That'll be great. We appreciate it, Mr. . . ."

"Graves," he says. "And you are?"

"Denny Younger, and this is Iffy."

"Iffy? What kind of name is that?"

"My . . . Christian name is Pamela," she says. "Iffy's just a nickname."

This seems to satisfy him.

After a brief pause, I ask, "You wouldn't happen to know what time it is, would you?"

He looks at me through his rearview mirror, a bit of the previous suspicion creeping back into his eyes. "No watch?"

"It, um, broke when I was looking under the car."

Again, the simple answer seems to do the trick. He looks at his own watch. "Just a little after five."

That would be 5:00 a.m. given his previous comment about morning.

The rest of the trip is spent mostly in silence, with just the occasional question thrown our way. Thankfully, all are easy enough to answer. A little more than twenty minutes after he picked us up, we arrive in the town of Lone Pine.

From the amount of lights we see as we drive in, I can tell it's not very large. The highway we're on seems to do double duty as the main street of town. Scattered businesses line both sides, separated by stretches of empty lots and here and there homes. An illuminated sign ahead catches my eye.

The Dow Motel.

I lean over the seat and point at it. "Can you drop us there?"

"Is that where you're staying?" Mr. Graves asks.

"Where we were supposed to stay if we hadn't broken down," Iffy answers quickly.

He pulls to the curb in front of the motel and looks back at me. "How much cash do you have, son?"

He must want some money for gas, I realize. "I—I—I'm sorry. I don't have anything I can give you. We really appreciate the ride, though."

"That's not what I mean." He fumbles with something out of sight and then hands me two one-dollar bills. "Won't get you a room, but should get both of you fed."

The look on his face tells me he was acting before and hasn't believed a word of our story. How he thinks we ended up stranded in the middle of nowhere without the proper clothing, I don't know. "Thank you," I say.

"You need to get yourself some warm clothes, too. I'd give you some more, but I didn't bring much money with me on this trip."

"No, that's fine. This is more than generous."

"If you give us your address," Iffy says, "we'll pay you back."

He studies us for a moment and then smiles. "I believe you just might. Now go on. I've gotta get back on the road."

◆ ◆ ◆

As much as I hate stealing, my ripped and bloodstained pants will draw far too much attention once the sun comes up. I need to find another pair. A jacket for Iffy would be nice, too.

Lone Pine's residents seem to live on the few blocks that spread out to either side of the highway, behind the businesses. Fences encircle a few of the homes, but most just have open yards. We walk quietly through the dark streets, scanning each property.

"Laundry machine," I whisper, pointing at a round tub sitting on four legs outside the back door of a house. The machine bears a striking resemblance to those the people in my caste still used in modern times.

I sneak over and carefully open the lid covering the tub, but it's empty.

Several more houses have machines, while others simply have big metal buckets and washboards. Nearly all, though, have lines strung out to hang wet clothes on.

I check every machine, approaching each house as quietly as my limp allows. Finally, I come up lucky, and discover a pile of clothes lying on a wood palette next to a tub. The pants I find are denim like mine and just about the right size, too, though a little short. Dried mud cakes each cuff, but I don't care about the dirt. It's certainly a lot better than the blood on mine.

I change as fast as I can so I won't freeze to death, and dump my pants in a barrel that looks like it's used to burn trash, three houses away. We then continue the search, hoping to find a jacket, but soon realize that's just wishful thinking.

Back on the highway, we find a diner that will open at 6:30 a.m., and huddle in the doorway as we try to keep warm until then. Fifteen minutes before the place is scheduled to open, a waitress inside spots us and unlocks the door.

"Dear Lord, where are your coats?" she asks. Her name tag identifies her as Winnie.

"Long story," I tell her.

She opens the door wider. "Well, come on inside. I can't have you dying out here. That's not the way I'd like to start my day."

Once we step inside, she hands us a couple of menus. "Take a seat. Any table's fine. I'll come take your order as soon as we're ready."

We choose the booth farthest from the door, next to the window, and sit pressed against each other. Even then it takes a few minutes before we thaw out enough to do more than just sit there and shiver.

"Are you okay?" I ask Iffy.

"I'll be fine. How are *you*?" She touches my leg.

"Sore. But I'll be fine, too." Because of the cold or the presence of Mr. Graves, there has been no opportunity for us to talk about more than what was absolutely necessary. "How did Kane grab you?"

She shrugs. "He was waiting outside the bathroom at the café after I finished. He flashed me the gun and said that if I didn't go with him, he'd kill all of us. I wanted to run, but . . . he seems a little, I don't know, off. I couldn't tell if he was lying or not. I'm sorry."

"Don't be. You did the right thing."

"What are we going to do now?"

"We're going to find him and get my chaser back."

"How? We don't even know when we are."

Something ticks at the back of my mind, but before I can examine the thought, our waitress approaches.

"Warmed up?" she asks.

"Getting there," Iffy said.

"Thanks again for letting us in," I say.

"You're welcome. Now, how about some breakfast?"

I grab a menu and quickly scan it. Turns out Mr. Graves was being generous.

"The country farm special sounds good." Fried egg, hash browns, two strips of bacon, toast, and coffee, all for forty-five cents.

"All right, and you, young lady?"

"That sounds fine for me, too," Iffy said.

"I'll be right back with your coffee."

"You wouldn't happen to have today's paper, would you?" I ask.

"The *Inyo Register* only comes out once a week. There might be a copy of last week's lying around. Would that do you?"

"Sure."

"Be right back."

As Winnie walks away, I look out the window. Beyond the businesses on the other side of the road is a line of majestic, snow-covered peaks. Though I know it's a beautiful sight, I can't really appreciate it. All I can think is, *how are we going to find Kane?*

Iffy, clearly having the same concern, says, "I don't know how big LA is at this point in time, but it's going to be a lot larger than this town. We could search for a year and never find him."

If he wants to be lost, we could actually search a lifetime, I think but don't say. "He can't go anywhere without us," I tell her, hoping to ease her mind a little. "If we don't find him, he'll find—"

I stop. The thought I had earlier pokes at me again. It's sitting there just an atom's width out of reach. I close my eyes and concentrate.

"Denny?" Iffy asks.

I hold up my hand, letting her know I need a moment as I continue to try to bring the thought forward. It's elusive, though, and as close as I am to it, I can't seem to grab on.

"Here you go."

Winnie's voice breaks my concentration, and I open my eyes as she's setting down two cups of coffee.

She then pulls out some folded newspapers from under her arm and says, "You're in luck. Not only do I have last week's *Register*, but a customer left a copy of the *Los Angeles Examiner* from two days ago. You want that, too?"

"That would be great. Thanks."

She sets the papers on the table.

"Your food'll be ready in just a bit."

The moment she leaves again, I snatch up the top paper, the *Examiner.*

"October 7, 1952," Iffy says, finding the date first. "Two days ago makes today the ninth."

I glance around. "Does it look like 1952 to you?"

"I guess. I only know the fifties from TV and movies. This is even before my mom was born. Feels about right, though."

I look back at the paper, and note stories about a forgery case moving through the courts, that day's still-to-be-played World Series game 7 between the New York Yankees and the Brooklyn Dodgers, and a missing boy in San Gabriel. But it's as I'm setting it back down that my eyes drift once more to the year.

1952.

I had seen a two in the date field of the chaser before we'd left 2015. There was something else I had seen, too—the last four digits of the location number. They had seemed familiar, but since I was trying to not get us killed and had no idea where in the world we might be headed, it hadn't connected with me.

This is the thought that had been nagging me: 3928. I have recently input those same numbers myself in that very order.

Which city? Kane had said. *Los Angeles! What do you think?*

"What is it?" Iffy asks me.

I run it all through my mind one more time before saying, "I know where he's headed."

CHAPTER TEN

Three-nine-two-eight. These are the last four digits for the locator number of Kane's house in Echo Park.

Sure, some of the digits that come before the final set could be different, meaning his destination was someplace else entirely, but I think it highly unlikely. He'd expected us to materialize in Los Angeles. The coincidence that he'd want to arrive somewhere else in the city with the same last four numbers is too much to believe.

"He's going home," I say and explain how I know this.

"Why would he do that?" Iffy asks.

"No idea. But we need to get to LA. How far away are we?"

"I'm not sure. A couple hundred miles, at least."

That's a problem. After we deduct the cost of our meal and a tip, we'll be left with only a dollar. I know prices are considerably lower in this time period, but I can't imagine that's enough to get both of us all the way to Los Angeles.

I start pulling everything out of my satchel and setting the contents on the seat between us. Med-kit, my notebook, a ballpoint pen that I'm not sure has even been invented yet, RJ's makeshift charger, my useless cell phone, Kane's knife.

"What are you doing?" Iffy asks.

Though the bag now appears empty, I run my fingers along the bottom. There's a lip under which I used to hide whatever time-appropriate money I was given by the institute when I went on missions. Since my last mission for them had been to eighteenth-century America, I had been given several Spanish dollars, the common tender of the time. I used some in those first weeks after I found myself in a changed 2015, but surely there were still a few left. My finger touches nothing until it's almost at the end of the space. I pull out what I find. Not a few coins, as I'd hoped. Just one.

"Denny? What are—"

Iffy cuts herself off and quickly slides the knife behind her back.

"Two country farm specials," Winnie says as she approaches our table carrying plates in each hand. She sets one in front of Iffy and then the other in front of me. "Can I get you anything else?"

"Everything looks great," I say, "but I have a question."

"Shoot," Winnie says.

"You wouldn't happen to know the best way to get to Los Angeles, would you?"

"Straight south on the highway. Can't miss it. Big city. Lots of people. If you reach the ocean, you've gone too far."

"I mean, is there a bus or something like that we can catch here?"

Her brow furrows. "No car?"

"It, um, broke down. But we need to get back to the city today."

"Today? Well, I believe the bus comes through between twelve thirty and one. You should check with Marsha over at the Dow Motel. She's got the schedule. Won't get you into LA until later tonight, though. A lot of stops between here and there."

"Do you happen to know how much a ticket costs?"

Another furrowed brow. "Please tell me you have enough to pay for your food."

"Of course." I reach into my pocket and pull out the two dollars Mr. Graves gave us.

Winnie relaxes. "I don't know how much the bus is these days, but if that's all you have, I don't think it's going to be enough."

"Thanks," I say.

"Holler out if you need anything," she tells us and then heads off to help a customer who's just arrived.

"Are you trying to get us arrested?" Iffy asks as she pulls the knife from behind her and shoves it in the bag.

"You heard her. We need money. I'm trying to find something we can sell."

Iffy looks at the things I've piled on the seat. With a frown, she shoves her hands into her pants pockets and pulls out some change, several bills, her ID, her phone, and her key chain.

She has twenty-seven dollars, but every bill bears a maker's date that's at least sixty-plus years in the future and is useless here. After she tucks them back in her pocket, she hands me the coins.

"Check those. We might get lucky."

She starts doing something with her keys while I quickly go through the change. The earliest date is on a penny from 1978.

When I tell her this, she says, "Hold onto them. I'm not sure what the vending machine situation is here, but if we run across some, those should fit."

As I put the coins in my pocket, I see that Iffy has detached the trinket that's been connected to her key chain since I met her. It's a character from a Japanese cartoon—Mikasa from *Attack on Titan* Iffy told me when I asked once. It's also not called a cartoon, but an anime, I believe. The figurine is about an inch high and is wearing a brown jacket and white pants crisscrossed with what I assume are supposed to be leather belts. It's actually quite detailed.

Iffy shoves everything I've removed from the satchel back inside the bag, then says, "Move over to the other side."

"What?"

"Just do it."

As I slip out from the table, Iffy follows right behind me, taking the satchel with her.

Before I can sit again, she says, "Give me the two bucks."

"What are you going to do?"

"Like you said, we need money."

I have no idea what her plan is, but I give her the dollar bills and then watch her walk over to the counter. The dining area is starting to fill up, and Iffy has to wait a minute before Winnie can get to her.

I then watch Iffy hand one of the dollars to the woman. A few moments of conversation is followed by Iffy placing the Mikasa figurine on the counter. The waitress picks it up, clearly fascinated. After the two exchange a few more words, Iffy reaches into my satchel, pulls something else out, and sets it down. Unfortunately, she's positioned so that I can't see what it is.

Winnie glances at the item but leaves it on the counter and calls back into the kitchen. The cook comes out a few seconds later. He's a man about the same age as our waitress, though clearly has sampled more of the restaurant's dishes. He picks up the item to examine it closer, and I now see that it's Kane's knife. The man opens it and inspects both sides, then he carefully touches the sharp edge. With a shrug, he says something to Iffy, puts the knife down, and returns to the kitchen.

Winnie, on the other hand, holds on to the Mikasa and gives back the dollar Iffy had paid her for our breakfast and adds a second bill from the register.

When Iffy returns to the table, she looks disappointed. "We're up a dollar, and breakfast is free. I was really hoping to sell the knife. The waitress said there's a store down the street that might buy it."

I'm not so keen to get rid of our only weapon, however.

We leave the diner after the town has woken up, and in less than an hour, we have held on to the knife but sold the Spanish dollar for more than enough to cover two tickets on the 12:40 bus to Los Angeles.

◆ ◆ ◆

Winnie wasn't joking about how long the ride south would take. Traffic in 1952 seems to travel slower than it does in 2015. It also doesn't help that the highway is only two lanes and in need of repair. And then, of course, there are all the promised stops we make on the way.

Both Iffy and I try to sleep as much as we can. She is considerably more successful at it than me. I'm not only plagued by my six-foot height, but also by my stitched-up leg. For the most part, the constant throbbing is bearable, but it's when the bus bounces over a pothole or a crack in the road that the pain shooting out from the wound temporarily blinds me.

The bus finally arrives at the downtown Los Angeles Greyhound Bus terminal located on the corner of E. Sixth and Los Angeles Streets at just after 10:00 p.m. While the area looks just as crowded as the downtown from our home time, what's missing are the tall skyscrapers that dominate the area in 2015. Though I noticed a few buildings in the distance that might be ten or so floors high, most aren't any more than five or six.

Iffy and I join the line exiting the bus and then work our way through the building to the street. The night is cool, but it's nowhere near the frigid temperatures we experienced in Lone Pine, and the clothes we're wearing are adequate enough for now.

"How far away is Echo Park?" I ask. While I would rather not walk, if the house is close enough, doing so would save money.

"Three or four miles at least. Maybe more."

So much for that idea.

At the curb are several bright yellow taxis. Curvy, bulbous things, with signs mounted behind the trunks advertising such places as Atlas Tires and Rexall Drugs. While some drivers sit inside their cabs, others are leaning against fenders, talking with each other. A few are wearing yellow hats with black bills, though the majority are bareheaded.

The driver at the front of the line perks up when he sees us. "Need a lift?"

My plan had been to catch a city bus, but a taxi would be faster.

"How much to Echo Park?" I ask.

"A buck and a quarter. A buck fifty. Depends on where exactly you're going."

We have $3.20 left. The ride will eat up almost half of that, but a quick glance at Iffy tells me that we are both thinking it's worth it.

We climb into the back and drive off.

As we go through the north end of downtown, I see a building I finally recognize—the city hall building. It towers over all the other structures we've passed, making it the giant of LA. Funny how later, after all the skyscrapers go up, it will be the one that looks small.

We're heading west on Sunset Boulevard when our driver asks, "You got an address?"

I know the address to Kane's place, but I don't want to stop right in front, so I only give the name of his street.

"Vestal Avenue? Where's that?"

I try to remember some of the other roads in the area, and say, "Echo Park Avenue and Baxter. Do you know where that is?"

"I ain't driving on Baxter," he says.

I'm not sure what his objection to it is, but I say, "That's fine. You can just drop us right there at the corner."

Several minutes later, we turn down Echo Park Avenue and drive into the narrow valley where Kane's future house is located.

Coming into the area this way instead of jumping right to his house gives me a better sense of the neighborhood. It feels almost as if a small, quiet town has secretly moved in a stone's throw away from the center of LA.

The taxi pulls to the curb in front of the Elysian Heights Elementary School.

"Echo Park and Baxter," he says, nodding at the intersection just ahead. "A buck thirty."

We give him a dollar fifty, and as soon as we've climbed out and closed the door, he pulls a quick U-turn and heads back into the city.

"Which way?" Iffy asks.

I think for a moment. I've seen a map of the area only on my phone, but unfortunately here, where there's no signal for my cell to grab on to, the device is just a glorified camera and flashlight.

I point across the street to where Baxter disappears behind the house at the corner. "That way, I think."

I take the lead, and as soon as we turn on to Baxter, I realize why the cabbie didn't want to drive on it. The road is very steep, and we lean forward to stay vertical. Thankfully, we only have to go up one block before we reach Vestal.

I look down toward his house and see that most of the dwellings are dark. Not Kane's, though—or more accurately, not the house that will one day be Kane's. The first-floor windows are all lit up, as are several on the second floor.

We cross over to Kane's side and head down until we reach the base of the stairs.

"Wait here."

Iffy grabs my arm. "What are you going to do?"

"Just take a look."

Reluctantly, she lets go. "Be careful."

DESTROYEЯ

As I move up the steps, I crouch farther and farther down so that my head stays below the level of the front yard. This is not something my thigh particularly enjoys doing, but I clench my teeth and ignore the pain.

When I'm as high as I can go without exposing myself, I pause a few seconds and listen. The drone of distant cars plays like background music on a loop. Somewhere a few blocks away, metal hits metal—the lid of a trash can closing, I'm guessing. A dog barks and then another and another, each successively farther away, like a message is being passed on. From the house, though, I hear nothing.

Very slowly, I raise my head until the home comes into view.

A shadow plays across the ceiling in the front room, but I can't see what's causing it.

I need to get closer.

Looking back at Iffy, I pat the air and mouth the words, "Stay there." Before she can try to stop me, I take the stairs the rest of the way up, and slink across the yard to the corner of the house.

I press my ear against the sideboard, and for the first time, I can hear something inside. Music. Instrumental, I think, but too low to follow the tune. I hold my position, hoping I might hear voices or movement, but there is only the wispy sound of instruments, sometimes there, sometimes not.

The front windows are just a few feet away, but though I want to look inside, it would be risky. Better to save it as a last resort.

I look down the side of the house. A chimney rises up the wall five feet from my position. I lean so I can see around it, and spot two windows between the fireplace and the house's back corner: a small one, higher on the wall—a bathroom, I think—followed by a larger one, though not as large as those at the front of the house.

I sneak along the building until I'm just a few feet away from the bigger window. The music is louder now. I was right about it

117

being an instrumental, though I don't know the tune. My knowledge of music in my new world is even worse than my knowledge of cars.

I move out from the wall enough so that I can see a sliver of the room inside. From my exploration of the house in 2015, this should be the kitchen and family room. It doesn't appear to be as bright as the front of the house, but it's not dark, either. Somewhere inside a light is on.

I take an arcing path that will put me in a direct line with the window, but far enough away that little to none of the illumination spilling through the glass should fall on me. When I reach the apex of the arc, the room inside comes into full view.

Immediately I freeze.

The renovation that will turn half of the space into a family room has not yet taken place, so for now there is only the kitchen and a small eating area, with a countertop separating the two. The rest of the future space is walled off, creating some other room beyond. What's captured my attention, though, is not the house's layout, but Kane.

He's near the counter, angled partly toward the front of the house, but I can still see his lips when they begin to move. Whatever he says does not come through the glass. A moment of stillness is followed by a nod and a few more words, and then he turns all the way toward me and walks in my direction.

I hold rock still, resisting the instinct to drop to the ground. Several feet from the window, he veers to his right. He is almost, but not quite, out of sight. If I were to move I'd risk drawing his attention, so I hold my position.

Finally he turns and walks in the other direction. When he reaches the far end of the room, he heads into the hallway that leads to the front of the house.

The second he's out of sight, I let out a breath. That was too close.

I need to get back to Iffy. Now that we know for sure that Kane is here, we can work out a plan.

With the kitchen currently unoccupied, I don't need to worry about being seen, and head straight for the house. My intention is to duck down when I get there and then retrace my steps back to Iffy, but as I get closer to the window, I catch sight of something on the table in the eating area that stops me.

My chaser. It's just sitting there, waiting.

Unable to stop myself, I inch forward until I am right next to the window so that I can confirm I'm not seeing things.

It *is* a chaser, though I'm now not sure if it's mine, because sitting just on the other side of it is a second, almost identical box.

CHAPTER ELEVEN

The house, the ground, the night, it all sucks away from me in a rush. Even my skin feels as if it's being pulled from my body.

A second chaser.

That can only mean there's another rewinder close by.

Who? Do I know him?

And how did Kane know to come here to meet whoever it is?

I'm struggling to come up with even an implausible theory to explain what's going on when I feel my arm shake.

"Denny?" Iffy's voice, so far away. "Denny, what are you doing? Someone might see you."

As I blink the world slowly returns around me—the stars first and then the grass that I seem to be sitting on and finally the house that's propping me up. At least I'm not still standing in front of the window.

Iffy is beside me, her face tense and scared.

"Denny, snap out of it," she whispers. "We can't stay here."

I nod and push myself to my feet. We sneak along the house, then quickly cross the front yard and hurry down the steps. Though we can no longer be seen, I don't feel safe. I lead Iffy to the closest intersection and turn onto the new road.

I slump down on the edge of the sidewalk next to an empty lot, my feet in the dirt.

Iffy sits beside me. "What happened? Did you see something?"

I nod.

"Kane?"

I nod again.

"Did he see you?"

"No."

"Then what's wrong?"

I hesitate. "The chaser."

"You saw it?"

"Yeah."

"That's, that's great! Do you think we can—"

"There were *two*."

She appears confused. "Two what?"

"Chasers."

Her eyes widen. "Are you sure?"

"Of course, I'm sure. I know what a chaser box looks like."

"I didn't say you didn't."

I take a breath. "Sorry." I'm not angry at her. I'm just frustrated and confused.

"Were the boxes open?" she asks.

I shake my head.

"Could one be empty?"

"Why would there be an empty one?"

She shrugs. "A decoy? In case you show up and try to get yours back?"

"That's impossible. Kane hasn't had my chaser long enough to make a copy of the box."

"Was he alone?"

"I don't think so. He said something to someone."

"Who?"

"I couldn't see who it was."

"Could he have been talking to himself?"

I think back to when I saw him standing in the family room, facing the hallway. "No. He was responding to someone."

Several seconds of silence pass.

"So, what do we do now?" she asks.

I've been pondering that question myself for the last several minutes, but there's really only one answer. "We get the chasers. Both of them."

◆ ◆ ◆

We find a spot next to several tall bushes from where we can see the house, but won't be noticed by any neighbors.

It's well after midnight when the lights in Kane's house start going out one by one. The lamp in the master bedroom winks off last. We give it another forty minutes before we cross the road and head back up the steps to the front yard.

Though my instinct is to avoid the front of the house altogether, we can't chance missing an opportunity to get inside. Very quietly, I approach the front door and try the knob. Locked.

I try the windows, but none moves more than a fraction of an inch, so we head around the same side of the house where Iffy found me, and try the ones there. While neither opens, I do see through the last one that the two chasers are still on the table.

We move around the corner and work our way slowly across the back of the house, checking more windows. As much as I'd rather do this quietly, if it comes down to it—and I'm starting to think it might—I can smash through a window, grab the chasers, and get out of there before anyone inside can react.

I almost feel foolish when I ease open the screen door covering the rear entrance, and reach for the knob. I'm under no illusion that it'll be unlocked, but then the knob twists in my hand. When it stops moving, I give the door a gentle inward push, sure that there will be a bolt or a chain holding it in place, but it slips from the jamb and swings into the house.

I glance back at Iffy and see that she's as surprised as I am. I then push the door until it's wide enough for us to enter. After I step inside. I pause, listening for any noise that might indicate we've been detected, but there's not even a creak.

I motion for Iffy to follow me. My plan now is that as soon as I get the devices, I'll input new jump parameters into mine and we'll leave from right there in the kitchen.

The screen door is on a spring so that it will automatically close. Iffy eases it back into place so that it doesn't slam, and then we step over to the table. It's too dark for me to see any of the wear and tear marks that would tell me which box is mine, so I reach down to pick them both up.

Before I can even touch them, though, a female voice from the corner of the room whispers, "I wouldn't if I were you. You'll never get it open in time."

From the hallway steps a giant of a man. He's at least another half foot taller than me, with the girth to match. Even in the dim light, I can see his face is hard and unsmiling.

I glance at the boxes again, quickly calculating whether I can grab them and escape out the back before the man can get to me.

"Pretty, aren't they?" the woman says, her voice still soft, almost ethereal. "Vincent?"

Someone steps into the house behind me, and as I'm turning to see who it is, Iffy yells, "Let me go!"

Kane has come in from outside and now clutches Iffy against his chest.

The unlocked door was a trap that we walked right into.

"Sorry, Denny," the woman says. "No way out this time."

I twist to the left and spot her shadowy shape sitting on a chair. Whoever she is, Kane has clearly told her my name. But she's wrong about one thing. There is still a way out.

I dive for the table and grab a box with each hand. Whichever is the fake should be the lighter one, but as I raise them up, they feel the same.

Just as I realize this, the big man reaches over the table and slaps a hand against my shoulders, slamming me down. My ribs collide against the table's edge, knocking my breath from my lungs. I gasp for air as the two boxes I'm still somehow clinging to are taken from me.

"Denny!" Iffy cries.

"Quiet!" Kane tells her.

"He needs help!"

"He'll be fine," the woman says, still rooted to the same spot in the corner.

The silent giant comes around the table and flips me over so that I face him. He puts a surprisingly light hand on my chest, and after a moment I begin to relax. As I do, the pressure under my ribs eases and my breath returns.

"Gentlemen," the woman says, "please take Denny and his pet into the living room, where we can chat."

The giant yanks me to my feet and ushers me toward the hallway once Kane and Iffy have gone past. As he and I near the doorway, I hear the strike of a match, and look over to see the woman lifting a flame to a cigarette sticking out of her mouth. The light flickers over her face, revealing a slanted sneer and features that I know oh so well.

"Hello, Denny. Long time, no see."

CHAPTER TWELVE

If the entire universe disappeared earlier when I realized there were two chasers, then there are no words to describe how utterly stunned I feel now.

Sitting in the chair in the corner of the kitchen is my training mate.

My fellow rewinder.

My tormentor.

Lidia Brewer.

The condescending, upper-caste waste of a human being is the walking definition of why our old world needed to go away. She'd tried to force me to change everything back to our original time line by kidnapping Iffy. We had struggled, and when she was momentarily dazed, I had sent her far into the past with my own chaser, while keeping hers—the one I have been using ever since then.

She shouldn't be here. I banished her to 1743. Even if her trainer had also taught her how to rekey a chaser, it shouldn't have mattered. My device had been desperately low on power, and had barely enough left to activate for that final jump. She should have lived out her life in the eighteenth century and never bothered anyone again.

The giant takes my satchel from me and dumps it on the coffee table, then shoves me onto the couch next to where Kane has put Iffy.

We sit there in the darkness for several seconds before the overhead light clicks on and Lidia enters the room.

I feel Iffy stiffen beside me in surprise. I reach for her hand, but the giant slaps my wrist away.

At first glance, Lidia looks exactly as she did the last time I saw her, but as she nears, I detect a tension in her face that appears to have taken up permanent residence, and a disturbing glint in her eyes that makes me want to immediately look away.

"Didn't think you'd see me again, did you?" she says as she takes the seat across from us. "Well, then, you should have sent me back farther than 1949."

Nineteen forty-nine? I sent her to the eighteenth century, not the middle of the twentieth.

Unless . . .

During my training I was never told what would happen if a device quit mid jump, but my old chaser running out of power is the only explanation that makes sense. Instead of dropping her 272 years in the past, it obviously only took her sixty-six.

"*I've* always known you'd come," she continues. "Even knew the date, too. That's called planning." She glances at Kane, then looks back at us. "You've met my grandson, Vincent."

Grandson?

"He's part of the plan, too," she says. "And the fun part is I haven't even had any kids yet."

"One kid," Kane says. "My mom."

She gives the grandson, who must be a decade older than her, a halfhearted smile. "Of course, dear, but it doesn't really matter. That time line is no longer relevant."

There's a flicker of confusion in Kane's eyes, but unlike him, I understand immediately what she means. The version of her that will give birth to his mother did so purposely only to put one of her descendants—Kane—in the position to create this very moment. Now that it's arrived, there's no need for this Lidia to have that child. Kane has unintentionally been party to the erasure of his own mother.

"And this guy?" I ask, tilting my head toward the giant. "Another one of your descendants?"

"Leonard? No. I found him here. He's been helping me get ready for your visit." She looks around. "How do you like my house? Nice, huh?" When I don't answer, she takes a puff of her cigarette. It's a habit I don't remember her having back at the institute. "Took me about six months after I arrived to figure out how to manipulate the system here. It's amazing what selling a few simple product ideas can get you. Don't worry, nothing too time line-destroying. After all, how would you ever know about it?"

"What's that supposed to mean?"

She continues as if I haven't spoken. "Maybe it should have taken less time, but as I'm sure you can imagine, I wasn't in the best mental state when I arrived."

If you ask me, she's not in the best of mental states right now.

"I could be super rich if I wanted to be, and live in a mansion three times the size of my father's," she goes on. "But I knew doing that might make me lazy. And God forbid I started to like it here. Can't have that." She motions to the room around her. "This feels temporary to me. Just the way it should."

There's no mystery in where this is going. Bringing me here has been for one purpose only. She wants to finish what she was trying to accomplish before I exiled her. She wants to bring the empire back, and to do that she needs me. "Sorry to disappoint you, but I'm never going to tell you where the trigger is."

"The trigger?" She laughs. "Seriously, Denny, do you think I haven't already figured that out yet? I've been here three years. I've had plenty of time to find it. The hardest part was remembering the history from our time line since, obviously, those resources are no longer available to me."

"I don't believe you."

"Fair enough. I wouldn't if I were you, either." She pauses, then says, "Cahill. You told me and the others the name yourself. He's important, but the rest of your story was a lie."

I hold perfectly still, not letting the panic I feel inside show. She's referring to the story I told when I tricked the few remaining rewinders into thinking I'd stumbled on the trigger that had erased our world, and I had then set things right. Cahill, indeed, was the catalyst.

"Robert or Preston or something like that," she says. "His first name has eluded me, but it doesn't matter. *You* know who I'm talking about. You kept him from turning George Washington in to the redcoats. So Washington lived, leaving us with this god-awful reality. Am I close?"

She's not close. She's dead-on.

I fight hard to keep my face neutral.

"All I would have to do is hunt around to find the exact moment." After another puff, she taps the cigarette out in an ashtray. "I bet you're wondering if I tried to make a jump the moment Vincent showed up with my chaser."

"You couldn't. It doesn't work for you." Her chaser isn't her chaser anymore. It's keyed to me.

She smiles. "Yes. That's a bit distressing. But for argument's sake, even if it did work, I wouldn't have gone. Ask me why."

I say nothing.

"Come on. Play along, Denny. Ask me why." When I again don't answer, she switches her gaze to Iffy. "You want to take a stab at it?"

"I don't care," Iffy replies.

"You should. But then again, soon enough it won't matter to you." Lidia looks over at Kane. "Vincent, why don't you take . . . Ivy, is it? Please take Ivy up to the room we've prepared for her."

"She stays with me!" I shout as I start to push myself off the couch. Before I gain my feet, however, Leonard shoves me back down.

I try again, getting all the way up before he pushes me again. This time, I stagger but don't fall, and shove at his arms in an attempt to knock them away.

"Leonard," Lidia says, "try his leg."

I look down to see what she's talking about and notice that blood has seeped into the denim above my wound. Before I can do anything else, Leonard whacks his knee into my thigh.

I fall back onto the sofa, my vision narrowing to a small circle surrounded by black. For several seconds that's all I can see. When my sight finally returns, Kane is at the base of the stairs pushing Iffy up.

I try to rise for a third time, but Leonard grabs my leg and gives it a quick squeeze. The tortured yell that flies from my throat is quickly muffled by Leonard's meaty palm slapping down across my mouth.

"Shut up and stay there." These are the first words he's said. His voice is gravely but more tenor than I would have expected.

When my rapid breaths finally start to slow, Lidia nods at Leonard, and he removes his hand from my face.

"I don't know what happened to you," she says, nodding at my leg, "but you might want to have a doctor take a look at it."

The bloodstain has nearly doubled in size since Leonard hit me, and is damp enough to glisten in the light. Though I can't see the wound, I'm sure several of my stitches have broken.

I level my gaze at Lidia. "If anything happens to Iffy, you will pay for it."

"That's her name," she says, looking relieved. "Iffy. Should have remembered that." She leans forward. "What happens to your girlfriend is up to you. Help me, and she'll be fine. Don't, and, well . . ." The mad glint returns to her eyes with a vengeance. "Here's what's going to happen. First, you're going to fix my chaser so it works for me again."

When she doesn't immediately go on, I say, "And then what?"

"And then the fun begins."

My chest tightens when Kane comes downstairs without Iffy. Following Lidia's instructions, he retrieves the two chasers and sets them on the coffee table in front of her and then moves over next to Leonard.

Though he's trying to look tough, I sense that he's preoccupied. Leonard, on the other hand, is focused entirely on me. I doubt I could get an inch off the cushion before he batted me down again.

Lidia picks up one of the boxes. From the nick at the top, I know it's the one that I've been using these past few months, the one that used to be hers. Which makes the other device my original chaser.

"How much power does it have left?" she asks.

I don't respond.

She huffs out an annoyed breath. "The way this works is that if you answer my questions, I don't send Leonard upstairs to hurt your girlfriend. Simple enough?"

I notice Kane glance at Leonard, troubled. Lidia's blood may run through the accountant, but I'm starting to think he's found himself in a situation he didn't expect. Unfortunately, I have a feeling the same isn't true about Leonard, so as much as I would like to, I know I can't ignore her question. Before I say anything, though,

I see the second chaser out of the corner of my eye, and an idea comes to me that that might at least give me a chance to get the upper hand again.

"It was around seventy-five percent last time I checked," I say.

"You're lying. It was well below that when you stole it from me."

As I hoped, she's taken the bait.

"You're right. It *was* lower, but I charged it."

Her eyes narrow angrily. "How could you do that? I didn't have a charging kit, and I know you didn't have one, either, or you would have never let your chaser get so low."

"Which is why I had one made."

She stares at me. "You had one made?" She snorts a derisive laugh. "Right. No more lies. How much power is left?"

"If you don't believe me, the charger's in my satchel."

She glares at me, eyes narrowing, and then motions for Leonard to give her my bag. Once she has it, she dumps the contents onto the table. I'm relieved to see that the knife in the side pouch, though, has not fallen out.

Lidia is immediately drawn to the solar-powered battery and the tangle of wires that make up RJ's charging unit.

"This?" she says, picking it all up.

"Be careful. It's just a prototype, so you can damage it if you don't watch what you're doing."

She twists the battery around, looking at both sides, and then follows the wires until she finds the not-quite-perfected connecter at the end. It's close enough, though, that the shape of it surprises her.

She holds it out. "Show me."

I scoot down to the end of the sofa, near her, and she slides my original chaser toward me.

"This one first."

The lock that holds the top flap in place utilizes a different battery than the one that powers the device, a safety precaution for situations just like this, so when I touch my thumb against the small identification screen, the flap unlocks.

As I push the lid all the way open, Lidia grabs the sides of the device, ready to snatch it away if I try anything. I open the charging port and stick RJ's connector in. Nothing happens.

"I knew you were lying," Lidia states.

Ignoring her, I jiggle the connector. Just as Lidia is about to make another comment, a blinking dot appears on the main screen.

"Oh," she whispers under her breath, stunned. She watches for several seconds until the battery meter appears and begins to tick upward ever so slowly. "How long does it take to charge?"

I explain in vague terms how the system works.

"Seems inefficient," she says.

"I've only had a few months to get this developed since we last saw each other. You've been here three years and what do you have?"

She tenses. "Do you think I haven't tried? They still use vacuum tubes in their electronics here, for God's sake!" She grabs the other chaser. "Open mine."

I so want to say, "Not yours anymore. Mine." But I keep the thought from my lips, and take the box from her.

Once the flap is open, the screen comes to life.

She studies it for a second. "Seventy-two percent. So you weren't lying."

Her finger brushes across the surface as if she's afraid it might disappear at her touch. It's a moment I'm sure she's been waiting for since she realized the other box no longer worked. Soon, though, the wonder in her eyes turns mischievous, and she begins rapidly inputting the coordinates for a jump.

She glances up at me and sneers, then touches the go button.

For a split second I fear that the machine might have some kind of residual memory allowing it to recall its former owner and take her away from here. But like what happened when Kane tried to do the same thing, the chaser doesn't activate.

Instead of turning angry like I expect, she shrugs. "Worth a shot. Now, how do we make it work for *me*?"

"It needs a sample of your blood."

"My blood?"

"For the genetic markers," I say. In Iffy's world it's called DNA.

"That's right," Lidia replies as if I've only reminded her of something she already knows. But I can tell she has no idea how the process works. "Let's do it right now."

"It's not that easy. We need to prep your blood first."

A pause. "Remind me."

"It needs to be dry."

She raises a skeptical eyebrow, all pretense forgotten. "Dry?"

"A couple drops on a surface that it can be scraped off of later should do it. Metal or tile would work. Leave it overnight and it'll be ready by morning."

She studies me for several moments before saying, "And how does this dried blood get into the chaser?"

I touch the faint outline of a rectangular panel at the bottom corner of the control surface. "Under here."

She pushes on the spot but nothing happens. "How does it open?"

"There's no reason to do it until your blood's—"

"I want to see."

I say nothing for a moment. "Okay. I'll need something thin, like a table knife. And a metal paper clip. They have those in this time, don't they?"

Once more I'm subjected to her scrutiny. Finally, though her eyes never leave me, she turns her head to the side and says, "Vincent, you'll find a knife in the kitchen. And there should be a paper clip in the drawer by the cutting board."

Kane glances at Leonard as if the giant should be the one to run the errand.

"Vincent, now please."

As Kane reluctantly heads into the back of the house, I notice a flicker of light near the bottom of my vision. I almost look at it, but I stop myself when I realize what it is. A full operating screen has replaced the meter on my original chaser. It means the battery has enough power now to make a jump. I doubt that it can go very far yet, but it is working again.

Lidia appears not to have seen it, and I'd like it to stay that way. My fear is that if she did, she'll disconnect it from the charger. My chances of getting out of this are much better if there are two working devices.

"How did Vincent find you?" I ask, hoping to keep her distracted.

"It doesn't matter how. What matters is he did."

"It was the journal, wasn't it?"

"Journal?" From her tone, she knows exactly what I'm talking about.

"The locator he used to bring us here was in it. *Your diary*, I assume?"

"Well, the diary I specifically created for him to find." She smiles coyly.

Though this admission is news to me, it's not surprising. Of course, she created a journal that she intended to be read and used by one of her descendants. No doubt it's packed full of lies and half truths meant to garner sympathy for a grandmother stranded in time.

In the kitchen, I can hear drawers opening and closing.

"Why 1952? Why not 1949, when you arrived here?"

She leans back and I think she's not going to answer me, but then she says, "I'm sure you can imagine that I was in no condition to do anything when I first got here. If Vincent had come to me then, I doubt I would have even believed him. I needed time to work things out and get my head on straight. When I finally did, I picked a date." She laughs to herself. "You're going to love this part. I decided to do a little experiment. Six months ago I decided that today would be the day I wanted him to bring you to, but I didn't write it down yet. No, I just kept it up here." She taps her temple. "When Vincent used the information in the diary, the ink was already over sixty years old. The thing is, I didn't actually write it in there until after he knocked on my door this afternoon. So in a way, you're all here because I merely thought it. Blows your mind, doesn't it?" She leans back. "What can I say? I'm a genius."

"Why this year then? Why not 1953 or 1954?"

"My grandson tells me that I'll be married and pregnant within a year. Better to have him come for me at a point where I can avoid all those unnecessary steps, but still have had plenty of time to prepare everything."

"Those unnecessary steps were part of your plan, too, weren't they?"

Her smug smile is all the answer I need.

The daughter she had (will have/will never have) was not conceived out of love or the natural desire to start a family. No, Lidia wanted to create a chain that would reach all the way to 2015, where she knew I would be. And now that chain is no longer necessary.

"Why didn't you tell him to help you when you were in 2015 trying to stop me?" I ask.

Her smile slips a little. "What makes you think I didn't?"

I suddenly recall the calendar in the future version of this very house, the date of April 4 circled. Kane *had* known. So why hadn't he shown up then?

"Nineteen fifty-two is your backup plan."

"You can never be too prepared."

I shoot a quick look at Leonard. "And what about him?"

"Insurance," she says, once more looking pleased with herself.

Of course. There was no way she could know the type of person who would be coming back to get her, but she *would* know they'd need my help. Leonard was to be the muscle in case her descendant turned out to be unable to handle the job. Which, I'm fairly certain, is the case.

A few moments later Kane reenters the room and hands Lidia a knife and a paper clip.

"Before I give these to you," she says to me, "I want you to describe exactly what you're going to do with them."

She asks a few questions as I go over the procedure, and once she is satisfied, she hands the two items over.

I uncurl one end of the paper clip and then use the knife to bend the tip into a hook. Next, I turn the chaser so that the side the hinges are mounted to is facing me. There's a small hole along the edge of one hinge. It looks like a gouge mark in the wood that might have been made when the box was created. It's not. I slip the hooked end of the paper clip into the hole and then close my eyes. I have only done this once before, and that had taken me several tries. This time, though, it takes only a few seconds to find the notch and tilt the hook into it. Once I'm sure it's correctly in place, I pull.

The rectangular cutout on the display panel rises a fraction of an inch. I slip the knife just under the raised piece and lift straight up.

At its height, it sits only an eighth of an inch above the control panel, like a raised terrace. On the long side that faces the display screen is a tiny tray. Using the hook, I pull it out.

"This is where the sample goes," I say, tapping a shallow indentation in the tray with the clip. The blood I put there when I took control of this device is long gone, destroyed by the very process that mated me with the machine.

Lidia snatches the paper clip out of my hand. "Let's see if it works."

She punctures the tip of her finger with the unused end of the clip, causing a bubble of blood to appear.

As she moves her hand toward the chaser, I say, "Wait. I said dried blood."

"And I don't believe you."

"Maybe you don't, but if you're wrong and I'm not lying, you'll destroy the whole device." While I have no idea if fresh blood will actually destroy a chaser, I'm telling the truth about its need for dried blood in the keying process.

She hesitates, her finger only a few inches from the tray.

"You've waited three years," I say. "What's another few hours?"

Though I'm pretty sure she still doesn't believe me, she pulls her hand away.

"Watch him," she says to Leonard and her grandson and then disappears into the kitchen.

They stare at me until Lidia returns carrying a saucer. She tilts it so I can see a spot of red where she's dabbed her blood.

"Is this enough?"

"Should be."

I reach over to the chaser and start to close the small panel.

"No," she says. "Leave it open."

"Unless you know how to fix these things if something goes wrong, I think it would be better to keep as much dust from getting inside as possible, don't you?"

She considers the question for a moment before giving me a reluctant nod.

◆ ◆ ◆

At Lidia's orders Leonard takes me to the upstairs bathroom. I had hoped I would be reunited with Iffy, but she's not there. My escort ties my hands behind my back and gestures for me to get into the tub. It's too small for me to stretch out, and I need to fold my legs to fit, something my right thigh is not excited to do.

"You know she's just using you, right?" I say as the giant secures my wrists to my ankles with another rope. He doesn't even glance up. "Do you even understand what you've gotten yourself into?"

He yanks on the rope, pulling it tight.

"Please. At least put me with my friend."

He checks the knots and stands. If it weren't for the fact I know otherwise, I would start wondering if he was deaf.

As he walks to the door, I say, "Lidia is going to take everything from you. *Everything.*"

Looking back, he says, "Good," then turns off the light and closes the door.

I test my bindings, but the giant has been thorough and has left no slack for me to work with. There's no chance I'll be able to slip them off. I could probably twist and wiggle my way out of the tub, but even if I manage it, I'd still be tied up. There's not even a cabinet in the room that might contain something I could use to cut myself loose—just a pedestal sink, a toilet, and the tub.

For a while, I hear creaking in the hallway and the occasional muffled voice, but soon enough, silence descends. My mind spins as it throws out idea after idea on how I can turn things around. Each plan I come up with is more outlandish than the last, and even the tamest is not something I'll likely be able to pull off.

I don't mean to fall asleep, but other than the sporadic naps I had on the bus, I've been awake for going on twenty-four hours. I'm deep in a dark dreamless nowhere when someone shakes me. My eyes shoot open, and for a moment I think I'm in my bed in San Diego. But why can't I move my hands?

Right.

Kane.

Nineteen fifty-two.

Echo Park.

The tub.

While the bathroom lights are still off, a glow of a twenty-first-century smartphone illuminates Kane sitting on the edge of the bath.

"Time to get up already?" I try to sound tough and disinterested, but doubt that I pull it off.

"Tell me about where you're from," he says.

Though my eyes might be open, my brain is still working at half speed. "From? I don't know what you mean."

"Where you and my grandmother grew up."

I hesitate. "She didn't tell you already?"

He nods with his chin toward somewhere else in the house. "*She* didn't. My . . . other grandma—is that how you say it?—she told me. But I want to hear it from you."

I should have made the connection before, but life has been running at light speed since Kane stole my chaser and lured us to Los Angeles. The few moments I've had to think, I've used to look ahead, not back, as I tried to figure out what to do.

The old woman who looked back at me from her chair in the front yard of this very house sixty-three years from now.

The one who wanted more sugar in her lemonade.

Lidia. Though the half dozen decades she lived through rendered her otherwise unrecognizable, that's why I saw something familiar in her eyes.

From Kane's tone it's obvious that the Lidia here in 1952 is nothing like the grandmother he knows.

"All right," I say. I take a few seconds to gather my thoughts, then as concisely as I can, I describe what life was like in Lidia's and my original time line. I talk about the monarchy and about the institute and the caste system and the crumbling edges of our society.

He listens intently throughout, and says nothing until I'm done.

"I've been hearing the stories since I was a little boy, but the way you describe it doesn't make it sound anywhere near as nice as the way Grandma did."

"That's because she's from a privileged caste."

"And you're not?"

"Not even close."

He's silent for a moment, then asks, "Is that why you changed things?"

"Believe it or not, it was an accident."

His brow creases. "She told me you did it on purpose."

"The first time, no. The second time, yes."

"Second time? I don't understand."

I tell him the story of the twelve seconds, and how I then used it to bring my dead sister back to life.

When I finish, he sits quietly for nearly a minute before saying, "I believed her stories when I was young, but as I grew up, I tried to convince myself it was all make-believe. But every once in a while, I'd start wondering again. What if the stories were real?" He pauses, seemingly lost in a memory, before going on. "Then I found her journal when I moved in to take care of her. I read her plan for her own rescue. I still didn't want to believe that she'd been telling the truth all along, but it was hard not to. I thought, I'll just go to where she wrote that you would be. I'll see for myself that you didn't really exist, then I could just move on."

"April 4," I say, thinking about the circled date on his calendar.

He nods.

"Where were you?"

He closes his eyes for a second as if he doesn't want to remember, then lets out a quick, humorless laugh. "On the boardwalk near the pier. I saw you running, but I still didn't believe it was you. Then suddenly she was there, rushing at you, and the moment she grabbed you, you both disappeared. I could hardly believe it. All her stories had been true." Another pause. "When I went back to LA, I showed Grandma the journal, and told her what I'd seen. You know what she told me?"

"What?"

He stares at his hand, saying nothing for a moment, then, "She told me it was just stories. That I should forget it. That it wasn't important." He looks over at me. "She said that she loved me."

It's easy enough to connect the dots from there. For weeks, he did nothing, but then his own love for his grandmother and his desire to give her a second chance finally drove him to return to San Diego, to find me, and to initiate the plan a much younger and—though I don't think he realized it until he got here—vengeful Lidia had thought up.

As he stands, I say, "She's going to leave you here."

He frowns and turns for the door.

"The moment she disappears and undoes what I've done, we'll all be erased. This time line will have never been. Your mother will never have been. And unless she takes you with her, *you* will never have been."

He opens the door and leaves.

CHAPTER THIRTEEN

Pale sunlight streams through the bathroom window when I open my eyes again, but it's the sound of raised voices that wakens me.

The confines of the tub make it hard to tell exactly where the noise is coming from. One of the voices is Lidia's so I assume the other is Kane's, though I guess it could be the near-silent giant.

The distance makes it almost impossible to tell what's being said. Words here and there are all I get at first, but then Lidia moves closer to the bottom of the stairs.

"Which one of us knows how this works?" she says, annoyed. "I do. So you need to trust I know what I'm doing."

"But—" Kane begins.

"But nothing! It'll all be fine. You'll see for yourself. I'm hurt that you even doubt me."

Whatever Kane says next is too low for me to hear.

"Good," Lidia says. "Now help Leonard bring them down."

Seconds later, two sets of steps pound up the stairs.

They come for me first. Leonard removes the rope from my ankles, but leaves my wrists tied. As I'm jerked up, I'm able to get my good leg under me, but my injured one takes considerable effort to extend.

After I awkwardly climb out of the tub, Leonard manhandles me out of the bathroom and shoves me against the wall, then glances at Kane. "Get the girl."

Kane enters the room across the hall and returns several moments later with Iffy. She looks scared but otherwise unharmed.

Still, I ask, "Are you okay?"

As she nods, Leonard yanks me off the wall and pushes me toward the stairs.

"Wait!" Iffy says. "His leg. We need to take a look at it!"

"Later," Leonard says, and gives me another push to keep me moving.

I stumble forward, nearly tripping, but save myself from tumbling down the stairs by quickly leaning into the wall.

Leonard taps my back again. "Keep moving."

When we reach the living room, I notice that my original chaser is still sitting on the coffee table with the charger connected. While I had wanted them to remain joined last night, I can't help but feel a sense of dread this morning. Lidia would have never left the machine hooked up that long unless she had something in mind.

Iffy and I are escorted to the back of the house, where we find Lidia sitting at the kitchen table, a plateful of eggs and sausage and fruit in front of her. Sitting at two of the other places are similar meals, but any illusion that the food might be for Iffy and me is quickly dispelled when we are led to the two chairs where no breakfast waits.

Once we're all seated, Lidia says, "Good morning. Did you sleep well?"

Neither of us answers.

She smiles, amused, and then looks past us to where Kane and Leonard are seated. "Boys, please eat."

As Iffy and I watch as the others dig into their breakfast, my stomach can't help but grumble. The last thing Iffy or I had to eat was the sandwiches we purchased just before we got on the bus in Lone Pine.

Lidia is the last to finish. The moment she sets her silverware on the plate, Leonard gets up and collects both of their dishes. Kane lifts his plate as Leonard nears, but the giant walks right by without stopping. Flustered and embarrassed, Kane gets up and buses his things over to the sink.

"Leonard, if you could bring the saucer back in with you, I'd appreciate it," Lidia says. "And, Vincent, there's a container of toothpicks by the stove. Grab them for me."

The men return with the requested items and set them in front of her before retaking their places. The blood on the saucer is now a dry, dark brown stain.

Lidia tilts it toward me. "Good enough?"

"It should do."

Perhaps it's odd, but I've been tied up since last night, and it's only at this moment that I feel the situation is truly starting to get away from me. Once the chaser is rekeyed to Lidia, I'll have little time left to do anything. The problem is, I have no clue what that anything should be.

Lidia uses a toothpick to scrape the blood loose. What she ends up with is more than enough material for the job.

A sense of inevitable failure pounds in my mind like the drums of an approaching army. I try to block it out, but the feeling refuses to go away.

Lidia says, "Vincent, could you be a dear and bring the other chaser in? And the charger, too, please. Don't forget that."

"Sure," Kane mumbles.

As he walks out, she reaches around the back of her chair, grabs the strap that's been slung over it, then pulls my satchel onto the table. From inside, she removes the chaser that had once been hers, and turns it toward me.

"Open, please."

"Can't," I say, twisting sideways to remind her that my hands are still tied behind my back.

"Leonard," she says.

The giant pulls a knife out of his pocket, opens it, and turns me in my chair so he can cut the rope. Once my hands are free, I flex my tingling fingers to get my circulation going again.

Lidia nudges the box. "Now open it."

I hesitate until I hear Kane coming back down the hall and then touch my thumb to the screen.

My timing is perfect. The lid unlocks at the very same second that Kane returns. Though Lidia is still looking at the chaser in front of us, I can tell that her grandson's arrival has distracted her.

Knowing this might be my only chance, I pull the chaser quickly to me, and move my fingers toward the emergency escape combination.

The blow that hits me in the side of the head knocks me to the floor. I lie there, not sure what happened, and for a few seconds not even sure where I am. A hand clamps down on my arm, lifts me straight up, and then deposits me back in my seat.

Leonard.

"Nice try, Denny," Lidia says. The chaser is once more sitting in front of her, now with the flap open. "Perhaps I should do this myself."

She goes into the kitchen and comes back with a table knife and the same paper clip I fashioned into a hook last night. She struggles with getting the panel unlocked, but she doesn't give up, and eventually the rectangular section pops up. Once she has pulled out the tray, she pushes the bits of dried blood into the dimple. She then closes the drawer and pushes the panel back down.

"Is that it?" she asks.

It is, but there's no need for me to confirm this as digital readouts on the display are all suddenly replaced by a single, blinking word: *STANDBY*.

This goes on for more than a minute before the screen goes blank and the machine reboots itself. I tense, knowing that all Lidia has to do now is push a few buttons and she could jump out of 1952, leaving us all here to be erased in her wake.

Lidia, however, does not immediately input a destination. Instead, she closes the lid and then tests if the rekeying has worked by pressing her thumb against the lock screen. As I knew it would, the lid clicks open.

While this clearly makes her happy, she still doesn't tap in a locator number. In fact, she sets the chaser to the side and grabs the one Kane has brought in. The lid is still propped partially open by one of the charger's cords. When she flips all the way to the side, the screen comes on.

My hope is that she's left the device plugged in overnight only to check how the recharging went, and I think I'm right when she says, "Forty-three percent. Well, I'll be damned. You weren't lying." She picks up the battery component of RJ's charger. "So, how do I recharge this?"

I'm done helping, so I remain silent.

Looking unperturbed, she shrugs and says, "Forty-three percent should be more than enough for now."

For now? What does that mean?

She begins scrolling through the menu options. Though I'm at an angle, I can easily see the screen, and am confused when she enters the area for instructor settings, a section used only during initial rewinder training. The highlight bar moves down the list, stopping at one I'm familiar with—slave mode. Once she selects it, there's some back and forth she does between both chasers before the function is fully activated.

It's obvious now why she wants both machines powered up and ready. What the slave mode does is link one chaser to another. Back in training this meant Marie would initiate a jump on her device, and my device—with me holding it—would instantly follow wherever she went. Lidia has made it so that my original chaser will mimic everything her device does.

She's going to take someone with her, and it's pretty clear to me who that will be.

I give Iffy a quick look. Though I know she hasn't figured out the details, she knows we're in serious trouble.

Lidia coils up the charger and slips it into my satchel. "Vincent, my bag is on the counter behind you. Please grab it for me."

Kane looks almost as concerned as Iffy does, but he retrieves his grandmother's black purse and gives it to her. From inside she pulls out a leather-bound journal. Though it's the same size as the one Kane referenced to get us here, it's nowhere near as aged and the design on the cover is different. I would bet everything that this is a journal her grandson has never seen.

She opens it to a page marked by an attached ribbon. I can see three handwritten columns. I can't make out the words in the first due to the messy scrawl and the fact I'm looking at it upside down. The second column is easier, though. Numbers only, written in the distinct order one uses when writing dates. The third column is as difficult to decipher as the first. But there's more than enough there for me to make a guess as to what she's looking at.

It's a list of jumps, at least a page long, though, who knows, maybe there are more pages after this one. What I don't understand is why she's compiled even a single page of jumps. All she has to do is go back to Massachusetts in 1775. A little hunting around, and she'd figure out how to stop me from interfering with the original path of the time line.

She traces her finger across the first line and then begins entering the information into her chaser, confirming that these are indeed jump coordinates.

"I'll never let you stop me," I tell her.

She looks at me, confused. "I'm sorry?"

"I won't let you stop me from making the change." When she arrives at the Three Swans Tavern, she'll find four of me, and I know two of them will quickly understand what's going on and stop her. At least, that's what I'm hoping.

But her expected grin confuses me. "That's adorable, and I appreciate your concern. I'll admit, there was a time when I first got here that righting your error is exactly what I had planned to do. In my rage, I wanted nothing more than to bring the empire back. But I eventually cooled down and asked myself, why? There was nothing waiting for me in the empire. And there's no way that I wanted to spend the rest of my life behind the walls of the institute. I realized that there's only one thing that interests me. Do you want to know what it is?"

She locks eyes with me, and I stare back, impassive.

"You, Denny," she says. "All I care about is you and destroying everything that you know or have known." She finishes inputting her jump coordinates and then looks at me again. "Have you heard of the Hindu goddess Kali?"

India was part of the empire I grew up in. I have read history books that touch on the Hindu deities and I have heard the name Kali, but I don't recall anything specific about her. As before, however, my lips remain sealed.

"She's the goddess of time and destruction. Don't you see? *I'm* Kali, and I'm going to fulfill my destiny by taking everything from you."

I've always known that a wide river of evil flows through Lidia, but now I think it's more than just that. She's insane. Temporary or permanent, I don't know, nor does it matter, but something has snapped inside her.

She is right about one thing, however. Being both crazy and in possession of a time traveling device *does* make her Kali.

After putting the book in my satchel, she picks up the slaved chaser, stands, and says, "Leonard, it's time."

As I suspected, she's taking the giant with her.

He rises from his chair, but instead of leaving me there unguarded, he pulls me to my feet and shoves me against the wall.

"Don't move," he says calmly.

He watches me for a moment to make sure I'm doing as told before he grabs Iffy and guides her around the counter into the main part of the kitchen. There, he tells her the same thing he's just told me and then returns to the eating area.

"Vincent, please make sure she doesn't move," Lidia says.

Kane gets up, but he remains on our side of the counter. "What's going to happen to me?"

"I told you, when I'm done, I'll come back for you."

"She's lying," I say. "You'll be erased, just like—"

I see Leonard's punch coming, but am unable to jerk completely out of the way. His fist grazes off my arm with enough force that I'm sure it'll leave a large bruise. I tense, knowing I won't be able to duck from a second swing, but Leonard grabs me by the front of my shirt, straightens me back up, and then gives me what I'm sure he thinks is a gentle tap on the face.

"Behave," he says.

"Is he right?" Kane asks his grandmother. "Am I going to be erased?"

"I'm changing his past, not yours," she says. "I told you before, I'm the one who understands this stuff, remember?"

He looks unconvinced.

"I'm your *grandmother*. Why would I lie to you?" The words would sound funny coming out of her twenty-two-year-old mouth if not for the fact that several of us are about to cease to exist.

He looks at Iffy and me. While I can tell he's having a hard time believing her, there's resignation in his eyes, like he knows what's really going to happen but is still hoping the grandmother he knows, the one who would never do anything to harm him, is inside Lidia somewhere.

"Okay," he whispers.

"I'll be back before you know it," she tells him.

She hands the other chaser to the giant.

"You can't do this," I say, desperately grasping for anything that will delay her. "You can't leave us here."

"Oh, Denny. Why would I leave you here? That would defeat the purpose, don't you think? You need to see what I'm going to do. That's how this works."

As horrifying as this sounds, it means that maybe all is not yet lost. If she takes me with her, I'll still have a chance to stop her.

She gives the giant a nod, and turns to the table to retrieve her chaser. Leonard reaches out for me with his massive free arm to pull me to his side so that I can be his passenger on the trip.

As he does this, he turns his back to Kane. Lidia's grandson, whom I'm sure Leonard no longer even gave a second thought about, suddenly does something none of us are expecting.

With a quick step to the side, he rips the slaved device out of Leonard's hands and shoves the unsuspecting giant into the wall. I slip out from under the man's arm, but the move causes me to stagger several feet away.

No! I think. I need to get in contact with Kane now that he has the chaser before Lidia hits go, or it's all over. But she's already pulled my satchel over her shoulder and is reaching for her device.

"Here!" Kane shouts. For a second time, he does the unexpected and throws the slaved chaser toward me.

In the blink of an eye, I see Lidia pick up the other device. I see Leonard pushing from the wall in an attempt to intercept the chaser heading my way. And I see Kane, already in motion, slam into the giant to keep this from happening.

What I know, though, is that there's no way the slaved chaser is going to reach me before Lidia is gone, meaning it will disappear in midair and take no one with it.

I do the only thing I can and leap for it, my arms outstretched.

I think I hear Iffy call my name. I want to look back at her. I want to tell her everything will be all right. But there's no time.

Just as my fingers wrap around the box, Lidia activates the jump.

CHAPTER FOURTEEN

I'm surrounded by black, and for a split second believe that I have indeed been erased. But the fact that I can even think this means I'm still alive.

That's when I become aware of the gray mist and know that I'm within a time jump.

I made it. Dear God, I actually made it.

It's Kane who deserves the credit, though. He sacrificed himself to give me a chance to stop his grandmother. No, that's wrong. The Lidia I'm currently bound to is not Kane's grandmother. Which is exactly what I think he realized at the end.

The relief I feel for making the jump dissolves in an instant as I remember that Iffy has been left behind. My heart seems to stop, and my throat feels as if it has constricted to the width of a hair.

I tell myself that in the grand scheme, it doesn't matter. Once I deal with Lidia and clean up whatever mess she creates, my final act will be to return to San Diego in 2015 and change the time line so that Kane never steals the chaser. As far as Iffy will be concerned, everything that has happened after that point will not have occurred. But as many times as I tell myself all this, I can't get rid of the thought that there's a real possibility I've lost Iffy forever.

And then there's my sister, too.

Oh, God.

The weight of it all feels as if it's about to crush me when the gray starts to fade and our destination begins to replace the mist around me. It's only at the last second that it dawns on me that I'm not arriving as I typically would. I entered the journey nearly horizontal and in midair. And while my chaser is able to accommodate for elevation, I materialize at a steep angle that has my toes touching the ground, but my head and my outstretched hands a good couple feet above it.

I thump down on a grass field with an *oomph*, and know that I've just racked up a few more bruises. The headache from the journey is annoying but not overbearing, and I'm able to quickly get to my feet.

I turn in a circle, knowing Lidia has to be somewhere near.

Wherever we are, it's night. Lidia has stuck to training in that regard. The field is surrounded on three sides by a U-shaped building and by a high fence on the fourth. As my eyes adjust, I realize it's not a typical building. While it has a roof, the side nearest me is open air and contains rows of chairs moving higher and higher, all facing the field.

A stadium, I realize. And I'm right in the center of it.

I turn toward the sound of movement off to my right and see the outline of a person push up from the grass fifteen feet away. Lidia. Since she hasn't traveled in several years, I'm guessing it's taken her longer to deal with the trip's side effects than it did in the past.

I rush at her, knowing that this will be my best shot to subdue her. But I only cover about a third of this distance, when everything disappears again, and we are once more in the grip of a time jump.

When traveling great distances into the past, the preferred method is to make a series of shorter trips. This is done to lessen the pain one feels, since the longer a jump, the stronger the headache. A trip of a couple centuries could even black you out for days. Go too long in one leap, and you'll arrive dead.

Given that Lidia has taken us on a second hop so quickly, I figure our ultimate destination must be a great distance from 1952. It wouldn't surprise me if she'd been lying about no longer being interested in resurrecting the empire, and that we're actually heading for the trigger point in 1775.

As the mist begins to clear again, I brace myself, knowing Lidia will be in front of me. I want to get to her before she triggers the next jump. The night is so dark, however, that I can't even see her outline this time.

I rush forward anyway, my hands blindly waving in front of me, ready to grab her. But she also hasn't remained still, and instead of knocking into her, I feel her brush by me going in the other direction.

As I'm turning, we jump again, and I am surprised to find that we're back in the stadium. I finish whipping around and see that Lidia is running toward the seats, already thirty feet away from me. I raise my foot, and—

Jump.

The deep dark of night again. I can see the stars above me, but little else. What I hear, though, is Lidia putting even more distance between us.

I start after her but am afraid of going too fast as I can still barely even see my own hand.

Jump.

The stadium again. Only Lidia is not on the field anymore. In fact, I don't see her anywhere.

Jump.

Darkness.

I can hear her running steps again. She's much farther away now, and no longer directly in front of me.

Jump.

Stadium.

I'm all alone and can hear nothing but the sound of vehicles on a road somewhere outside the complex. Having no idea now where she could be, I remain where I am, anticipating another jump. But several minutes pass, and I'm still here.

I've been a fool. My chance to grab her was before she ever rose from the grass. It's clear what she's been doing. She can't unslave my chaser from hers without accessing the device in my possession, and therefore knows wherever she goes, I will go, too. What she can do, however, is put enough distance between us so that when she does jump, she won't need to worry about me being right behind her.

If I can't locate her, she'll be free to do whatever it is she has planned, while I can only witness the deeds her hatred of me has sparked.

I must find her.

Not for my sake, or Iffy's, or Ellie's, or even Kane's.

For everyone's sake.

I have to—

Jump.

◆ ◆ ◆

I'm someplace new. A quiet city street, streetlamps on—electric, I think, not gas—and most of the houses dark. As I turn for a look around, I see that the horizon to my right is an orange and yellow blend more representative of a sunrise than a sunset.

I look at my chaser to find out for sure. It's 5:47 a.m. Surprisingly, we've come back to 1952, only a week before Kane, Iffy, and I are to arrive. A check of the log reveals that the two jumps we had been alternating between were to 1927 and 1903.

I cradle my chaser to my chest, wishing I had my satchel to put it in, and approach the cars parked along the side of the street. The license plates are all black backgrounds with yellow characters. Embossed across the bottom is CALIFORNIA.

Could it be that we're back in Los Angeles? Back where we started?

I wonder if Lidia has returned to her house, but a quick look around makes me think this isn't the case. The Echo Park area where her house is located is extremely hilly, while the area around where I stand right now is flat. She can't be more than a few blocks from where I am. There just hasn't been enough time to get any farther away.

We've already been here longer than any other place we've jumped since leaving Iffy. Instead of just standing around to see what happens next, I decide to try and figure out where we are. If I can find an area where there are more businesses, I should be able to locate a newsstand or something else that will clue me in. After a quick study of my choices, I decide my best bet is to head north.

Though it's still not six o'clock, I can sense the city coming to life around me as I walk—a door opening here and there, a light coming on inside a house, an engine roaring to life. The sky continues to lighten above me, and the slight chill of the night is giving way to what feels like will be a pleasant October day.

I turn left three blocks up, thinking this will give me a better shot at finding what I'm looking for, and indeed it does, though not in the way I expected.

Lidia stands on the sidewalk at the other end of the block, staring at me. I hesitate a moment before starting in her direction. I'm sure that she'll start running again, but she holds her ground. I pick up my pace to a lopsided semi-jog.

I'm about fifteen feet away when she raises her chaser, her finger over the go button, and says, "Perfect."

Down she presses, and away goes the city street.

The jump is so short, though, I never see the mist. Suddenly I'm in a room, running toward a wall dominated by a large window. I skid across the floor and crouch down so that I slam into the concrete portion of the wall instead of crashing through the glass. I hit shoulder first, and nearly drop the chaser.

"Denny?"

I whip back around at the sound of Lidia's voice and scan the room behind me, but it's empty, not just of another person but of anything.

"You didn't hurt yourself, did you?" Her voice is coming from higher up than it should. I look to the ceiling and see a speaker mounted in the exact center.

As I stand up, I look around for the exit, but there isn't a door anywhere. The walls to the back and sides are solid. I turn to the windowed wall.

Lidia stares at me from the other side in a room that looks similar to mine except that there's a table against the back wall and next to it a door. Something is on the table, but it's too dim back there to see what it is. From the ceiling hangs a wire attached to a microphone, which dangles just above Lidia's head. I look above me and see there's an identical mic in my room, too.

Looking back, I study the glass for a moment. It's thicker than a normal pane, and through it spiders a mesh of wires. I have a feeling even if I had crashed into it, though the glass might have cracked, I wouldn't have broken through it.

"Where are we?" I ask.

"Do you like it?" She looks around and then back at me. "I didn't know if I'd ever get the chance to use it."

"*Where* are we?"

"Just outside of Los Angeles in an area I think you know as the Shallows."

The Shallows? My original home.

"I thought it would be fun putting this someplace you were familiar with. I contemplated having a window to the outside installed, too, but there's really not that much to see. Just trees and bushes. Hardly anyone lives out here yet."

"You built this place?"

"I had plenty of time to make my plans and prepare for any contingencies. I had this place built especially for you. Just in case. The walls are a foot thick. Concrete slab ceiling. And this glass?" She walks up and raps on the window in front of my face. "One of the strongest they make in this era. You might be able to get through it, but it'll take you a long time."

"Let me out."

"What are you talking about, Denny? No one's keeping you there. All you have to do is unslave your chaser and you can jump anywhere you want."

I would like nothing more than to jump into her room, grab her chaser, and get out of there. Unfortunately, I know full well that the moment I unslave my device, she'll activate her own jump, and leave before I can get to her. If that happens and for some reason I'm not immediately erased, I'll never be able to find her. She could be anywhere in time. My only option is to keep my box connected to hers and hope that she makes a mistake.

"No?" She laughs after several seconds. "You're a coward. Your kind always are."

She turns away from me, walks back to the table, and lifts the mound I noticed earlier. As she returns to the glass, I see that it's a simple-looking rucksack that, like my satchel that hangs across her torso, could fit into most eras without drawing attention.

"Like it?" she asks. "My bag of presents. If the institute was still around, boy would I get in trouble for traveling with this. But they're not an issue anymore, thanks to you." She snickers as she pulls my satchel off and puts it inside the rucksack. She then dons the larger bag. "I haven't properly thanked you for helping Vincent come back to me."

"Don't bother."

"No, really. Thank you. Without your assistance, I would have had to go through childbirth and raising a baby and . . . ugh. Not something I'm interested in." We stare at each other for a few moments before she says, "Well, I guess we should get things started. I would hold on to your chaser if I were you. We'll be going soon. I just need to put a little distance between us."

"Where are we going?"

"Thought we'd start off small." She walks toward the back of her room.

"What are you planning, Lidia?"

"I told you already. I'm going to destroy everything you have known."

If she really wants to get to me, there's an obvious way. "It's Iffy, isn't it? What are you going to do? Erase her whole family?"

Lidia reaches the door, but instead of opening it, she looks back at me, shaking her head. "Denny, Denny, Denny. Do you really think I'm that petty?" She motions to the room around her. "That I'd build all this only to change the fate of one insignificant girl? If that were my intention, it certainly wouldn't have taken three years to plan. I could have figured that out in an afternoon. Perhaps that might have broken your heart, but that's not enough for me. I want to rip it to shreds." She pauses. "When I was daydreaming about how I could get back at you, I thought about those months we were in training at the institute, and I remembered how you spent most of your free time in the library, studying, and how you always got the top score on the tests. And I realized the way to crush you is to destroy your greatest passion. It's not some girl you met in a bastardized time line." The side of her mouth ticks up in a half smile. "It's history, Denny. Your love for it was why the institute stooped so low to pull you out of your caste."

She opens the door, letting in a stream of bright sunlight, and hesitates on the threshold for a moment before looking back at me again. "I'm glad you're coming along to witness the bloody mess *I* create. But make no mistake. Everything that happens from this point forward is your doing."

She steps outside and the door closes behind her.

"Lidia!" I yell. "Lidia!"

But she's gone, and I fear that I will never set eyes on her again.

CHAPTER FIFTEEN

My guess is that along with building this doorless containment cell, Lidia has stashed a car somewhere nearby. By the time we jump again, I figure she could be as many as twenty or twenty-five miles from me.

The jump is so short that once more the gray never forms. The cement floor that had been under my feet is replaced by sloped ground covered with dry grass. Instantly I start to slide downward, and am able to stop my descent only by falling against the hillside and grabbing a rock.

This action nearly causes me to lose my hold on my chaser. I quickly readjust my grip, and know one of my top priorities is finding something secure to carry it in. After a look around, though, I realize I won't be able to accomplish that where I am.

The hillside is steep. Below me another forty feet, it becomes nearly vertical. From where I've stopped, I can't see how far the cliff drops, but I'm sure it's long enough for me to have broken more than just a few bones if I'd gone over.

Above me the terrain continues at the same angle for another 150 feet. Climbable, perhaps, but one missed step and down I'd go. My best bet is to stay where I am until Lidia decides it's time to travel again.

There is some consolation, though. At least my vantage point overlooks the ocean. Given that the coastline looks very much like that just north of Los Angeles and that the sun appears to be moving in a downward arc leading toward the water, I feel it's safe to assume that I'm looking at the Pacific. I could access the chaser's location map to check, but with my precarious position, there's no sense in taking a chance.

To make myself a bit more comfortable, I clear away some grass and start to level a small portion of ground to use as a seat. Naturally, before I can finish, we jump again.

This trip seems even shorter than the last, and I find myself on the exact same hill, just about a hundred yards to the left of my previous position, and thankfully, in an area with a much gentler slope.

I take a seat on the grass and check the date. It's May 29, 1952, and the time is 8:47 a.m. Now that I'm able to check the map without worrying I might drop the device, I confirm that my hunch was correct. I'm in the coastal mountains about a dozen miles west northwest of Santa Monica.

Ten minutes pass, then twenty, and then thirty. It's growing warm, and I wish that there were some shade nearby.

In my caste Eight childhood, waiting seemed to be part of every day—waiting for the doctor to see if he had time for us, for the grocer to put out his inferior goods, for the teacher to finally dismiss us for the day.

For my father to talk to me.

Always waiting for someone else, just like I'm doing now.

I spend three hours weaving between concern over what Lidia might be doing and thoughts about how I might trap her. For each scheme, I plan out every step, and try to ignore the glaring problems they all have. But finally I must face it. I can do nothing if I'm not close to her. I need to find a way to trick her into coming to me.

As I think this through, something tickles the back of my mind. A memory, I think, but before I can extract it, Lidia presses her go button again.

Yet another quick trip. This time, however, I don't arrive on the side of the mountain but in someone's backyard. Lucky for me, the occupants of the house haven't noticed me, and to keep it that way, I duck down and hurry around the side, out of direct view.

I look at the chaser. It's still 1952, just one day later, and late afternoon.

I look down the side yard toward the front of the house, and spot a nook between the chimney and the trash cans. The perfect place to hide if this ends up being another multi-hour stop.

Once I settle into my new position, I do my best to pretend the smell coming from the cans isn't as bad as it really is. I'm there for just over forty-five minutes when—

"Hanging in there, Denny?" Lidia's voice comes from the other side of the gate, just beyond the trash cans.

Before I have a chance to wonder how she found me, the house disappears, and in the blink of an eye, I'm standing between the wall of a concrete building and a field of drying brush. This lasts barely five seconds before we jump again, and I'm back inside the doorless cell.

"Did you have a good time?" Lidia asks from her side of the glass. "See anything interesting?"

"What was that all about?"

"See for yourself."

She nods past me with her chin. Turning, I see two newspapers stacked on the floor behind me.

"The one on top's the original," she says.

The concrete wall I'd been standing near moments ago must be right outside this building. She used that short amount of time to deposit the papers in here. Then we had hopped again, like rabbits, she moving from this room to the one she's now in, and me from outside to here.

I walk over and pick up the papers. They're both copies of the *Los Angeles Examiner*, and, in fact, both are dated May 30, 1952. On the front pages are the exact same articles. "What am I looking for?"

"Page three, at the top."

Since there are no tables in the room, I kneel down and open each paper on the floor. While everything on page two matches, the articles at the top of the page threes are different. In the one she called the original is a story about a robbery at a grocery store in downtown. In the other one, the headline reads:

WOMAN KIDNAPPED, FORCED TO DRIVE OUT OF TOWN

The story is about a woman named Felicia Andrews. On May 29, while I was getting sunburned on the mountainside, Miss Andrews had apparently been kidnapped in her own car and made to drive nearly thirty miles out of town. The story describes the kidnapper only as a "mystery woman." Miss Andrews was then freed, and the kidnapper disappeared.

"You?" I ask.

"Guilty," she says, holding up her hands.

What she's done probably won't make a large impact on the time line, but who knows? Perhaps this Andrews woman had originally been destined to do something important, but now will live the rest of her life in fear.

I walk over to the window. "Why?"

"Getting a little practice in first, having some fun."

"You don't need to do this," I plead, trying to come up with something to stop her from doing anything else. "Just . . . just exile me somewhere like I did to you. That would be fair. You don't need to destroy everyone's lives. You just need to destroy mine."

She responds with a scoff and then takes her rucksack off, puts the chaser inside, and pulls out a hardback book. She approaches the window again, and presses the book against the glass. Printed on the cover is:

WORLD WAR II: A COMPREHENSIVE HISTORY

"What are you going to do? Change the war?"

She smiles but says nothing as she slips the book back in her bag. "Sit tight. You'll be out of there soon."

Like before, she leaves by the door, no doubt to put distance between us again. As soon as she's gone, I turn to the question that's been bothering me since she brought me back here. How did she find me in the side yard of the house? The question triggers a return of the thought poking at the back of my mind. Now, though, I am able to pull it into the light.

Back in my first week in Iffy's time line, right after I had accidentally triggered the switch that kept Washington alive, Lidia had found me in downtown Los Angeles, outside the public library. She had *found* me.

She'd said Bernard, her supervisor, had showed her how to "tune" her chaser so she could locate other devices. Obviously she had used that method again just a little while ago to find me at the house.

I sit cross-legged with my chaser in my lap and scroll through the menus. I'm sure I've seen every function before, and don't remember any that would activate this ability, but maybe I missed a special setting or something similar. I work my way screen after screen through all the menus, but nothing even hints at detection possibilities.

I *must* figure this out. I know in my heart there is truth to what Lidia said to me earlier. Perhaps what she's planning on doing isn't 100 percent my fault, but I can't help feeling I share in the responsibility. I'm the one who caused her to step over the edge into insanity. I'm the one who took away everything she understood.

If it's not a single function, then perhaps it's a combination of different functions that by themselves can't locate another machine, but working together might. Yes, of course. That's got to be it, right? Because the last thing I want it to be is something physically I need to do to the device, like rearranging wire connections. First off, I'd have no clue what wires or components needed to be tampered with, and second, I'd have to assume that the moment I opened the machine, the slave mode would be deactivated. That's something I can't chance.

I start going through the screens again, slower this time and with an eye to what functions might be needed to create a makeshift chaser detector. The answer has to be here somewhere; it just has to—

Jump.

◆ ◆ ◆

My arrival at our new destination isn't greeted by the safety of night but by bright sunlight. Worse, there is noise everywhere. Engines and horns and voices.

As soon as I fully materialize, a shriek fills the air only a few feet away from me, and is quickly joined by several others. Without even thinking, I close the chaser's lid as I look around. I'm in the middle of a busy sidewalk. The first scream came from a woman who had been about to walk through the space I now inhabit. She has witnessed my arrival, but she's not the only one, and I'm quickly surrounded by a circle of fearful stares and shouts.

A man hollers a question at me. At least I think it's a question. I don't understand him. He's not speaking English. It sounds like—

Another yell, this from someone outside the circle trying to push through.

—German, I realize.

The crowd parts for a man in a uniform. Around his arm is a red band with a white circle containing the black symbol I recognize from research I've done on Iffy's world. In light of the book Lidia showed me, I guess it should be no surprise that we're in Nazi Germany, either in the period known as World War II or the years just before it. A glance at my chaser would tell me for sure, but I can't open the box and reveal what's inside with all these people focused on me.

The uniformed man starts to ask me a question, but the woman who almost ran into me cuts him off and begins talking rapidly in what I'm sure is a detailed description of how I appeared out of nowhere.

Even if the officer doesn't believe her, I must assume he'll still take me in, and likely separate me from my chaser. Being detained is not an option. I must stay free. So while his attention is momentarily on the woman, I lunge through a narrow gap in the crowd.

A few of the bystanders try to grab me, but most jerk away as if I'm diseased. Those that do get a hand on me are easy enough to shake off, and soon I'm in the street running for my life.

There are several shouts behind me, but I keep my focus on my path ahead, and cut through the traffic, then duck into the crowd moving along the opposite sidewalk.

The shouts continue as I push through the crush of pedestrians, and soon the voices are joined by the shrill blast of a whistle.

I turn down the first street I come to. It's at least as crowded, if not more so, but instead of forcing my way through, I slow my pace a little so that I can blend in more and not draw as much attention.

Unfortunately, it's not working, as many of those I pass still look me up and down.

My clothes. Most of the men here are wearing button-down shirts and slacks or uniforms. My bloodstained jeans and dark T-shirt must make me look like I've escaped from some kind of hospital.

I hear the whistle again, but it's farther behind me now, and sounds as if whoever is blowing it—the officer, I assume—is still on the street where I originally arrived. Whether he is or not, I can't afford to ease up, so at the next street I turn right.

Every few blocks after this, I randomly change directions again. I have long stopped hearing the whistle when I reach a park and finally allow myself to rest on an empty bench among several trees and bushes. In the grassy area at the other side of the park, several women are gathered together watching their children play. Except for an older couple walking down the stone path, there is no one near me.

When the beat of my heart starts to slow, I look at the chaser. The date is July 23, 1939. I'm still not sure if that's before any fighting has begun. I just know it's a few years prior to when the United States will join the war.

So what is Lidia doing here? Killing their leader?

I think for a moment. Hitler. The guy with the small mustache.

From all the accounts I've read, ridding the world of him would be a great thing. Though that would definitely change history, in Lidia's current state, I can't see her doing something that might *improve* the time line. So what then?

My mind explodes with dozens of different possibilities, all of them equally horrendous, but there's no way for me to really know the answer right now. I tell myself I need to focus on what is in my control and note as much about this reality as possible so that once

I do figure out what she's done, I'll have a familiarity with this time that will help me when I come back and fix things.

I check my chaser for location information, and discover we are in the city of Berlin—the capital of Germany in both this time line and mine.

I close my eyes and try to remember what I've read about this era, but it's really only been overviews, with little specific information about Berlin, other than this is where Hitler ruled from. The little I know continues coming back to me in dribs and drabs. If I'm remembering correctly, at this point Hitler has been in power for several years, and has basically turned the country into a military state.

As my eyes open again, my gaze falls on my bloodstained pants. I'm in need of another change of clothes, and it would be best to do it soon for my own safety. Unfortunately, I don't think I'm going to find any washing machines sitting outside like I did in Lone Pine.

I look beyond the park, wondering where people of 1939 Berlin buy their clothes. Not that I have any money, but it will be easier to take from a business than to break into someone's home.

Stone buildings surround the park. Perhaps there's a store in one of them I can sneak into. I scan the area to make sure there are no military or police around and then head off in search of a new outfit.

I discover a handful of clothing stores and two tailor shops down a side street four blocks away. Unfortunately, one of the tailor shops is locked up tight, while the other shop and the clothing stores all have several customers inside. Fewer people will give me a better chance of getting away.

I slip into an alley with the intention of waiting until one of stores is less busy, but then I spot something white fluttering from a back window three floors above me. A shirt. I scan the rest of the building and spot hanging in a higher apartment window several dresses and a couple pairs of pants. There are other windows where clothes are drying, but these two straddle either side of an iron fire escape that runs up the back of the building, making them much easier to reach.

I loathe the idea of stealing from another residence, but this is an opportunity I can't pass up.

After tucking my shirt in and sticking my chaser inside it so I can use both hands, I maneuver an empty barrel below the fire escape and use it to reach the ladder sticking down from the second-floor landing.

My leg throbs as I jump up to grab the lowest rung. I need to attend to my wound soon. If it becomes infected, it could derail what I need to do. It's a problem for later, though.

I head up to the third-floor landing, making as little noise as possible. The metal structure isn't designed to be silent, though, and the best I can manage is to minimize the intensity of the clanking. Every few steps, I glance over at the building across the alley, convinced that I'll see someone staring out a window at me, but so far my presence has gone unnoted.

I move to the railing along the right-hand edge of the third-floor landing. The window I'm interested in is three feet away, and the shirt one foot farther. I lean out over the rail, stretching my arm as far as I can. My fingers touch the shoulder of the shirt, but I'm unable to grab on to the material.

Propping myself on my good leg, I raise my bad one higher. This helps me to extend my length by a few more inches, and I'm able to clamp my thumb and first two fingers over the shirt and give it a pull. It easily slips from the nearest wooden clip holding it to the wire across the window. The other clip, though, isn't so eager to give up. When I give the shirt a hard yank, the clip pops off the shirt and flies into the air.

I curse to myself. If the clip falls inside the house, I'll be discovered. But instead of flipping through the window, it hits the stone outside it and then tumbles through the air to the alley below.

Careful not to let my new possession touch my bloody pants, I pull myself back onto the landing, then head up one more floor. The window the pants hang in is closer to the fire escape, and the pants should be easier to obtain than the shirt. As I reach for them, though, I hear a shout behind me.

A woman is leaning through a window of the opposite building, pointing at me. She continues to yell at me in German, and though I can't understand her words, I get the meaning well enough. More people look through their windows, and a few join in with shouts of their own. I see a man on a lower floor duck back inside, and I'm sure he'll be in the alley in moments.

I reach for the pants, intending to grab them and then make my way up to the roof. There should be another way down, which will allow me to avoid those who've already spotted me. But as I'm pulling the pants free from their clips, a hand reaches out and grabs my wrist. It's old and small, but squeezes tight like a vise. I hear a door open down below, and see the man who'd been looking out his window rush into the alley.

I give my arm a yank, but the hand does not let go. Realizing that my best option is no longer to go up, I swing one leg over the rail that surrounds the landing and then the other leg, and jump through the window into the apartment.

The old woman who'd grabbed my wrist stumbles backward, but she quickly gets over whatever shock she may have had and starts talking loudly at me in what I'm sure is some kind of lecture about the flaws of my character.

"I'm sorry," I say as I scan for the door.

The apartment is stuffed with furniture that's even older than the woman. On the walls are a few dusty paintings and some framed photographs.

The woman steps toward me again and tries to grab the pants away. I can't help but feel like a complete jerk as I move them out of her reach, but it's not like she'll understand me if I tell her that I need the pants so I can save the world as she knows it.

The only exits from the room are on either side, open doorways to elsewhere in the apartment. I move toward the one on my right, hoping it will lead to the way out, but I find myself in a bedroom. There's an old man on the bed, sleeping. These, I think, must be his pants, and I feel even worse.

The woman comes in behind me. She's still berating me, but her tone is now a harsh whisper.

"Excuse me," I say as I push past her back out of the room.

I hurry over to the doorway on the left. It leads into a small kitchen and dining area, but more importantly, there's a door that looks like a main entrance.

I glance back into the other room and see the woman walking toward me as fast as she can. I wish there was something I could leave for her to pay for what I'm taking. But I have nothing of value, and all I can do is say, "I really am sorry."

I pull open the door and enter a long dark hallway. There seem to be exits at either end. I go left and limp-run past a handful of other doors by the time the woman enters the hallway and yells after me. I worry that her neighbors will rush out to help her, but it's not until I reach the end of the hall that I hear the first door open somewhere behind me.

Stairs lead both up and down. I head to ground level, the old woman's shouts fading fast. When I reach the bottom floor, I peek into the hallway. The closest section is a mirror image of the fourth floor, but then, maybe ten doors down, the left side opens up in what I assume is the lobby of the building.

I want to run again, but I worry that if someone comes out and sees me, it will make them curious and could cause problems, so I keep my pace to a quick walk.

A mother and two young children are entering the building when I arrive in the small lobby. I grab the door for them, and she gives me a relieved look as she herds the kids inside.

"*Danke,*" she says.

This is a word I do know. I'm also pretty sure of what the response should be, but I don't want to risk messing up the accent, so I just smile and nod as I scoot by them and exit.

I clasp my ill-gotten garments against my shirt to help keep the chaser tight to my stomach, and head down the street. Thankfully, the sidewalk here is not as busy as the others I've been on.

A couple of minutes later, I find another alley. This one is surrounded by mostly businesses, and there are few windows along it. I head down it until I reach several bins that will block me from view of anyone who might wander into the area.

I pull off my T-shirt and jeans and then take a moment to examine my wound. I'm happy to see that though a few of the stitches have popped, more than I expected remain. It's a dirty mess, though. I wipe what I can away with the jeans and then tie the T-shirt around it like a bandage. This won't keep blood from staining my new pants forever, but at least it should slow the process.

The white shirt fits well enough, but the pants are at least two sizes too wide at the top and nearly that much too short at the bottom. I look around for something I can use as a belt, and find a length of twine from a discarded package in one of the bins that will do the job. Set now, I head back toward the street.

I make it within a dozen feet of the end when Lidia moves us again.

◆ ◆ ◆

A second later, I find myself in the backseat of a car. Since I was standing when the jump occurred, my chaser's safety functions detected the obstructions and forced me to arrive in a crouch. It's an unnerving sensation, but not the first time it's happened. Thankfully, there are no other occupants.

It's night again, and the vehicle appears to be parked along a residential street, with no one currently using the sidewalks. Satisfied there's no immediate threat, I check my chaser. We've traveled about ten hours to 3:00 a.m. on July 24. Since this makes it unlikely the owner of the vehicle will be returning anytime soon, I decide to stay where I am. It's a perfect opportunity for me to figure out how to get a fix on Lidia's exact location.

I start methodically going through the menus again. The mapping function would have to be part of any search tool. But what else? I scroll through a dozen other menus, but nothing stands out to me. Returning to the master sections list, I'm about to select the category covering maintenance functions, when my attention is drawn to the line item several below it: *COMPANION*.

Back at the institute, using a companion was an integral part of every trip. Companions eased the trip effects rewinders felt by taking much of it on themselves. They also helped with the accurate arrival at destinations. I've grown used to jumping without a companion since I disconnected the function soon after I'd exiled Lidia. My first chaser had somehow linked to Iffy, and I didn't want my newly appropriated one to do the same and force her to take on my pain. But the fact that the machine could reach out through the companion function makes me think there might be something there that can be used as part of this detector.

I look through its menu and identify two additional functions that I have a feeling are relevant. I think I'm close now, maybe one or two more functions to bring the tracker to life.

As I return to my search, though, I'm yanked out of time again.

◆ ◆ ◆

I'm starting to feel like a dog on a leash that never knows when and in which direction its master will pull.

It's night and a city again, though if this is Berlin, we are in a totally different district. The buildings along the street I'm on are much taller. Not quite the skyscrapers of 2015 Los Angeles, but working on it.

The time and date on my machine put us at 11:30 p.m. on June 1, 1950. I use the map function to decipher the location number, and discover that we're in New York City, on the island of Manhattan. That explains the buildings. What it doesn't explain, however, is the complete lack of activity. The New York I've read about, seen in movies, and experienced on a small scale myself seems to be in constant motion. Even in this earlier decade, the city was supposed to always be hopping. But the street is deserted. Even the intersections that cross it are empty.

It could be that I'm just on a minor road in a part of town that is more active during the day. Whatever the case, I have more important things to worry about. I sit on the curb and pick up my examination of the menus again.

Though I hear a car turn onto my street, I stay focused on my task. I have no interest in the occupants, and assume they'll have no interest in me, either.

"Hey!"

I look up, startled. The sedan rolling to a stop across from me is not just any vehicle. It's a police car.

As calmly as I can manage, I close the lid of the chaser and say, "Yes, officer?"

He stares at me, waiting, but I have no idea what he wants.

"It's after eight," he finally says.

"Um, okay. I know."

Again the stare.

"What?" I ask.

With a growing scowl, he opens his door and climbs out. I can see his partner now, behind the steering wheel, looking bored. The first cop opens the back door and then motions me toward it. "All right, let's go."

"Go where?"

"Come on, buddy. Let's not make any trouble."

"I'm not trying to make trouble. I haven't done anything."

"Is that right? Well, I hate to tell you this, but you're three and a half hours over. As much as I'd like to ignore that fact, you know I can't do that. Now get in the back, or I'll put you there myself." To emphasize his words, he takes a step toward me and sets a hand on the gun hanging from his belt.

"Three and a half hours over what?"

"Enough already. Get in the damn car!"

He flicks off the tab holding his gun in place and starts to pull the weapon from its holster.

A few times I've been in a situation where there are no good options, just ones that are slightly less bad than others. This is one of those times, and at the top of my current list of bad options is being trapped in the back of a police car.

So I take off running down the street in the direction from which the police car has come.

A gunshot rips through the night. I don't know where the bullet's gone. I'm just grateful it hasn't hit me.

I'm fifty feet from the nearest intersection when the cop shoots again. This time I actually hear the bullet pierce the air a few feet above my head and then smash through a window of the building to my left.

Just as I reach the corner, I hear a door slam and then the engine of the cop car roar into reverse. I take the turn, hoping there's another intersection close, but it's a long block without any breaks. I sprint—if you can call it sprinting—knowing I will never make it to the next corner in time.

Behind me, I can hear the cops nearing the corner. They'll be behind me at any second. Now would be a *great* time for Lidia to take another jump. Apparently, though, she's otherwise occupied.

I scan ahead, looking for anything I can hide behind. That's when I spot the storm drain along the curb. I don't know if it's wide enough for me to slip through, but I run to it, and drop to the ground beside it.

My feet and legs go through without a problem. My waist rubs against both sides, but also doesn't slow me. The police car's tires squeal as it takes the corner. I'm unsure if they can see me or not, so I continue to push my way through the opening.

It's my head that proves to be the biggest problem. I have to turn it sideways and can feel the skin scraping off my ears as I pass all the way inside. At this point, the cops have already driven by me. I hear them screech to a halt in the middle of the next intersection, and can imagine that they're looking in all directions, wondering where I've gone.

I figure it's only a matter of time before they decide to check the drain, so I follow the spillway into the main tunnel and then head down the tube. I randomly turn down other pipes, and don't slow until I am well away from where I started.

When I spot another spillway, I grab the lower lip and pull myself up so I can peek outside. The road in front of me is wide, and I can see darkened stores on the other side. While this is clearly a main thoroughfare, what I don't see is a single moving vehicle or pedestrian. It's as quiet as the street where I arrived.

I try to remember if June 1, 1950, is some kind of special day in Iffy's time line. There are a few of those in her history, I know, where the whole country seems to shut down for twenty-four hours or more. Perhaps this *is* one of those occasions, but if it is, I can't remember its cause. The truth is, I should be right in the middle of America's postwar boom, when the country was going nonstop.

I move back into the tunnel until I come to a ladder leading up to a manhole. I know if Lidia were to jump now, the chaser's safety buffers would deposit me at ground level, but I'd feel better just the same not to be underground when the journey begins.

The manhole cover is extremely heavy, and I have to push up with my shoulders to unseat it. Moving the lid proves nearly as difficult. Once there's enough room for me to wiggle around it, I do. To close the cover again, I sit on the ground and push it with my feet against until it drops into place.

As I stand up, I notice a pair of headlights several blocks to my left—the only ones on the road—heading in my direction. There's a fountain in front of the building on the far side of the street. I hurry over to it and duck behind the retaining wall, where the water pool would be if there were any water.

The vehicle drives by without slowing. I chance a peek as it moves off, and see that it's another police car.

It's after eight . . . you're three and a half hours over.

Now that I have time to process what the officer had said, it sounds like he was talking about a curfew. That would certainly account for the shutdown. I've read about political and social protests sparking curfews in the latter half of the twentieth and the early twenty-first centuries. Did those stretch as far back as the beginning of the 1950s? And if yes, then wouldn't a curfew in New York City have been a major event?

Stop it, I tell myself. *It's unimportant.*

What I need to do is finish working out how to find Lidia. Everything else is just noise.

According to the chaser, we've already been here six minutes shy of an hour. I can't imagine we'll be hanging around for that much longer, but I feel exposed here by the fountain.

I spot what looks like an alley a half block to the right, and I head toward it. On the way I notice that there are banners hanging from most of the streetlamps. While they are all similar, they are not the same. I give the closest one a look.

An American flag is printed at the top, but otherwise it is all white with black letters.

We

Will

Never

Stop

The next one reads:

Victory

Is Only

Possible

If We

Work

As One

Wouldn't today's date be around the time the Korean War begins? It must be what the signs are referring to. At least that's what I think until I read a third:

If Himmler

And His

German Machine

Are Not

Defeated

Evil

Triumphs

Buy War Bonds

Today

Himmler? German machine? War bonds?

But it's 1950. The war in Europe should be five years finished. Himmler, who I believe was one of Hitler's closest advisors, should be dead or, at the very least, on the run. He certainly shouldn't be in charge of Germany.

We were in 1939 for no more than a few hours. What was there in that history book Lidia showed me that she could have used to cause this? Did she kill someone whose removal from history paved the way for the Nazis' success? Maybe she *did* kill Hitler. From what I've learned, his ego certainly didn't help his country in the end.

I am still staring at the banner, dumbfounded, when I hear the sound of a car around a nearby corner. I race into the alley and huddle in the dark, hoping I wasn't seen.

It turns out it wouldn't have mattered much if I had been.

Fifteen seconds later—jump.

CHAPTER SIXTEEN

I half expect to end up back in Lidia's doorless room, but that's not the case. Instead, we travel considerably farther back, to August 8, 1874, at 3:00 a.m.

I check the chaser's map twice to make sure there hasn't been a mistake. According to my device, I am just off the south coast of England on the Isle of Wight, between the towns of Newport and Cowes. More specifically, I'm in a field filled with rows of tall crops that I can't identify that block my view. Rising on my toes, I can just get my eyes above the plants, but I barely start scanning around when Lidia yanks on my chain again.

The jump feels as if I've been standing in a dark room and someone has simply turned on the light. The sun beats down on rows of plants that look exactly those from the field where I'd just been. I stick my head up for a peek and am positive that I'm in the same field, though probably about ten yards south of my previous position.

I'm pretty sure we've just performed a textbook rewinder insert. Lidia brought us in under the cover of early morning, took a look around, and then jumped several hours forward to a position close to where she had been that would hide her when she arrived in the daytime.

Which probably means it will be some time before we travel again while she completes whatever evil task she has come here to do. I sit on the ground and finish my search through the menus, not allowing my mind to start down the worrisome road of trying to figure out why we've come to this place at this time.

Once I finish, there's one thing I need to do before I can start testing combinations to get the tracker working. For any of the companion functions to work, I must reconnect the companion wires. Doing so makes me very nervous, however. While there are no trained and official companions in this time line, the box could connect to someone else, like mine did with Iffy back in late March. Also, I worry that opening the specialized area of the box might disconnect the slave mode.

I take a deep breath and then perform the task as quickly as I can. As soon as I close the panel again, I check the training functions to make sure the device is still enslaved to Lidia's. Thankfully, it is. As for a companion, the status function under the companion menus reads *UNCONNECTED*.

I begin the testing phase. The initial attempts yield either error messages or nothing at all. I keep at it, though, positive that I'm on the right track.

I've been at it for nearly ten minutes when the screen suddenly goes dark. For a half second I fear that I've somehow disabled the device and I'll be stuck here in the nineteenth century. But then it flicks back on, a map now displayed on the screen.

There are two glowing dots. One hovers over the spot where I am now. The other is in the town of Cowes.

It has to be Lidia's chaser. What else could it be? I touch this other dot, and a callout appears beside it, containing a locator number.

If I wanted to, I could jump right to where she is, but that would mean deactivating the slave mode, a move that I'm pretty sure would alert her device that our machines were no longer tethered and allow her to make a jump I could not follow. What I can do, though, is shorten the distance between us the old-fashioned way.

Staying low, I move down the row to the end of the field, where I find a path. This leads to another and then a third, which eventually meets up with a narrow muddy road that, if my map is not misleading me, will take me to Cowes.

If we stay in this place and time for a couple hours, I should be able to reach her.

Take your time, Lidia, I think over and over as I limp down the road.

I've gone about a half mile when I hear the slow but steady clomp of hooves and the creak of wood behind me. Glancing back, I see a cart pulled by a pony heading my way. The driver is a middle-aged, balding man, with a gray-speckled brown beard. Stacked high in the cart's cargo area are several canvas-covered bundles.

As he nears me, he slows his already moderate pace. "Are you lost?"

"I, um, I'm heading to Cowes."

His eyes narrow suspiciously. "Don't think we've met before."

"No. I'm not from here."

"Clearly. So where would you be from?"

His accent makes me think about the British Empire of my youth, and I stop myself at the last moment from saying New Cardiff. "America," I tell him.

"You're a long way from home."

"Yeah, I guess I am."

"Headed to Cowes, you say?"

"Yes."

"That leg of yours isn't doing you any favors."

I glance down at my pants, thinking they've become bloody like my jeans, but while there are a couple dark spots, they're small and not obvious. It's my limp that's drawn his attention. "No, sir. It's not."

He pulls on the reins, stopping the pony. "Well, hop on then. Unless you'd rather be on your own."

I grab the side of the cart and start to swing into the back.

"No, no," he says. "Up here. More room."

I pull myself onto the bench seat next to him. "Thank you. I appreciate it."

He gives the reins a shake and calls out to the pony, and the cart starts moving again.

"Here for the boats, I assume," he says.

"The boats?"

"The regatta. Cowes Week. Why else would you be here?"

"Right, yes. The regatta. I'm here for that." Perhaps I'm not lying about that. Though I know nothing of this regatta, there's a good chance something connected to it is what's drawn Lidia here.

"So what were you doing way out here?"

"Friends."

"Played a trick on you, did they? Got to drinking a little too much and they dumped you out here?"

I smile guiltily, but say nothing to confirm his guess one way or the other. His theory isn't the story I was going for, but I like it better.

We ride on silently for a few minutes before he nods at my lap and says, "What's in the box?"

Instinctively my grip tightens on my chaser. "Just . . . my things." I pause, then add what I hope sounds appropriate. "Pens, paper. That kind of thing."

"You're a writer?"

"Only letters."

"Got a girl back home, then."

Iffy, I think, my heart tightening. "Yes."

"Good for you. If you love her, hold on to her tight."

"I'm trying."

"Sure you don't have any tobacco in there?"

"No, sir. Sorry."

"Oh, well. Worth a shot."

Several minutes later, I wonder if I should have just told him the box was a time travel device. That way he'd have had something to ease his shock when I suddenly disappeared.

◆ ◆ ◆

The jumps start blending into one another—three minutes here, ten minutes there, a few times over an hour. Thankfully, the coordinates for each stop are automatically stored in a list on my chaser. I will need them later when I undo Lidia's messes. What those messes could be and what possible atrocities they are causing press down on me like thick sheets of lead that I'm finding harder and harder to ignore.

I've noted that there's a discernible pattern to the trips. We go back several decades, hop around a little bit there, then jump forward a few years before heading even farther back, like a weird game of checkers. My guess is that the initial backward trip is where she does whatever it is she has planned, after which we move forward so she can see the results. Then repeat and repeat and repeat.

And it all makes appalling sense.

Layers upon layers, starting at the most forward point in time that she wanted to affect—either the kidnapping in Santa Monica, or, most likely, the change she caused in prewar Berlin.

See, if she were to change the outcome of World War II and then go forward to the 1950s to do the same with the Korean War, she would likely find that ripples from the first break with the time line have altered the future so that perhaps there is no Korean War. What she's doing instead is making each change farther back in time than the last. So she could remove a world leader from the 1950s, then alter the financial collapse of the 1920s, then throw a wrench into World War I, and so on.

It doesn't matter if the World War I change negates the financial collapse change. Once her World War I damage is reversed, then the Korean issue she created reappears. Remove C, and B comes back. Remove B, and A comes back. Only there are a lot more layers already than just three. The only way I'll get things back to the way they should be is if I eliminate each change she's made in the reverse order that they've been created.

It chills me how disturbingly well she's thought things through. It's an insane and admittedly brilliant plan. If I'm unable to figure out just one thing, there is the very real probability that I'll never see Iffy or my sister again.

Each time we jump, I try to close the physical gap between us. Sometimes we stop only long enough for me to get a dozen feet. Sometimes I can go much farther. The problem is Lidia is also on the move, and every few jumps the distance grows larger instead of smaller. I'm gaining on her, though, and by the time I find myself in a wooded Kentucky wilderness in 1786, I am within a half mile of her position. We jump in this general location four separate times, my arrival spot moving up to fifty yards each trip, until finally Lidia seems to have found a place she's happy with. If the overall pattern holds, we should be here for at least thirty minutes, and likely much more.

It's time to eliminate the remaining distance between us.

The forest floor is covered in thick brush, and it takes longer than I like to find the path of least resistance that keeps me headed in the direction I want to go. Thankfully, I procured something to carry my chaser at one of the previous stops. It's a burlaplike bag I found just inside the open back door of a general store. I dumped out the few bits of grain it still contained, and fashioned a strap out of the top portion. Some of its fibers are already wearing a little thin, so I keep an arm wrapped around it as much as possible in case it suddenly falls apart, but it's better than carrying the box in the open.

I keep expecting the trees to thin and reveal a village where Lidia will be, but so far the vegetation has yet to back down. After ten minutes, I pause and check the map again. I've more than halved the distance between us, and know that if I were to yell out, she'd hear me. That, of course, is not something I want to do. I proceed with caution, carefully moving branches out of my way and then easing them back into position without a sound.

Three hundred yards. Two hundred. One hundred and fifty.

I stop when I hear a crunch ahead and to the left. I'm not sure if it was a footstep or something falling to the ground. What I do know is that it didn't come from the direction of Lidia's chaser. At least not according to my tracking map. Of course, it's possible the map isn't as accurate as it could be and the glowing dot is merely an approximation of her location, making me torn whether to keep moving forward or to alter my course toward the noise.

Best to stay on track, I decide after a few moments. If she's not where the map says she is, then I'll adjust.

I move forward in a crouch, rolling my feet from heel to toe on each step. As I do, I diligently scan the ground ahead for anything that might snap under my weight, and redirect myself around these traps.

Finally, when I'm within a hundred feet of her presumed position, I see an opening in the trees ahead. A meadow. It looks as if Lidia has stopped just short of it.

I continue creeping forward.

There are four people in the field. Two are kids, boys from their clothing, though I could be wrong. One is a man of perhaps forty. The last I think is a man, too, until he turns and I can see his face. While he has the height of an adult, he has the features of a young teenager. They appear to be clearing the area.

A father and his sons working the land together is my guess.

Lidia should be about forty feet away from me now, just a hair to the right of the direction I've been headed.

This is it, I think. *I can put an end to her madness right now!*

I adjust my path and take another slow step.

A scream, not of fear but of rage. It doesn't come from Lidia nor those in the field, but from the same direction in which I earlier heard the crunch.

The man and his boys stop what they're doing and look toward the noise just in time to see someone run out from the trees. A native, by the looks of his outfit and darker skin. Three others follow.

The man shouts out at his boys. The tall one grabs the arm of the brother that is closest to him in size and says something in the boy's ear. The boy then takes off running in the opposite direction from where the natives are coming—to hide or get help, I have no idea which.

The tall one yells something to the littlest boy and then runs diagonally across the meadow to what looks like a small cabin.

The native reaches the older man, and with what looks like a single, bloody blow, drops the man to the ground. The native then turns toward the cabin, and he and his friends start after the older boy.

The small boy hasn't moved since his brother ran away, but the attack breaks his paralysis and he races to his father, drops to the ground next to him, and shakes the man's shoulder. There's no response nor will there ever be again. There's just too much blood.

One of the natives has noticed the boy and has turned toward him. I press my lips together to keep from shouting out a warning as I'm sure the boy is done for. But when the native is only a few feet away from him, the boom of rapid-fire gunshots cracks across the field.

I think at first that the tall brother has taken a shot at the native to keep him away from the smaller boy, but one of the bullets has slammed *into* the woodpile by the cabin that the older sibling is using for cover.

The result is the boy ducks down farther, and the natives running toward him break for the woods, scared off by the shots from an unknown assailant. Only the assailant isn't unknown to me. The hail of bullets came from Lidia's position. Somewhere on our journey she's obtained an automatic rifle, a weapon over a century away from even being built. In Germany, probably.

One of the natives, though, has not fled for the trees—the one headed for the little boy.

He raises the same weapon he killed the father with over his head as he nears.

"Shoot him," I whisper. I know that would be messing with the time line, but Lidia's already pulled the trigger once, so who knows what's right and wrong anymore?

But instead of shooting the native, she sends a single bullet toward the tall brother to keep him down as the native delivers to the small son the same sentence he gave the father.

I know that Lidia could have killed the boy and his father herself before the natives attacked. That would have been the efficient way, but I know none of this is about efficiency. It's about manipulating history to do her dirty work.

I stare at the bloodied bodies, unable to move, unable to think, and barely able to breathe.

Jump.

Brett Battles

♦ ♦ ♦

I materialize at the edge of a group of buildings. Lidia should be in front of me somewhere, but there's a structure between us, and I can't see her.

All is quiet, though. It's the dead of night. Which means we're about to—

♦ ♦ ♦

When the world reappears it's daytime, though the sun is hidden behind a thick layer of clouds that foretell of rain soon to come. I'm next to a copse of trees just behind one of the buildings I had seen during the night moments earlier. I check the tracking map. Lidia is actually *inside* the structure.

Hearing voices coming from around the front of the building, I slip into the trees and move through the cover until I have a better view. There are maybe a dozen buildings strung along a wide central road. I'm not sure I'd call it a town. A village perhaps, if even that.

Several people are about, and others are coming into the settlement on horseback via a trail that leads from the woods. The few women I see are all wearing black dresses, while the men tend to be dressed more in work clothes, though some have covered these with black jackets. They all seem to be heading into the building where Lidia is.

I cross a short, open expanse to a group of bushes that will give me a view of the front of the structure. A man standing outside the main entrance and greeting everyone as they go in tells me all I need to know. A church, but one that's still under construction.

Why would Lidia be in a church? I doubt she's sitting with everyone else. A stranger would stick out in a small place like this. Besides, I'd be willing to bet some people were inside already when we arrived, and if Lidia had appeared in front of them, people would be running out of the building screaming instead of calmly waiting as others walk in.

When the preacher follows the last of the arrivals inside, I decide to move closer. After crossing to the front of the building, I peek around the edge of the door, look around, and then quickly pull back when the preacher begins turning in my direction. There are at least thirty people seated inside. As far as I could tell, though, Lidia was not among them. What dominates the room—and is obviously responsible for the mood of the crowd—are two wooden coffins sitting up front, one considerably smaller than the other.

The father and son from the meadow—why else would we be here? The town is so small I wonder how the events that took the two lives can possibly be important enough to be of interest to Lidia. And yet they had. Obviously she knew the attack was coming and that the father would die. It's the son who is really the key here, I realize. I'm pretty sure he was supposed to live. Lidia's meddlesome hand has kept that from happening.

The preacher begins talking. There are prayers and quotes from the scriptures and then, ". . . we pray for Bathsheba Lincoln and her children Mordecai, Josiah, Mary, and Nancy to find peace in knowing that their husband and father Abraham and their son and brother Thomas are now in the arms of the Lord . . ."

Whatever else he says becomes background noise to my thoughts.

Bathsheba Lincoln . . . husband Abraham.

Could it be?

Abraham Lincoln is a giant in the history of Iffy's time line. But something's not right. That Abraham Lincoln rises to fame in the second half of the nineteenth century. This Abraham Lincoln, if he'd been allowed to live, would still be long dead by 1850.

And it's Thomas Lincoln whom Lidia has murdered, not Abraham.

My breath catches in my throat as a possibility strikes me. A child sees his father killed but survives the attack himself. Would it not make sense for this child to grow up and name his own son after his dead parent?

Have I just witnessed the erasing of the man who is supposed to end slavery long before he would take his first breath?

When I hear someone moving around inside, I quickly retreat back to the brush in case they come out for some air, and it's from this hidden place, a half hour later, that I'm whisked even farther back in time.

CHAPTER SEVENTEEN

I look at my chaser twice to make sure I haven't misread the date. I haven't.

I'm at the edge of a dark, treelined road. A look at the map confirms what I already know. Though I've never been at this exact spot before, I have been in this area on this very day in 1775 several times.

Has it all been a ruse? Have the seeds of destruction Lidia has been sowing simply been a game? Has she just been teasing me? Playing a little joke before doing what she really wanted to do all along?

We are near Cambridge, Massachusetts, no more than a ten-minute walk from the infamous Three Swans Tavern. This is the night and the tavern is the place where I made the twelve-second mistake that wiped away the world I was born in.

Clearly Lidia lied to me when she said she was no longer interested in bringing the empire back. The only reason we are here must be to stop the earlier version of me from changing things. Why else?

I check the tracker and see that Lidia is in the woods off to my right and already moving toward the tavern. There's no way I can sneak up on her without making a lot of noise, but the road provides a clearer path than the forest she is working her way through, and even with my limp, I should be able to reach the tavern before she does.

I set as brisk a pace as possible. Though I can feel a dull throb in my thigh, for the most part it's numb. I'm not sure if that's good or bad, but it *is* allowing me to move faster than I had thought I could.

It's my fault Lidia has found this place. When I was executing my plan to bring my sister to Iffy's world, I tricked the other rewinders who had survived the initial time line change into thinking I wasn't the one who caused the break but that I *had* discovered where the deviation had occurred.

Mixing a bit of truth with a larger lie, I told them that Richard Cahill—the man who should have turned George Washington over to the British—had disappeared from history, his mother killed before he was born.

Oh, God, I realize as I nearly stumble on the path. The death of the two Lincolns and the likely erasure of the man who should one day be president.

She's taunting me with my own story. A story that was all made up because Cahill's death had nothing to do with his mother and everything to do with the twelve-second delay I created. That tiny change to the time line caused Cahill to be killed by a pair of British soldiers before he could report on Washington, an event that will be happening in just about ninety minutes unless Lidia interferes.

She's had three years to check my story. There would be records showing that, unlike what I told her and the others, Cahill had indeed been born, and there would be more documenting the night he died. She could put the pieces together, and while she might not know the exact details of the evening, she had clearly figured out enough to get us here on this night.

It's those details that I hope will be my savior. I know them intimately. All the events of this night, the multiple trips I made here, are all only a few months in my own past, and still vivid in my mind.

I push my pace even more, and tell myself she's finally made a mistake. I just hope to God I'm right. I'm about halfway to the tavern when I hear horses on the road behind me. Two, coming fast.

I step into the trees, more to keep from being hit than to hide. Though the riders don't even glance in my direction as they race by, I'm able to get a good look at their faces. I've seen them both before, inside the tavern. These are the two British agents who will instruct Cahill to report on Washington's whereabouts.

As I watch them disappear into the darkness, I realize that I just discovered a second place where the time line could be altered. All I would need to do is keep them from reaching the tavern, say, flag them down and warn them of a waiting ambush at the Three Swans. Simple and more than enough, I would think, to get them to flee back the way they'd come. It's not perfect. Cahill would still be alive, so who knows what he might do in his altered future, but I file it away, just in case I need to call on it later.

It's the strong smell of cooking meat from the tavern's chimney that lets me know I'm getting close. After making sure there's no one on the road either behind or in front of me, I check at the tracking app. Lidia's still heading straight for the tavern, but as I'd anticipated, her progress has been slower than mine.

I'm just about to turn the screen back off when a new dot appears, indicating the presence of a third chaser, this one maybe fifteen yards in front of the tavern. I check the time. It's 8:00 p.m. exactly, which means the new arrival is me. Specifically, it's the one I think of as Scout Me, a naïve junior rewinder at the beginning of the mission to observe Cahill. Scout Me's job is/was to record all the comings and goings at the tavern.

I take a moment to plot a course that will keep me well away from him, but then I pause.

Scout Me's chaser.

It's not slaved to Lidia's.

I could hide my slaved chaser in some bushes, and use Scout Me's device to hop back a few minutes and be in the woods waiting for her to arrive at the tavern. Since I wouldn't need to turn off the slave mode, she would think I'm still here and would be unaware as I sneak up on her.

I enter the woods about fifty feet shy of the clearing where the tavern is, and carefully circle through the trees toward Scout Me. As soon as I get a glimpse of him, I pause and check to see where Lidia is.

She, too, has neared the clearing, but has stopped about half a dozen feet within the trees on the side where the wagons are parked. The position gives her a front-row seat for the little shell game the other versions of me are about to play to save my sister and Iffy's world. In just over a minute, there will be three Dennys near the wagons—Original Me, who is destined to go inside the tavern and cause Cahill to delay his departure; Off Switch Me, whose job it is to stop Original Me and leave the empire's time line intact so that I could return there to kidnap my sister; and finally, On Switch Me, who's tasked with stopping Off Switch Me after Ellie is safe. It's all very complicated and confusing, I know, and I'm sure it's about to get even more so now that Lidia's set to join the party.

My plan, what little there is of it, is to wait until Lidia makes her move. I'm sure she will engage the other versions of me, which means Scout Me will see this, taking his attention away from his satchel, which I know is lying at his feet. I'll grab it, hop back, and stop Lidia before she even gets to this point, ending her march of terror.

I creep through the brush, moving in as close to Scout Me as I can without giving myself away, and then huddle down. All his attention is on the arrival of a new customer, and he is completely unaware of my presence. I want to check on Lidia again, but I don't dare open the chaser for fear that the light will be noticed. Instead, I look past the wagons, toward the woods where she should be hiding.

On Switch Me is the first to appear. If I didn't know he was coming, I wouldn't have picked up on the slight change of shadows at the back of the wagons. Scout Me hasn't noticed him at all, just as planned. I'm sure Lidia, on the other hand, can't help but see him.

I tense, my gaze on the clearing, ready to make my move the moment Scout Me sees her break from the forest. But all remains still.

I can't help but glance over my shoulder to see if she's decided to sneak up on me. At some point, I know she's going to want to separate me from my chaser and break our connection so she can roam free through time. It would be poetic to her, no doubt, if this were that moment. But the woods behind me are quiet, nothing moving.

Looking back at the field, I know that by now Off Switch Me should be at the wagons. On Switch is probably moving in behind him to tell him Ellie is safe so there's no need for him to do anything; as soon as this conversation is over, Off Switch will leave the area. Still no sign of Lidia, though.

What's she doing? Has the fact that there are two of me caused her to sit tight? If so, she's about to get another jolt.

In the field beside the wagons, directly in my and Scout Me's view, appears yet another version of me—Original Me. If Lidia really wants to bring back the empire, now is the time she needs to act. In less than a minute, it will be too late.

No movement. No Lidia running from the woods to throw a wrench into things. No yells to draw everyone's attention. No nothing. Just the night playing out the way I had designed it.

I have no choice. I need to know where she is, so I crack open my chaser's lid just far enough for the screen to come on. There are now six dots on the tracking screen. Lidia's hasn't moved from the spot I last saw it. Did she only come here to witness what I'd done before? Or did she leave her chaser and is right now moving toward my—

The screen changes to the main jump screen without me doing anything. I've never seen this before, but it can mean only one thing. My device is receiving information for a new jump.

My plan to use Scout Me's chaser is shot, but that doesn't mean I can't use it at some future point. There is no time for me to finesse it from him, though. I launch myself forward, wrapping one arm around him to move him out of the way as I reach for his satchel with my free hand. My fingertip is a fraction of an inch away when 1775 disappears.

◆ ◆ ◆

The jump is longer than any Lidia has taken me on yet. When the mist finally falls away, I tumble forward, my head pounding with the effect of the lengthy trip. My fall, however, is cushioned by a body below me.

Though it wasn't my intention, Scout Me has come along for the ride. Unfortunately, his satchel has not come with us.

He rolls out from under me and scrambles to his feet, ready to either fight or flee. But as he takes a couple backward steps, he looks at me and freezes.

"What . . . wha . . . what are . . . what?"

"Grab on to me," I whisper as I push myself up and stumble toward him. It's pitch-black out, and given recent patterns, I know it's extremely likely Lidia is following protocol again, and at any moment, we'll be jumping to daytime.

But Scout Me shirks back. While the person I've become has had plenty of experience talking with other versions of me, this is Scout Me's first time, so he's understandably freaked out. "Where's my chaser?" He desperately looks around. "Where's my chaser?"

"Don't worry about it right now," I tell him. "Just—"

"Don't worry about it? How can you say that?" He pauses. "What are you doing here? Which . . . where . . ."

I have to remind myself that he is still a junior rewinder working for the institute. Keeping my voice low, I say, "I need you to hold on to me. We're not going to be here long."

He looks around, as if just realizing we're no longer outside the Three Swans. "Where are we?"

I swear under my breath and then grab him just above the elbow and yank him over, then wrap an arm around his chest so his back is to me.

"What are you doing?" he asks. He struggles with me, but it's only halfhearted, his confusion making him unsure what he should do.

"Don't you think you should trust me?" I say.

"But—"

Lidia hits the go button again, and the deep night suddenly dissolves into the yellow light of daybreak.

Scout Me pulls away again, but this time he doesn't go far. "Where have you taken me?"

"Keep your voice down," I whisper. At last check, Lidia was about a hundred yards away. It would be to my advantage if I could keep her from knowing I brought someone with me.

His jaw tenses, but he speaks more softly when he says, "Answer my question."

"*I* haven't taken you anywhere."

"What do you mean by that?"

I pause for a moment. "A lot has happened since I was you."

"What do you mean since—" He cocks his head, his eyes narrowing. "You don't look any older than me."

I give him a quick humorless smile as I open my chaser and switch it back to the tracking app. Lidia is moving to the northeast, away from our position. I then check to see where exactly we are.

Europe. East of Vienna in an area I know as one day being part of the Russian Empire, and in Iffy's world would be Slovakia, I think, or maybe Hungary. The year turns out to be 1242.

I've never been this far back in time before, and I'd be lying if I said I'm not experiencing an irrational sense of unease. Home, whether Lidia has destroyed it or not, is so far away.

Now that we are earlier than 1775, we are in the part of history that I loved to study growing up. I close my eyes and try to remember if there's any historical significance to this time and place.

Yeah. There *is* something, but my mind is too scattered with all that's been happening to function the way I need it to, and I'm having a hard time remembering.

Frustrated, I say, "Stay close," and start moving in the direction Lidia has gone.

"Where are you going?"

I look back and see that Scout Me hasn't budged. As much as I'd rather not waste the energy, I limp back to him. "You need to come with me. We need to stop her."

"Stop who?"

"Lidia."

His eyes widen. Perhaps I didn't hate her as much at his point in my life as I do now, but I never liked her.

"She's trying to destroy everything," I say, attempting to push him over the edge.

"What do you mean?"

He's having a hard time connecting the dots, so I give it to him straight. "She's changing the time line. She's already done it probably a dozen times."

Blood drains from his face. "Why would she do that?"

Because you did it first, I think. But those words will do nothing to help me at the moment, so I say, "It's complicated and I don't have time to explain it to you. You're free to stay here, but if I suddenly jump, you'll be left behind without a chaser."

A whole other type of fear fills his eyes. "Why would you do that?"

"Because my chaser's slaved to Lidia's. I go where she goes."

When we start off, I tell Scout—as I've decided to think of him—to keep a hand on my shoulder, in case Lidia decides to jump. I'm not sure this will be enough contact to guarantee he'll be pulled into the mist with me, but before long, it's no longer an issue. I've been going nonstop, and my leg has decided it's done being numb and starts throbbing again. Seeing me wince with every step, Scout puts his arm across my back and takes some of the pressure off my uncooperative thigh.

"What happened?" he asks.

"Knife accident."

"Lidia?"

"Her grandson."

He looks at me as if I've gone crazy. "What?"

"I told you it's complicated."

My chaser guides us after Lidia through a patch of densely wooded hills. That's another surprise for Scout. He had no idea the device could locate another one. But I have no doubt his day of being shocked is only just beginning.

Though we are steadily moving, we can go only so fast traveling in tandem, and much to my dismay Lidia is increasing the gap between us. Finally, fifteen minutes into our hike, she stops moving.

I want to hurry so we can make up some ground, but we're walking through an area where the terrain rises and falls like static waves in the middle of the ocean. The downward slopes are hardest for me to negotiate, and if not for Scout's support, I would have fallen and hurt myself worse long ago. When we reach the top of what turns out to be the final ridge, we stop, both of us taken aback by the beauty in front of us.

We are on much higher ground than I had thought. The ridge where we are standing falls off in a long gentle slope down to a wide grass-covered valley. To our right, the valley continues on to what look like distant hills, though it's hard to tell for sure. In the other direction, though, the expanse quickly narrows down and funnels into a pass between the forested hills we are on and those directly across from us.

Deep in the valley I see thin columns of controlled smoke that hint at civilization, but excluding that, there are no signs of people anywhere.

I check the map. Lidia is approximately seven hundred feet to our right. It's impossible to see her through the trees, but I'm certain she is on the same ridge we are.

I look back at the valley, once more trying to figure out what it is about this place and time that has brought her here. I feel as if I should know this. History's my thing, after all, but I'm still trying to pull whatever nugget I can from the depths of my memory when we jump.

Interestingly, the only thing that's changed is time. We're still on the ridge above the quiet valley, just forty-eight hours forward on the time line. As I turn to tell Scout this—

Jump.

Same place. An additional seventy-two hours ahead.

Jump.

We've gone ahead a week this time, our feet anchored to this spot as if we're rocks that have been here forever.

Jump.

Another week.

Jump.

Another.

Jump.

A month.

Jump.

We pause.

There's been a change to the valley. While it's still empty and quiet, much of the grass has been churned up, creating a corridor of destruction that continues off to the right as far as I can see and into the pass on our left.

Something has moved through here. Horses, I would guess, thousands of them.

A light flickers dimly in my mind, a marker taunting me that I should know what's going on.

"Why is she doing this?" Scout asks.

I open my mouth to tell him to be quiet while I think, but then I pause.

Not only is he me, he's the innocent version of me who hasn't lived through the chaos that has rained down through the additional months I've lived. His mind is not clouded in the same way as mine.

"Twelve forty-two," I say. "Eastern Europe. What's the significance?"

His face scrunches in confusion. "Is this some kind of test?"

"Just answer the question."

He looks at the ground in the way I often do when I'm thinking.

This is the pose he's in when we jump again. For the first time since our initial arrival, we move backward in time, a week. The valley floor is still trampled into a muddy mess.

"Well?" I ask.

"Where in eastern Europe?"

We jump back again, another week. No change in the scenery below.

I almost tell Scout Slovakia, but that's not a name he'd be familiar with. "Not far from Vienna. Between it and Budapest."

Another jump, another week. Only this time the grass has returned. Whatever force will come through here has not yet done so.

Lidia takes us on a series of four quick micro jumps, each moving us twenty-four hours in a forward direction again. The first three are mirror images of one another—the silence and the grass and the wisps of smoke in the distance.

Day four, though, is something else entirely.

About a quarter mile below us, moving from the valley into the pass below us is a vast army. Almost everyone is on horseback. Both Scout and I stare at the mighty sight as they ride on.

"The Mongols," Scout whispers and then looks at me. "It's the Mongols. You said 1242, right?"

I nod, unable to speak.

"That's the year they retreat from near Vienna."

His words open the dam holding back the identical information in my mind. Retreat is not the right way to describe it, though. Their leader back in their homeland—not Genghis Khan, but one of his sons . . . Ögedei, I believe—has recently died. When word gets to the khan's army in Europe, something that takes months, the advance will grind to a halt not far from Vienna, and the troops will return to the steppes, while the leaders head all the way back for the gathering that is supposed to choose a new khan.

One of the many history tests Marie gave me during my training was loaded with questions on this very subject. I curse myself for not remembering sooner.

Of course, Lidia in her altered state would be drawn to this place and time. It's a linchpin moment in the story of the whole human race. The Mongols had Europe by the throat. If they had not suddenly turned back east, there is no doubt they would have not only conquered the continent, but the British Isles beyond. Everything in both Western and Eastern cultures would be different from that point forward.

Everything.

But once they went back to select their new leader, they never returned, and the potential of not just ruling a vast empire but the entire world never came to pass, leaving scholars with probably the biggest what-if question in history.

I'm sure Lidia's plan is to find out the answer. What I can't imagine is how she could possibly go about it. The task seems far too massive. To keep an entire army from turning around due to the death of a khan that at this very date has *already happened?* That seems as likely as her being able to go to the Mongol capital and keep Ögedei from dying.

Forget that she's a woman in a decidedly male era; she can't possibly speak thirteenth-century Mongolian. Even most of her modern English wouldn't be understood by anyone anywhere.

But whatever her plan is—and I know she has one—we need to get to her before she can execute it. I'm already daunted by all the changes she's made that I must undo. Adding a monstrous one such as this feels as if it's a step too far, and if she succeeds, I will never be able to make anything right again.

In the woods just behind us, we hear a horse snort.

Scout and I whip around and see three soldiers riding through the trees about fifty feet away. They don't look Mongolian, but then again, the Mongols often forcibly recruited into their ranks those they didn't massacre as they moved westward.

Before we can dive behind cover, one of the men yells and points in our direction.

"Come on," Scout says as he turns me downslope and starts off in a half run.

But even if I were uninjured and we were able to sprint, we are no match for the horses. As it is, we're only a dozen feet down the slope when the soldiers reach the ridge.

A couple of them laugh, maybe all three. I don't know. I don't turn to look.

They let us continue for several seconds, then I hear movement behind us. Not horses—men. This time I chance a look. Two of the soldiers have dismounted and are working their way toward us at a leisurely pace.

My leg has finally betrayed me to the point that I am done for.

"Take the chaser," I say to Scout as I reach for the strap of my makeshift bag. "Find Lidia. You have to stop her."

Before I can get the strap over my head, though, Scout jerks it back down. "I'm not leaving you."

"You have to!"

"I don't even understand what's going on."

"You don't need to understand. You just need to stop her."

I start pulling at my strap again. Though Scout won't be able to undo all the havoc Lidia's unleashed, he can at least keep her from causing this colossal shift. A small victory in the face of otherwise total defeat, perhaps, but I'll take what I can at this point.

I love you, Iffy, I think as Scout reluctantly takes the bag from me. *I love you, Ellie. I'm sorry.*

When he doesn't leave, I try to push him away and then fall to my good knee so that I'm out from under his arm, but it's too late. The soldiers are upon us. One of them twists Scout around, punching him in the face.

The Mongol army is notoriously ruthless, and I fully expect to feel the blade of a sword slicing through the back of my neck at any second. Instead, though, the other soldier wrenches me to my feet.

Scout is brought up alongside of me, blood flowing around his mouth from his broken nose. The soldiers look back and forth between us, surprised by our identical looks.

One of them finally shouts something at us. When we don't respond, he rips the bag holding the chaser out of Scout's hands.

The other man says something, and then they circle around us and push Scout and me back toward the ridge. Scout props me up under his arm again, and we start walking.

Halfway up, I stop to rest. I could make it all the way, but if I'm heading to my death, I might as well stretch things out. The soldiers try to keep us moving, but I gesture at my leg and wince, hoping that doing so will buy us a few seconds.

The man who stayed on the ridge yells down to his companions. They yell back, and then the one who has my bag opens it and pulls out my chaser. Thankfully, the lid is closed, but it's little comfort when they possess the box and I do not. As much as I don't want it to happen, I can't help but wonder what Lidia's reaction would be if she hit the go button right now and then finds out she's now hauling a Mongol soldier with her.

The man turns the box over, tries unsuccessfully to open it, and then says something to us.

"Sorry. I don't understand," I say.

Looking at me oddly, he says something that I'm pretty sure is just a repeat of his previous statement.

"You want to know what's inside?" I ask, miming opening the lid.

A short word this time, confirmation, I assume.

I hold my hands out. I'm more than happy to unlock it. If there was ever a time for me to deactivate the slave mode tying me to Lidia, it's now. The question is, can I distract him long enough to do it and jump Scout and me out of here?

The soldier laughs, though, and says something I take to mean that he'll open it. I just need to show him.

I point at the security pad on the side. Though it looks like wood, the small rectangle is actually a type of glass. When the soldier touches it, he pulls his finger back in surprise. He then shows it to his friend, who taps at the plate with equal fascination.

The first one pushes the pad and then tries sliding it side to side. When none of these methods works, he looks at me and says something again.

"It only opens for me." Since they can't understand me, there's no reason not to be honest.

I hold my hands out again. This time, after hesitating a moment, the soldier gives it to me.

Looking right at them so they think I'm speaking to them, I say, "Don't let go of me."

Scout responds by tightening his grip around my back.

I turn the box and place my thumb against the pad. As it always does, the lid pops up a quarter inch. Before the soldier can grab it back from me, though, I open the lid all the way. The screen lights up, and, as I have desperately been wishing would happen, both soldiers pull away in fearful surprise.

When I touch the main screen so I can navigate to the slave menu, the first soldier yells.

"It's okay," I say, holding up my hand in what I hope he takes as a peaceful gesture. "I'm just showing you how we're going to escape from you." I finally get to the list of training functions, and scroll down to the item *SLAVE MODE*. The two soldiers move in a bit, their curiosity overcoming their wariness. "So in a moment, we're going to disappear, and you're going to freak out. Sorry. Can't be helped."

I'm just about to open the slave mode function screen when the display reverts back to the main jump screen.

"She's moving again!"

We remain on the side of the hill just long enough for me to see that one of the soldiers has reacted to the change in my tone before we enter the jump.

CHAPTER EIGHTEEN

The black is short like before, a quick trip, but unlike the past several hops, when we arrive, we are no longer overlooking the large valley, but on a different slope surrounded by woods. And by we, I mean Scout, myself, and the Mongol soldier who grabbed my arm just as we winked out. Apparently a simple touch is more than enough to come along for the ride.

The soldier's hand remains locked around my wrist until he realizes that everything around him is not as he thinks it should be. He backs away, his eyes wide, and then he draws his sword and starts reciting something that has a pattern like a poem or, more likely, a prayer. Scout and I are unable to hear the end of it, though, as Lidia jumps again, and we leave the soldier behind.

We are back in a pattern of short time hops, our position changing no more than twenty or so feet from the first to the last.

Finally we stop long enough to work our way to a nearby clearing. From there we can see a mountain pass below us, the same pass that started at the valley churned up by the Mongols. I know this for a fact because the army is below us, too. But though it's barely midday, the mass of soldiers isn't on the move. Instead, they seem to have made camp.

The slope between us and them is thankfully steeper than the one before, and in places almost vertical, and while I stay alert for the sound of soldiers on watch, I'm confident the terrain provides us relative safety.

This is as much as Lidia allows us to see before we travel backward twenty-four hours. We are in the same spot, but instead of thousands of camped soldiers below, there are only a few hundred, those in the lead milling around while the others gradually catch up.

Jump, ahead this time, eight hours.

The sun is getting low, and deep shadows cover the pass. But it's not so dark that I can't see that the number of soldiers has swelled.

Backward jump, ten hours. It's late morning. There are no soldiers below us yet, but I can hear the rumble of the horses coming. Depending on how fast they're moving, I think the head of the army could be anywhere from ten minutes to an hour away.

The tracking map shows me that Lidia is just a little more than a hundred yards from our position.

"We have to keep moving," I say. I nod to my right. "That way."

I'm surprised, though probably shouldn't be, by the fact Scout isn't bombarding me with questions. He's obviously grasped the seriousness of the situation and has chosen to help instead of hinder. I'm strangely proud of this, like a parent of a deserving child.

Many of the trees around us are scarred, and the ground is covered by deadwood and new growth. A fire has moved through here in the last few years, and the rejuvenation is in full flourish. Unfortunately this slows our progress, as there's no clear straight shot to Lidia's position.

A small clearing, no more than thirty feet across, gives us another glimpse at the pass as the first soldiers are riding into view, their pace steady and unhurried, confident even. And why not? No one has defeated them since before Genghis Khan rose to power.

We are about to press on when I detect a flurry of activity coming up the pass. Half a dozen horsemen are riding fast along the edge of the advancing army, and don't stop until they reach the soldiers at the forefront. Conversations are held and the force begins to stop.

This is the start of the camp of men we have already witnessed, I realize, so I'm not in the slightest bit shocked when the world disappears again.

Six jumps in all, each giving us a new vantage point, but we stayed nowhere long enough for Scout and me to get any closer to Lidia. When we finally arrive at a spot we don't almost immediately jump from, I check the time and location. We've gone backward again, this time to 8:00 a.m. that same morning, and have retreated along the pass about a third of the way back in the direction of the valley.

Below us is the army again. From its appearance, I would guess we are near the back end of the mass of soldiers. Out of the dust that followed the Mongols emerge a couple dozen riders moving fast. I think at first they must be part of the group we just witnessed stopping those at the front of the parade, but instead of heading to the side, they gallop straight down the middle, the soldiers in front of them parting to let them through.

Clearly this is unusual. Though we are too far away to see the expression on anyone's face, the way the men who have parted begin to cluster in small groups after the riders have gone by evokes a sense of confusion.

I pause as the reality of what I'm witnessing hits me. This must be it, the moment when the Mongol tide that's poised to wash over Europe receives the news that stops it literally in its tracks. I'm positive these are the messengers who have come all the way from the Mongol homeland bearing the news of Ögedei's death.

The riders stop when they come to a group of soldiers who stand their ground. My guess is that they have reached the leaders of the army. Minutes pass, minutes Scout and I could be using to gain ground on Lidia, but I can't tear my gaze away, and neither can he. This is a monumentally historic moment.

Suddenly from the gathering, several mounted soldiers break from the group. They ride to the edge of the still-moving column and then take off along the side toward the front of the pack. *They must be the riders we saw farther down the pass.*

If I had any doubt before what we have been witnessing, it's gone now.

After I nudge Scout, we move back into the woods and close to within a hundred feet of Lidia before we jump again.

We arrive all the way back at the familiar spot where the wide valley funnels into the pass, exactly an hour and a half earlier than the moment in time we had been at moments before. A small group of riders is in the valley no more than ten minutes from the pass's entrance. From their clothing I recognize them as the messengers.

Barely ten seconds after I realize this, Lidia starts us on a series of jumps. It's immediately clear that we're following the riders farther and farther back into the valley—in a sense, watching a real-life movie in reverse.

Most major events in history are caused by many elements coming together at once. Remove one of these elements, and the outcome may not change at all. But on rare occasions, there is what Sir Gregory once referred to as a switch moment. A single event that, if either prevented or allowed, results in two massively divergent time lines. One is the Cahill switch I found in 1775. And in the valley below us, I realize, rides another even more devastating switch.

Lidia doesn't need to contend with the whole Mongol army to keep them marching on. She need only stop the messengers from reaching them. If that happens, the Mongols will continue sweeping across Europe, and by the time their leaders back home send more messengers, it will likely be too late. This switch, though, will not be nearly as easy to flip as the one that allowed Iffy's world to come into existence.

When we finally stop our quick jumps, it's nighttime. A near-full moon provides more than enough illumination, however, to see that the valley is gone.

We seem to be in a group of rolling hills, dotted with trees. Scout and I are at the bottom of a slope just a few yards away from a rutted trail that could have just as easily been made by wild animals as by man. I can smell smoke in the air, coming from a campfire or fireplace, but as I take a quick look around, I'm unable to locate the source.

The chaser says it's 11:00 p.m. I check Lidia's position. She's directly ahead of us, but on the move again. She's traveling at an angle that roughly parallels the path, so we use it to follow her.

The smell of smoke grows stronger, and I worry that she's going to walk us directly into the messengers' camp. I have no desire to interact with the Mongols again.

"Horses," Scout whispers.

We pause and then I hear them, too. A few snorts, but no running hooves. There are voices, also, low and a bit distant.

"We need to get off the trail," I tell him.

The woods here are not nearly as dense as those near the mountain pass, which makes them easier to move through, but more difficult to find someplace to hide.

A glow of flames tickles the top of a rise just ahead. Pausing, I motion for Scout to take a look around while I check on Lidia again. She's also stopped, but much closer to the camp.

We creep up the rise and then drop to the ground when we reach the crest. There's a clearing just ahead, and in the center, a campfire with maybe four or five men sitting around it. In the light of the flames, I can see the lumps of at least a dozen other riders sleeping on the ground.

Scout taps me and points ahead at a spot just inside the trees. Another human shadow, this one kneeling behind a bush.

Lidia.

She is within thirty feet of the nearest Mongol, and it'll be near impossible to grab her without drawing attention. While it's a concern, it's not a deterrent. All we need to do is get our arms around her, unslave my chaser, and then jump out of here.

Scout scans the area for anyone else who might be awake and walking around as I work out my plan. When I'm ready, I mime to him what I want to do. He looks dubious, but nods, deferring to me.

Slowly we push back to our feet, but remain in a crouch—well, for me, as best a crouch as my leg will allow—and move along an arc that puts us behind Lidia.

It's weird. I've had a few glimpses of her here and there as we've jumped around, but this is the first good view of Lidia I've had since we were separated by the glass in the doorless cell she built, before we'd even gone to 1939 Germany.

As much as I know she'd hear me coming, it's hard not to rush forward and try to grab her. *Closer first,* I caution myself. There's still a good hundred feet between us. Twenty would be okay to stop worrying. Ten would be better.

As I pick my way over the ground, I see her reach toward a shadow sitting against a tree next to her. Her rucksack, I realize after a moment. Her hand clasps around a stick jutting out of the top, and pulls it out. Setting it on her lap, she fusses over it for a moment. Then I hear a metallic click, the same metallic click I heard in Kentucky, where a man named Abraham Lincoln and his son were killed.

The automatic rifle.

I had forgotten all about it.

I break from Scout and start to run toward her, my adrenaline drowning out any protest my leg might be making. But I'm not even halfway to her when she pulls the trigger.

The sound of automatic gunfire rolls across the clearing like a continuous thunderstorm. I stumble forward and fall to a knee as bullets fly.

The men by the campfire are the first to go down, not a single one of them able to get to his feet before being hit. Those who'd been asleep jump up among shouts of confusion and anger, but their bodies are no more bulletproof than their companions' were. It is the most direct role Lidia has taken in affecting the time line that I have witnessed. Clearly she's decided to take things more into her own hands than she has in the past. Why, I don't know, but it's a turn in events I don't like at all.

"No!" I shout. "Stop!"

But Lidia doesn't even flinch.

I'm up again and moving toward her when the shooting and the shouts suddenly stop.

Lidia twists around and points her rifle at me. "Not a foot closer, Denny."

I halt.

At the sound of a footstep in the trees behind me, Lidia jerks her rifle a few inches to my left and sends three rounds flying into the darkness.

"Don't shoot!"

Lidia looks at me, her eyes narrowing. Though the voice is mine, it didn't come out of my mouth. At least not the mouth of *this* me.

"Lidia, please. Don't," I say.

She raises her voice. "Come out where I can see you."

DESTROYEЯ

The look of disgust on her face tells me the exact moment Scout comes into view.

"That's far enough," she orders him.

She glances back and forth between Scout and me. It must be the bloodstains on my pants that give me away as the one who brought her grandson to 1952.

She sneers at me. "Picked up a little help, did you? Cute."

Just then, several mounted soldiers ride into the clearing— sentries, no doubt, responding to a noise that they've never heard before.

Lidia takes a quick peek in their direction and then looks back at us and mouths, "Don't move."

She keeps her weapon trained on us until the sentries pull to a halt at the campfire and jump off their mounts. Once she has a clear shot at all three, she whips the rifle back around and fires a burst that takes down not only the sentries but their horses, too.

Even if I'd been able to move, I couldn't have taken more than two steps before the weapon is pointing back on me. But the massacre before me in the meadow, the unimaginable deviation to the time line she's caused, cements me in place.

Behind the rifle, Lidia smiles. "It's been a fun time, hasn't it, Denny?"

"Put the weapon down, Lidia."

"I think not." The hint of laughter. "Have you enjoyed the journey?"

"What's next? You take down Rome? Maybe the Greeks?"

"Oooh. Good suggestions. But I'll be honest. This has been exhausting. Fun, but I could use a little time off. Thinking I might find a deserted beach somewhere. Relax for a while. What do you think?"

"That sounds great. Let's go." At least she wouldn't be able to do any harm there.

There's no hiding her laughter this time. "Oh, Denny. Really? Do you think you're going to piggyback with me forever? I'm glad you've been able to witness the work I've been doing, but it's almost time for you to get off."

I hear something, faint, beyond the field on the other side. At first I think it's just the wind, but then it's there again, loud enough this time that Lidia notices it, too. It's the pounding hooves of a single horse heading our way.

"Almost?" I say, hoping to distract her.

But she's having none of it. "On the ground, both of you." Neither Scout nor I move. "I have no problem killing either of you."

I believe her so I lower myself to the ground and nod to Scout to do the same.

"Good. Now stay," she says.

The horse comes in fast from the other side of the meadow, but pulls up as soon as its rider sees his dead companions. In the split second before Lidia sends a burst of bullets flying in his direction, the sentry gives his horse a kick and they gallop off to the left. The shots miss their mark by only feet. The sound has terrified the rider, but instead of trying to figure out what has caused it, he veers his horse into the trees.

Lidia pulls the trigger again, but there's only the click of the hammer closing on an empty chamber. With a frustrated growl, she throws the gun to the ground and rips her chaser out of her bag.

I brace myself, ready to jump again, but then realize I don't have my device.

"Denny!" Scout yells.

He reaches out to me, and I throw myself at him, making contact just a second before everything disappears.

I hear a voice as soon as we come out of the jump. Lidia's, but it's coming from behind me, yet I can see her thirty feet in front of me. A quick scan reveals that physically we've only moved into the woods on the other side of the body-filled meadow, and I realize that the Lidia I hear is the one who's about to tell me that our travels together are almost over.

A horse comes through the forest carrying the messenger Other Lidia will try to shoot but will miss in a few moments. The Now Lidia, the one in front of me, starts running for the clearing.

"Here," Scout says, and hands me back the chaser. Though I'm sure he'd rather keep control of it, he knows I'm the only one with a handle on what's really going on here.

Lidia is maybe a dozen feet from the meadow when the messenger and his horse emerge from the trees. As before, he pulls up the moment he sees his dead colleagues, but this time, just a few seconds before Other Lidia is about to shoot, Now Lidia begins shouting, "Over here! Over here! Over here!"

The messenger yanks his horse around and starts moving toward her voice, bringing him closer to the campfire. This time when Other Lidia pulls the trigger, she doesn't miss.

Now Lidia laughs in triumph and then looks back at me in a way that tells me we are about to jump again.

I throw my hand behind me, my fingers spread wide, and feel the slap as Scout's palm connects with mine just a few seconds before we vanish from the site of the Mongol massacre.

◆ ◆ ◆

Momentum carries us forward a few steps as we come out of the jump. The pain, though, causes us to stop and cringe. A good-size jump. At least a hundred years, I think.

Through squinted eyes I check the chaser. Double what I thought. Two hundred exactly. 1442. And according to the map, we're only thirty miles outside of London, England.

I force myself to look for Lidia. While she's clearly in pain, she's already running toward some smoke rising above the trees to our left.

I yank on Scout's hand and we take off after her.

The smells of civilization hit me in waves of cooking meat and human sweat and waste of both man and animal as we near the town. Both coughing, Scout and I pull up our shirts over our mouths and noses to filter the air, but it's a wasted effort as it only adds our own stink to the other scents.

"Lidia! Stop!" I yell.

She continues on without a break in her step. Though she hasn't been able to add any more distance between us, we haven't been able to gain any ground on her, either. Ahead and to the left, I spot a building through the trees maybe fifty yards away. Another appears to my right. Then more and more.

I know the smell is probably stronger now, but while my nose still feels as if it is under assault, my body has adjusted my tolerance levels enough that I can continue on without retching.

A road emerges from the forest, running right into the town. Lidia turns down it, and we follow. Though this doesn't appear to be any kind of fortified village, the dirt road soon transitions into one of cobblestone. As the buildings begin to surround us, I notice something else strange, too. Maybe half the structures contain architectural elements that I've always associated with the Chinese Empire—upturned rooflines, ornate designs, and the use of bright colors. These are small things in the grand picture of the world, but they speak with the power of a god.

Kali, to be specific.

It's all the proof I need to know that Lidia's attempt to keep the Mongols on their march through Europe was successful.

It must be the adrenaline coursing through my veins because I'm not feeling any pain and am able to run almost as fast as I do when I'm not wounded. I feel like it's now or never, that I can't stop running until I capture Lidia.

Scout's feet slap the cobblestones beside me. At the moment, we're not currently in physical contact, but we're both keeping a close eye on Lidia, and if she makes a move toward her chaser, I know Scout will grab on to me again.

The street grows more crowded with villagers the deeper into town we get. As our little parade races down the center of the road, we draw stares of confusion and even fear. Our clothes, our shoes, our hair, even the color of our skin stands out. These are not the Anglo-Saxons I have known. Their blood has been mixed with not just the Mongols but the other races the Mongols swept along in their move west—the Chinese, the Persians, the Arabs, the Moors.

A large Eurasian man in a gray cloak shouts words at us that— with the exception of maybe one or two—I don't understand. Others begin doing the same, and I worry that a mob will form that will take Scout and me down before we can get to Lidia.

Thankfully the village is a small one, and I can see the buildings petering out ahead. But as we near, I spot several oxcarts entering the town and completely blocking the path.

Scout's hand is on my shoulder before I realize Lidia is yanking up her chaser. We keep running, though, gaining a foot or two by the time she hits her go button.

We stumble over uneven ground as we come out of the jump, heads pounding with intense pain. While I'm able to stay on my feet, Scout hits the ground.

I look back, but he shouts, "Keep going. I'll catch up." So I do.

The reason for his fall is that we materialized in a field that has been recently plowed. Chunks of mud lie in lines that slow all of us.

Lidia glances back at me. At first, her eyes blaze with the same wild anger they have had since the chase began, but then something else creeps in, and she almost seems to smile. At that moment she whips up her chaser and starts inputting a new jump.

"Grab on!" I yell.

I thrust my hand behind me, but when I glance back, I see that Scout's ten yards away.

"Hurry!"

Panic fills his eyes as he sprints across the field. To help, I reverse direction, and run toward him. Scout leaps the final few feet and hits me just as the jump takes hold.

◆ ◆ ◆

Upon arrival we topple onto hard ground. More cobblestones, I realize. My shoulder aches where it's slammed into the surface, but I can't let that stop me.

I stagger to my feet more than spring and then help Scout up. If there is such a thing as fate, it has once more been working against us, and the gains we've been making on Lidia have been lost.

"Stay with me," I say and then start running again.

Heavy gray clouds fill the sky. It hasn't started to rain, but it won't be long, which is probably the reason why there are only a handful of people about. As much as I'd like to, checking the chaser now to see when and where we are would just slow me down. A town somewhere, probably in Europe. It has that kind of feel, though who knows in this infinitely changed world? As for the time, it doesn't matter.

Lidia turns a corner up ahead, momentarily disappearing from sight.

Without either of us saying anything, both Scout and I pick up our speed. From the dampness on the leg of my pants, I know that my wound has started to bleed again, but my adrenaline is still keeping me from feeling anything.

When we turn the corner I expect to see Lidia on the road ahead of us, but she's not there. I have no choice but to consult the tracking map, which means we must slow to about half speed. The dot indicates she's ahead and to the left, but when we get to the point where her path diverges from the road we are on, we find not an intersecting street but a building that's been ravaged by a recent fire. The front door is missing, and much of the stone that surrounds the entrance is black with soot.

The signal from Lidia's chaser is coming from deep inside the structure, but we enter cautiously nonetheless. The front portion of the building is open all the way to the sky. A stone stairway runs up one wall to the ghost of a second floor. What doesn't still stick out from the walls lies before us in piles of ash and chunks of partially burned wood. A stone wall divides the building in half, making it impossible to see the back portion, where Lidia should be.

Two soot-encrusted doorways lead through the wall. We approach the one on the left, and look through. Another big room, though here, with the exception of a few burned-out holes, most of the second floor has survived. Several piles of debris scattered around give me the sense someone has started to clean this place up so it can be rebuilt.

A walled-off room sits in the back right corner, the door that once covered its entrance burned away. The map tells me that Lidia is inside it. Quietly we enter the big room and cross toward the corner. No movement from the dot. Is she waiting there for us? Why doesn't she just jump if there's no way out of there?

I hear a wet patter behind me, and jerk around, thinking maybe she's sneaking up on us. But the sound is only raindrops falling unimpeded onto the floor of the front room.

I stop Scout no more than ten feet from the point the map tells me Lidia is. Finally, this is all but over. Whether she comes out or jumps, it doesn't matter. We're too close to her now. We will take her down, and then I'll start mopping up her mess.

"Come on out," I say. "It's over, Lidia. There's nowhere for you to go."

Something skitters across the floor inside, small, like a pebble. This is Lidia's only response, so we move into the doorway.

There aren't any windows and the roof has escaped damage, so the only light getting in is what flows around Scout and me through the entrance. Someone has filled much of the space with what I'm guessing is the salvageable furniture from the fire—cabinets, both tall and short; a few chairs; and a long thin table turned on its end.

According to the tracker, Lidia should be just behind a tall cabinet directly in front of me.

"Enough, Lidia. Get *out* here!" My tone isn't as neutral as it probably should be given her mental state, but I'm tired of playing hide-and-seek. I just want to go someplace where I can rest for a little bit before I start detangling the changes she's made layer by miserable layer.

Another pebble, but not so much scooting across the floor as bouncing on it. I barely notice the difference, though, as I weave through singed furniture, and circle around the cabinet.

I stop dead and stare, surprised. The only things there are Lidia's rucksack and beside it my satchel, the chaser clearly inside, both sitting on the floor against the wall.

I barely register this, though, before she jumps off the top of the cabinet and onto my back, tumbling us both to the floor. I try to push up, but she knocks me back down and grinds her knee into my kidney. She starts choking me with one hand while hitting me with the other.

"Get off him!" Scout yells.

I can't see what's going on behind me, but I can feel him pulling at her. She stops hitting me, and replaces the hand around my neck with her arm. I hear the two of them struggle, but unlike me and Lidia, Scout has never been in an actual fight before, and soon she's yanked him to the ground. I twist left then right then left again, and at last succeed in turning enough so that I'm lying on my side instead of my stomach. This finally loosens her hold, and I'm able to suck in some precious oxygen.

With renewed strength, I slam my elbow into her ribs over and over and over until I'm able to roll away.

Lidia then turns her full fury on Scout. He covers his face with his arms to block her blows, but this opens his midsection to a brutal kick that sends him flying backward through the doorway.

My own breaths are still coming hard and fast, my wounds both old and new all screaming for attention, but I know I'm a helpless target if I stay on the ground. I pull myself up with the help of the tall cabinet and then turn to face her onslaught. Instead of coming *at* me, however, she dives past me.

I turn as she grabs my satchel and sticks her hand inside.

"No!" I yell. I whip back around and lock eyes with Scout. He's on his elbows a good fifteen feet away. I'll never get to him in time. "I'm sorry."

He shakes his head. "It's my—"

Those are the only words he gets out before Lidia activates her chaser and she and I leave Scout Me behind.

◆ ◆ ◆

Lidia clearly pre-entered the jump coordinates prior to setting the trap that would separate Scout and me, because she's chosen our destination well. The trip has taken us to an empty desert that goes as far as the eye can see in every direction, on a journey that was at least as long as the two-century jump that took us away from the dead Mongol messengers.

I arrive a huddled mass of pain. When I hear movement, I pry open my eyelids to thin slits and see Lidia coming at me. The only defense I can mount is to turn my head away and hope I can weather her attack. But though I feel a tug at one of my arms, she doesn't actually hit me.

I force myself to turn and look at her again. Instead of hovering over me, she's moved back several dozen feet.

I get up, thinking the whole time she's going to rush me, but she never moves.

Once I'm standing, she smiles and raises her hand. Dangling from it is the makeshift bag I created to carry the slaved chaser. Reflexively I look down, as if she couldn't possibly have it, but mine is gone, and she is now in possession of both devices.

It's a hot day, but the sweat seeping from my forehead is not caused by the sun. One push of the button, and I will be alone here forever.

I guess I should be grateful that if she does leave me, it will be only a matter of days until my death, because there is no way I'll find water in time. But grateful is not what I feel.

As dire as the situation is, I can't give up. I *won't* give up.

"Don't do this."

She snorts. "Do what?"

"I know you have a problem with me. I know that I took the world you knew away. I can accept whatever personal punishment you decide, but everything else you've done, all the changes, you've been damning billions for the guilt of one person." I tap my chest. "I'm the responsible party. Just me. I'm the only one who should pay the price."

"You want to pay the price? Sure, good idea. Let's start with this."

She swings her arm so that the burlap bag flies high above her, and then she brings it quickly down again and smashes it into the ground. It's impossible to miss the crunch of wood and metal. I take a step forward but stop as she swings it up again and repeats the maneuver. Though the machine is surely destroyed by now, she does it again and again and again. After she finally stops, she turns the bag over and dumps the contents on the desert floor. All that falls out are bits and pieces that can never be put back together again.

The only way out of here now is the chaser in my leather satchel, hanging at Lidia's side.

I run at her without thinking. If she can get to the chaser and disappear before I reach her, so be it, but I'm not going to just stand around and let her wink away without a fight. She makes no play for the bag, though. Instead, she sets her feet and leans slightly forward, anticipating my arrival.

At the last second I duck to the right to go under her arms, but she's anticipated this and steps farther to my left and shoves me on the back as I fly by.

I lock my knees and skid across the dirt to a stop. When I turn back, I half think she'll already be gone, but she's still standing there, grinning at me.

Fighting has always been Lidia's thing, not mine, but having no other choice I charge again. This time she grabs me, and we twist around in a tense dance of shoving and wrestling as we each try to get the advantage.

"I can smell your desperation," she whispers in my ear. "That's the kind of odor you inherit from your parents."

She flings me away.

"I have to admit, though, I thought you'd have given up jumps ago. All your gutter-dwelling friends would have. I guess I should be impressed, but I can't seem to muster up the energy."

I know she's trying to goad me into a mindless attack, but I'm not that naïve anymore. I circle to the right, staying just out of her reach.

She raises an eyebrow as she pivots her head to match my movements. "Already taken your best shot? Now I'm really disappointed."

I continue to move around her, saying nothing. Though I don't look at it directly, my attention is really on my old satchel resting against her right hip. I just need to get it and run. Unfortunately, her arm rests over the top, her hand clutching the strap just above where it's attached to the bag.

As I pass behind her, Lidia whips her head from one shoulder to the other, taunting me to attack her from the back. I have no intention of doing that, at least not yet, but her arrogance has caused her to make a mistake. In that moment when she's moving her head and her eyes aren't on me, I glance at the bag and see my opportunity.

Peeking out of the flap covering the smaller side pouch is the hilt of her grandson's knife. If I can get it out, I can cut the strap like I did before and get away.

I circle around in front of her again, my eyes once more locked on hers.

"What are we playing at here, Denny?" she asks. "Ring around the rosies?"

I say nothing, and continue past her left shoulder. Like before, once her head has gone as far as it can, she starts to turn it back the other way. The moment her eyes are off me, I charge.

Sensing I'm up to something, she immediately drops into a crouch and tries to hurl me over her head. It's a move we both learned during defensive training at the institute, but in this case it plays to my advantage. I jerk to the right as she reaches up for me, and slide across her back instead of flying over her head.

As my right arm rubs against the satchel's strap, my hand is already searching for the pouch. Unfortunately, while I'm able to pull loose the tie holding the flap down, I'm moving too fast to grab the knife, and instead sweep past Lidia's shoulder and onto the ground.

I quickly jump up before she has a chance to come after me.

"Nice try," she says, grinning wider than ever. "But you're going to have to do a lot more than—"

I launch at her again, throw my arms around her torso, and tackle her to the ground. I shove a hand over her neck to distract her and use my other to free the knife. I find the flap first, and move it out of the way so I can grab the blade. Only the pouch is empty.

A harsh, choked laugh escapes Lidia's throat. "So predictable."

I feel the blade cut through my shirt and slice the skin over my shoulder blade. Groaning in agony, I push myself away, but Lidia is having none of it. She jumps on top of me, her knees on my chest, and presses my newly sliced shoulder into the ground. As I yell in pain, she presses the knife against my throat, the blade nicking at my skin.

"This was fun and all, but it's time we take one last trip together." I must not be able to hide my confusion, because she then adds, "Someplace I'm sure we both would like to see. Well, I would, anyway."

Since she has only the one free hand, it takes her a moment to pull the chaser out of the satchel and unlock the flap. She doesn't input a destination, though.

I realize now that this desert was never to be my graveyard. That Lidia has had something else in mind all along.

That her *mission* won't be complete until she's shown me the hell she has wrought.

CHAPTER NINETEEN

A temporary paralysis seizes a person when inside a jump. One usually doesn't notice it because the mere fact you are traveling in time makes you not want to move. But as my own experience has demonstrated more than once in the last twenty-four hours of my personal time line, someone in motion before a jump remains in motion after arrival. So if I'm running, I continue to run, and if I'm falling, I don't stop just because I find myself somewhere else.

As Lidia moves her finger to the chaser's home button, I tense my arm and start it on an arc that will collide with the hand Lidia's using to hold the knife. It's barely off the ground when we enter the mist.

One of the longest jumps I've ever taken landed me in a New York hospital for several days. This jump is not quite that long but close. No matter how torturous, I need to hold on and subdue Lidia. Unconsciousness can take me after she's no longer a threat, but not before.

The dimming of the mist finally signals that our journey is coming to an end.

As the black of the jump fades into a dark night, my arm flies up and smacks Lidia's hand. I'm not even sure she notices. I barely realized what's going on myself as my brain feels as if it's on fire.

Hold on, I will myself.

I flop onto my belly and force myself up on all fours, then look around. Lidia lies on the grass beside me, eyes closed and moaning.

Crawling toward her, I tell myself, *Get . . . the chaser.*

I'm almost to her when something bites my palm. I snap my hand up, and can feel blood oozing from the puncture. I scan the ground, looking for the animal that attacked me. But the bite didn't come from an animal at all.

Shimmering softly in the dull starlight is the knife.

I grab it with my bloody hand and continue over to Lidia. My mind is working at only a fraction of what it should, and I'm already moving the blade under the satchel's strap to cut it free when I realize the chaser isn't in the bag at all but lying on the ground next to her. I grab it, and then, since she's obviously in no condition to put up a fight, I work the satchel over her head and pull it off.

She moans again as I do this, her eyes fluttering but not opening. Once I've strung the bag across my chest, I put the chaser inside. My hand brushes against a coil of wires and for a moment I wonder what else she's put in the satchel until I realize it's RJ's charger.

I use Lidia's limp finger to unlock the lid of the chaser and then wrap one of the charger's cords around it several times so that it doesn't close again. Now I'll be able to rekey it once I can concentrate enough so that I don't screw it up.

As I close the satchel's flap, I breathe a sigh of relief.

It's over. I'm the one in charge now.

While there's still much work for me to do, Lidia can cause no further damage. I'll start with the Mongol messengers and then slowly work my way forward through time.

But not yet. Rest first. A good long rest.

I stagger to my feet. I need to get as far away from Lidia as I can so that when I do collapse from exhaustion, she'll never find me.

We seem to be in a shallow depression covered by tall tufts of dried grass. Nothing looks familiar, but that's not surprising.

The home button was created to give rewinders a quick way of returning to the institute—the preprogrammed location—at the point that corresponded with one's date of birth and how long he or she has actually lived since then.

Where we are, though, is not the location that equates to where the institute would be had the institute existed in this world. Once I committed to living in Iffy's time line, I reprogrammed the home location coordinates to the living room of Ellie's and my apartment. Even so, given the distance Lidia and I have just traveled, all without a companion to keep our path true, a displacement of several hundred miles is not out of the question.

I check the chaser and see that we are a little bit north of where San Diego should be. What surprises me, though, is that we're not in 2015. The date on the device reads: October 12, 2018.

That's impossible. I can't go to 2018. I haven't lived long enough. That's three years past my home time. It must be some kind of mistake. It has to be an—

Wait. *Lidia* has lived an extra three years. Instead of being nineteen like I am, she's twenty-two now. And the chaser has been keyed to her. Could it be possible that the time barrier is in effect only in relationship to the person who is connected to the chaser?

Another wave of pain rushes over me. This is too much for me to figure out right now. I need rest. I can figure out what's going on when my head clears.

I weave up the slope, my hand touching the ground with every step to steady myself. In the distance, I hear a hum that sounds a lot like the drone of traffic, but there are no other noises.

Good. The farther away civilization is, the better.

As I climb out of the dip in the land, I see a glow rising above a jagged horizon in the general direction of where San Diego should be.

Good. Maybe the change hasn't affected things as much as I feared.

Off to my right is a line of vehicle lights on a road—the source of the hum. Scattered here and there are other lights, too, homes I'm guessing, but none are closer than a few miles.

My luck seems to be holding.

I randomly choose a direction and start walking. I can't describe how utterly exhausted I feel. I don't think there's a single atom in my body not pleading for me to lie down and close my eyes.

In this condition, it's no wonder I don't hear the footsteps behind me until a moment before I'm hit in the back. I trip over my own feet and take a slow tumble to the grass. I have enough energy to roll onto my back, but not enough to stand.

Lidia sways a few feet away, her face twisted in fury and pain.

"Where do you . . . think . . . you're going?"

"Go away, Lidia. Leave me alone." To be honest I can't help but wonder if this spot might be where I lie forever.

A growl starts low in her chest and becomes a scream the moment she throws herself at me. I curl to the side to protect the satchel and chaser a second before she smashes into me.

She claws at my shirt, at my neck, at my hair. A fingernail rips a gouge across the skin just above my collarbone.

"Get off!" I yell as I throw back an elbow.

It connects with her jaw, knocking it into her skull while at the same time causing my arm to feel like it's been rung like a bell. The sting is so acute, I look at my arm, thinking it must be broken, but instead of seeing bone sticking through my skin, I see Kane's knife still in my hand.

I pull away from Lidia and am somehow able to get my knees under me. From there I lurch to my feet. "Go, Lidia. You're done. Go and enjoy what you've created while you can."

She pushes herself up and rubs her jaw. Her gaze flicks to my hand, and she huffs, "What? Are you going to cut me?"

"I said go."

She starts walking toward me. "Or what?"

"Just go!"

I take a backward step, but she keeps coming until she's only a few feet away. Holding her arms out wide to her side, she says, "Go on, Denny. The first slice is free."

I don't want to do this. Why can't she accept the fate that she's created for herself?

After a few seconds, she drops her arms and laughs. "I knew you didn't have it in you. You caste dregs are all the same."

She sneers as if she thinks she can simply take the knife out of my hand.

Ellie.

Iffy.

The billions and billions who now have never been.

Yes, I've done my share of erasing, but my crimes pale compared to Lidia's. I did what I did for love—for my sister and for Iffy. Lidia? Her motivation has been spite and anger and jealousy. The only one she's contorted history for is herself.

In a burst of speed that surprises even me, I rush at her. Her eyes widening, she reaches for the knife, but I jerk my hand so that it flows under her outstretched arm and drive the blade into her chest.

Confusion is the first emotion that rolls over her face. Her hands go to the wound, and when she sees blood on her fingers, fear rushes in. She takes a staggering step before falling backward.

"Wha . . . what . . ." She loses her train of thought as she looks at her hands again.

Slowly, as if she is just going to bed, she lowers her back all the way to the ground. Her eyes, however, remain open as she stares between blinks at the night sky.

I didn't want it to go this way, but she's left me no choice.

She is Kali, the goddess of time and destruction, to the end. Because though my hand is holding the knife, she has destroyed herself.

When I kneel beside her, her lips begin to move, but she emits not even a whisper.

I stay there, my bloody hand holding hers until the life finally fades from her eyes.

Gently, I shake her just to be sure. "Lidia?"

No reaction.

"Lidia?"

It is truly and finally over. I have stopped her in the most permanent way.

I lay her arms beside her and close her eyelids. The last is for me, a final gesture that proves to me she's gone, and perhaps, to a lesser extent, that in killing her I haven't lost all of my humanity.

What I really should do is dig a grave. There's no way to know who might live around here, and I certainly wouldn't want some kids stumbling upon her body. The problem is, I don't have enough strength to even start.

Doesn't matter anyway, I remind myself. Once I jump out of here, I'll change the past, and Lidia's body, along with whatever reality this 2015 (or 2018 or whenever this is) has become will disappear.

Right.

Good.

Not an issue then.

The next thing I know, I'm stretched out on the grass beside her. I don't remember lying down, but, well, it does feel good.

Maybe I'll rest for a few minutes, just get a little strength. Five minutes, tops, and then I'll find someplace else to hole up, where I'll be out of the sun when it rises.

Good thinking.

A few minutes. That's all.

Just . . .

. . . a . . .

. . . few—

CHAPTER TWENTY

Voices.

Sunlight.

No, close your eyes. Don't let it in.

A dream. The same one that has been wrapped around me for what feels like forever. Iffy and I on a pier overlooking the ocean. Ellie is there, too. We're having hot dogs. Or maybe ice cream.

Voices.

My body shakes.

I say something, though I'm not sure if it's in my mind or aloud. Pressure on my thigh. And then a sting at the cut on my back.

Voices.

A prick on my arm, near my elbow. It hurts only for a moment so there's no need to open my eyes and check . . . not that I could if I wanted to.

The dream. Iffy and I in her car. Well, it's not *her* car. It's Marilyn's. Only it's not Marilyn's, either. Music on the radio that Iffy sings to as we drive and drive and drive.

A song I've never heard.

With lyrics I don't actually understand.

◆　◆　◆

Waking seems to take forever. It must be evening, though, because I no longer feel the heat of the sun on my skin.

Sun? Why would I be sleeping outside?

For a while the question ebbs and flows in importance. But as the tendrils of unconsciousness continue falling away, I begin to remember everything.

Lidia.

The Mongols.

My satchel.

Oh, God. The knife.

She's dead.

I've stopped her. That has been my primary goal up until now, and with the knowledge that it has been achieved comes a huge sense of relief, despite what it ultimately took for me to accomplish it.

I then try to recall where I moved to after I left Lidia's body, but I don't actually remember getting back up. Am I still beside her?

The thought causes me to wrench open my eyes. I look left and right, confused.

I must still be asleep. I must still be in the dream.

I'm not outside at all. I'm on a bed in a room with soft green walls. There's a black, very solid-looking door on the wall past my feet. In the upper half is a small window, but I can see nothing through it.

I try to sit up, but I can't seem to move. Have I hurt myself worse than I thought?

No, wait. I can move. I moved my head to look around, remember? I lift my head again, but this time examine my body. The good news is that I don't think I'm paralyzed. The bad is almost as disconcerting, though. I'm being held in place by straps across my chest, arms, and legs.

Panicking, I push at them, hoping they're loose enough for me to slip out of them, but it quickly becomes clear they're not.

My chaser! Oh, God, my chaser!

I scan around. My bag is definitely not on the bed with me, nor is it anywhere in the room, as there's not a cabinet or table where it could be stashed. In fact, the only other item in the room is a chair sitting against the wall.

"Hello?" I yell toward the door. "Is there anyone out there? Hello?"

I'm either being ignored or no one can hear me.

Think! I tell myself as I close my eyes. *What happened?*

My last memory is lying next to Lidia on the grass. Whatever happened after that is nothing more than jumbled images that very well could only be part of my dreams.

I didn't jump, did I? I mean, I'm still where Lidia brought me, right?

I can't tell from anything in the room. The chair and the bed look as if they could be from 1915 as easily as 2015.

I lie in my ignorance for what seems like hours before I finally hear a *clank* from somewhere outside the room. A moment later, the door swings open, and three people enter—two women and one man.

The man and one of the women, the taller of the two, are wearing some sort of uniform I have never seen before. The other woman is dressed in a light gray pantsuit, I guess you'd call it. Their skin tones, though not identical shades, are all browner than mine, and there's a slight Asiatic look to the women's eyes.

The woman in the uniform starts talking. If she's talking to me, as her gaze would indicate, I don't know what she wants as I can't understand what she's saying. There's the occasional word that sounds familiar, but I can't be sure of their meaning because every-thing else is completely foreign to me. When she finishes, she stares at me, obviously waiting.

I hesitate for a moment to see if anyone else is going to speak up before saying, "I'm sorry. I don't understand."

Stone faces all around.

The uniformed woman says something else to me, and again waits.

I shake my head and then ask, "Do any of you speak English?"

This causes the three to huddle together, each rapidly talking over the top of the others. The man gives me a suspicious sideways glance and then says something to the woman in gray.

With a nod, she approaches the bed and starts checking me over. From the attention she gives my wounds, it's pretty clear she's a doctor. As she moves the sheet away from my leg, I can see that the wound has been resealed, though not with sutures as far as I can tell. There's also less redness around it, which I take as a good sign.

She has to loosen the strap across my chest to look at my shoul-der, but immediately tightens it again when she's finished. The last thing she does is place a square on my neck that looks kind of like a piece of thick paper, but is cold like metal. She looks at it for a moment and then says something to her colleagues.

More conversation, and then the three leave without engaging me further.

I try not to theorize about what kind of society I've found myself in. The only thing I need to concentrate on is finding my chaser and getting out of here.

Barely a minute passes before the door opens again. This time I have five visitors, all in uniform. One is the woman from before, but the others are all new. She directs them as they unshackle me from the bed and roughly pull me to my feet.

As I'm guided down a series of white hallways, I try to keep track of each turn and draw a rudimentary map in my head.

At the end of a particularly long corridor, they take me through a doorway into a small room we all barely have enough space to stand in. The moment the door is closed, I feel the room move downward and realize that we're in a lift. There were none of the usual indicators when we entered—no gap between the doorway and the car, nor any selector buttons on the wall.

When it stops moving, the man closest to the door opens it, and I'm ushered out again. No white hallways here. Dirt, with wood and rock supports. Almost like a mine shaft. We are definitely belowground. How far, I'm not sure, but I don't like it. They take me along a windy route before turning down a new tunnel. Unlike those we'd just come through, the walls of this tunnel are made of what appears to be concrete. The passageway dead-ends about thirty feet down. Spaced evenly along each side are black doors—three to the right, three to the left.

I'm taken to the farthest door on the left. When one of my escorts opens it, I try to peek inside, but there are no lights so all looks black.

The woman says something to me and waits. I don't even try to respond. After several moments, she says something else, and one of her colleagues pushes me in the back.

As soon as I stumble into the room, the door shuts behind me, plunging the space into complete darkness.

I stand still, temporarily unable to move.

Whatever relief I'd been feeling at the knowledge that Lidia was no longer a problem is gone. Unless I can get out of this cell, the havoc she has sown will stand.

And at the moment, I'm not feeling particularly optimistic about my chances.

Something scrapes against the floor to my right. I whirl around to face it, but in the pitch black, I can see absolutely nothing.

"Is someone there?" I ask.

The movement stops for a second before starting again.

"Hello?"

The punch that hits my face comes without warning. I fall onto the floor, my mind barely clinging to consciousness.

"Confuto," a deep male voice says.

The scraping returns to the place from where I first heard it, then all goes quiet again.

The word the man has spoken feels familiar, like I should know what it means. But my mind has shattered into a million shards, and all it wants is to turn off.

A final stray memory guides me into unconsciousness.

RJ standing in my living room with a big grin on his face as he says, "May you live in interesting times."

He said a friend told him it was a curse, but RJ wasn't so sure.

I could tell him now, without hesitation, that his friend was right.

ABOUT THE AUTHOR

Brett Battles is a Barry Award–winning author of more than twenty novels, including the Jonathan Quinn series, the Project Eden series, and the Alexandra Poe series—the latter of which he wrote with Robert Gregory Browne. Battles draws on his extensive world travels to infuse his thrillers and science fiction stories with rare cultural and historical authenticity, bringing people and places to vibrant life. He lives in Los Angeles. You can find him at www.BrettBattles.com.